"You're getting red," Nate said. "I think you should probably reapply your sun lotion."

Sydney felt his cool touch against her lower back and she had to force herself to breathe. His fingers moved up her spine and found her shoulders, kneading them softly, causing her eyes to close. It was the most amazing thing she'd felt in a long time. Nate had always been great with his hands.

It was as if he were releasing the stiffness that had been there all the years she'd been without him. She opened her eyes as she felt him take the sandwich and wine from her hands and set them down, before returning his hands to her shoulders. She let her head drop, her shoulders slumping as he continued working his fingers, under the tie on her swimsuit and along the large muscles on her back.

She was aware of his body closing in behind her, his breath near her ear, and the lightening of his touch to a soft caress, making her breathing become shallow. He nuzzled against her neck, his hands dropping to her waist, his fingers moving around her until he was embracing her from behind.

"I miss you, Syd," he whispered into her ear.
"I miss you so much it hurts."

Praise for Jenny Hale

"Jenny Hale writes touching, beautiful stories."
—RaeAnne Thayne, *New York Times* bestselling author

CHRISTMAS AT SILVER FALLS

"Hale brings the beauty of the Great Smoky Mountains alive in this heartwarming Christmas romance...Authentic, dimensional characters enhance the emotionally charged love story. Fast-paced and brimming with holiday spirit, this is sure to please."
—*Publishers Weekly*

SUMMER AT FIREFLY BEACH

"A great summer beach read."
—*PopSugar*

IT STARTED WITH CHRISTMAS

"This sweet small-town romance will leave readers feeling warm all the way through."
—*Publishers Weekly*

THE SUMMER HOUSE

CHRISTMAS WISHES AND MISTLETOE KISSES

the
house
on firefly
beach

ALSO BY JENNY HALE

the
house
on firefly
beach

JENNY HALE

FOREVER

NEW YORK   BOSTON

Forever
Hachette Book Group
1290 Avenue of the Americas
New York, NY 10104
read-forever.com
twitter.com/readforeverpub

Originally published in 2020 by Bookouture, an imprint of StoryFire Ltd. First Forever Edition published in trade paperback in May 2022.

First Mass Market Edition: July 2023

Forever is an imprint of Grand Central Publishing. The Forever name and logo are trademarks of Hachette Book Group, Inc.

The publisher is not responsible for websites (or their content) that are not owned by the publisher.

The Hachette Speakers Bureau provides a wide range of authors for speaking events. To find out more, go to hachettespeakersbureau.com or email HachetteSpeakers@hbgusa.com.

Forever books may be purchased in bulk for business, educational, or promotional use. For information, please contact your local bookseller or the Hachette Book Group Special Markets Department at special.markets@hbgusa.com.

ISBN 9781538756515 (mass market)

Printed in the United States of America

OPM

10 9 8 7 6 5 4 3 2 1

the
house
on firefly
beach

Prologue

Sydney Flynn skipped along the beach road toward Nate's house, her auburn curls pulled into a ponytail to combat the swell of afternoon pre-summer heat. It was their senior year in college, and they were both graduating in a week, the clear, humid days of summer quickly approaching. Having spent four glorious years together, much of their winters separated by a lengthy drive between their two universities, Sydney couldn't help but feel the excitement of their uninterrupted future together bubbling up.

She fiddled with the purple stone of the toy ring Nate had given her as a placeholder for the real diamond he promised once they graduated—she wore the ring every day. Nate had called her this morning before she'd awakened and left a message to come see him right away. He'd sounded oddly breathless and nervous, and she wondered what the surprise could be. He wasn't usually this mysterious.

The sun was already beaming in a gloriously blue sky, birds flying overhead, the waters of the gulf that rippled by her side shushing relentlessly onto the Florida shore as she walked the familiar path toward the one person in this world that she adored the most—it was the perfect day to start the rest of their lives. She didn't want to jinx it, but she did wonder: Would he propose today? Could that be it?

Of course, she wanted it to happen in his time, but she was so in love with him that she was ready to start their lives together right now. Last night they'd celebrated her incredible news that she'd been invited to travel around the U.S. for three months, as a writer, documenting the work of a famous humanitarian. She didn't even want to go if she could start planning her wedding right now, but Nate had convinced her to follow her passion to be a professional journalist, so she'd decided to take the trip. If they had a year before the wedding, she could still get all the planning done if she started after she returned. Her excitement made her laugh because she knew she was getting ahead of herself.

Sydney came up the drive, bounding with the thrill of seeing Nate and hearing what he had to tell her, but she paused, the sight in front of her baffling. "What's going on?" she asked, as Nate hurried out, locked the door behind him, and stopped cold, his arms fumbling with a pile of boxes as he picked them up off the drive. He lumped them into the back of his truck, which was completely full of his things.

Were they going somewhere?

"I'm leaving," he said, his gaze fluttering up to her, but only briefly.

"Where are you going?" Her heart was beating uncontrollably, as if her body had caught up to the situation before her mind could process it.

"I don't know," he nearly snapped. "New York? LA? Somewhere I can write my songs and make something of myself." He shifted a box in the back and secured it with a bungee cord, his movement swift and focused. "I'm getting out of here. There's more to life than Firefly Beach," he said. "I just wanted to say goodbye."

A cloud drifted in front of the sun, casting a gray shade on everything, but she barely noticed through the tears that were forming in her eyes.

"I'm not coming with you?" She already knew the answer, but she was pleading with the heavens above to help her by casting some kind of reconsideration onto his heart before he broke hers into pieces.

"No."

"Why not?" she asked, her body beginning to shake all over, her world crumbling in front of her.

He swallowed, not answering or meeting her eyes. "I wanted to say goodbye, but... There's no good way to do this."

"Nate, what are you doing?" Why was he hurting her like this? "Explain to me what is going on," she cried, unable to keep her emotions from coming through.

He pushed another box into his truck and lifted the tailgate, shutting his belongings into the back.

"Talk to me!" When he didn't respond, she tried to push herself in front of him, but he darted out of her way. "I deserve an explanation! You can't just leave like this after four years. What happened between last night and now?"

He didn't answer, leaving her to wonder if he, too, had given thought to forever with her, and suddenly realized that it wasn't at all what he wanted.

"Sorry," he said quickly without even a look in her direction.

He paused in front of her and stared into her eyes, the hint of something in them, as if he wanted one last chance to make sure this was the right decision. Then before she could say anything, he got in his truck, starting the engine and shutting the door. She stepped back instinctively when he put the truck into gear, his face like stone. He pulled away, leaving her standing there, struggling to clear the tears from her vision enough to see him look back at her in his rearview mirror, but he never did. Sydney stood in the driveway of his dark, locked house, and watched his truck pull further away from her until it disappeared. Nate was gone, taking her happiness with him.

Chapter One

In her conch-shell-pink chiffon bridesmaid's dress, Sydney stood with the rest of the wedding party, at the end of their beloved family's pier, and locked eyes with Nate Henderson. She barely noticed the unseasonably perfect weather or the lapping of the sparkling Gulf of Mexico behind them, all of it fading away at the sight of Nate. Nate was the man whom Sydney had always considered to be the true love of her life. And now, with his Valentino suit and over-priced haircut, he was someone she barely recognized.

His cell went off. He quickly left his seat and bowed his way down the aisle, stepping off to the side to answer a call right in the middle of the service. *Mr. Hollywood can't even shut it off for a wedding?* she thought, irritated already. He had seemed slightly mortified, but it hadn't stopped him from answering. He slid back into his seat.

Knowing every rocky detail of their break-up and the scar it had left on Sydney's heart, Sydney's sister Hallie and Hallie's fiancé Ben Murray had warned her that Nate would be invited to their wedding. Ben had tried to convince Sydney that she'd misunderstood Nate all these years and that she should give him a chance to explain himself, that it would help her get through the wedding at the very least. Sydney had assured the couple she'd be just fine with him there whether she spoke to him or not. She was completely over it. Not until this very moment, under strands of summer twinkle lights and festive bouquets of hydrangea, had she felt like her knees were going to buckle.

Nate smiled at her guardedly from his aisle seat, while tucked in to the row next to him were the two women in his life: the plus one that had been written on his wedding RSVP card—an international supermodel and reported girlfriend named Juliana Vargas—and his sister Malory. If Nate was expressing his happiness to celebrate Hallie and Ben's wedding, that was one thing, but if that smile had been his feeble attempt to bury the hatchet with Sydney, given their history, he was completely delusional. She pushed herself to focus on someone else, her gaze landing on her friend Mary Alice, who gave her a tiny wave. Sydney smiled back at her before breaking eye contact. But her thoughts remained with Nate, her stomach in knots.

It had been years since she'd gotten her heart broken by Nate, and both of them had moved on with their lives. But two things had lingered, spiking her emotions when it came to him: the first was the fact that all those years ago, his leaving had made her feel like she wasn't good enough; the second was the overwhelming loss of the person he'd been and the gaping hole it had caused in her life. The four years she'd dated him, he'd been amazing, perfect for her, actually—he'd been her best friend.

Now, no longer Nate Henderson, he was known to the world as Nathan Carr, most eligible bachelor and songwriting superstar, not even his name recognizable to Sydney anymore. And he'd had the audacity to smile at her like everything had been mended between them. Wouldn't "I'm sorry" come first, at the very least?

"Benjamin," the preacher said, pulling Sydney back into the present where she should be: her sister's wedding at their gorgeous family beachside retreat, Starlight Cottage.

Sydney gripped her bouquet to steady herself and tore her eyes from Nate to focus on her sister and her soon-to-be brother-in-law. This was their moment, and it couldn't be more perfect. Hallie gazed up at the love of her life while Sydney looked on, under the cedar-shingled roof of the enormous gazebo, the southernmost point of the dwelling. The gazebo sat at the end of a pier that reached up to the shoreline where it met the boardwalk leading to the house Sydney and Hallie had spent the entire season renovating.

Growing up, Sydney had spent every summer at Firefly Beach, and when her divorce was finalized, she'd moved back for a few months to recharge, but returned to where she'd grown up in Nashville, since Hallie and her mother lived there. Then last summer, when Uncle Hank had been struggling with Aunt Clara's death, and Sydney had been given Aunt Clara's dying wishes to follow her heart, she'd moved back to Firefly Beach full time. Her mother divided her time between Starlight Cottage and her home in Nashville, but this summer she'd been there full time to help with renovations.

The gazebo where Sydney stood had been remodeled especially for the evening, widened to accommodate the throng of wedding guests in their rows of white chairs. The wedding had given them a timeframe, but their love of this place had been their motivation for restoring it.

Starlight Cottage was the home that had seen them through all their ups and downs. It had been revived originally with love and magazine-worthy décor by their great aunt Clara, designer extraordinaire, and when she'd passed it had fallen into disrepair. Now Sydney, Hallie, and their mother, Jacqueline Flynn, took care of it. With the grief that had been filling the hallways, her sister's wedding was like a warm coastal breeze flushing through the whole property, breathing life back into it again. The family's energy buzzed through the entire place, laughter filled the empty rooms, footsteps and banter tickled the hardwoods, and it was becoming the retreat that it had always been for them.

The ever-present salty air blew Hallie's veil despite the fact that they were all sheltered from the wind and the setting sun in an orange and pink sky. Ben's Labrador-spaniel mix, Beau, sat at his master's side, sporting a coral-colored bow tie. The dog tilted his head, his ears perking with interest as the preacher spoke.

"Will you take this woman to be your lawfully wedded wife? And whatever the future may hold, will you love her and stand by her, as long as you both shall live?"

"I will," Ben said, Hallie's hands in his as he peered down at her adoringly. Ben leaned toward her, clearly lost in the moment and ready to press his lips to his soon-to-be wife's.

"Wait," the preacher said, gently placing his hand on Ben's shoulder to stop him. "I have to get the rest of my lines out before you kiss her... That's my job."

The crowd chuckled and Ben looked back at the preacher, playfully impatient.

"Hey, I didn't write the rules for the wedding," the preacher added. "You two did."

Everyone laughed again, and in her amusement, Sydney let her eyes roam the front row of the guests, searching for her mother, to share in the moment of humor, but her attention was pulled toward Nate once more. This time, he was whispering something to the supermodel, the woman's eyes hidden behind her enormous designer sunglasses. She nodded at whatever he'd said and then fanned her perfectly smooth and professionally made-up face with one of the programs that Sydney had picked up from the printers herself yesterday to allow Hallie time to attend a final meeting with the wedding design team before the big night.

As if he could feel her gaze upon him, Nate looked back at Sydney, and his interpretation of her mood was obvious. This time, there were silent words in his stare. He had something to say, and the minute the ceremony was finished, she knew, by that look, that he'd find her to tell her whatever it was. Her mind wandered to places she could go to avoid him. She wasn't going to let Nate derail this evening. Sydney turned back toward her sister, basking in the happiness on Hallie's face as she and Ben continued their vows.

Sydney's eight-year-old son Robby, dressed adorably in his little tuxedo, his light brown hair combed perfectly to one side, held up the lace ring-pillow made from a swatch of Aunt Clara's vintage honeymoon gown that had been meticulously preserved over the years, in the back of her great aunt's closet. Their Uncle Hank had offered the dress to Hallie as a wedding gift, telling her that Aunt Clara would've wanted her to have it, and that he knew she could do something amazing with it. The soft blue satin had floated like the waves of the gulf over Hallie's arm when she held it out that night, deciding right then and there that it would be her "something blue" at the wedding.

Robby held the pillow above his head, just like he and Sydney had practiced all week, as the preacher untied the rings.

While Ben's friend from college sang the couple's song, "Marry Me" by Train, about knowing beyond a shadow of a doubt that The One is right there in front of him, Sydney tried to sort out the best way to avoid Nate at the reception while still being able to enjoy her family. She had planned to spend the entire night celebrating with her loved ones, rather than reliving old wounds. But what alarmed her was the pattering of her heart, just knowing Nate was out there. It was an involuntary response that she used to have every time he met her on the front porch of his parents' small beach cottage, bare feet, sun-kissed hair, those stormy blue eyes that used to swallow her like he couldn't get enough of her. . . .

She looked back at the bride in an attempt to refocus, but her racing mind wouldn't allow her to. Life seemed to move along neatly for her sister Hallie. Sure, she'd had her moments of uncertainty, but she was a successful designer, and she'd found the love of her life. Sydney's path wasn't quite so obvious. She had wanted to be in a better place before she'd come face-to-face with Nate again, but as fate would have it, she was still at her aunt and uncle's estate, Starlight Cottage, in Firefly Beach where he'd left her, the dreams of writing that they used to share now a distant memory for her, just like those long-ago days with Nate.

Memories floated into her consciousness, one in particular lingering: she and Nate were on a blanket in the sand one night. She was tired from too much sun and the rum-and-pineapple cocktails they'd been drinking. With their writing notebooks strewn out around them, he sat cross-legged on the blanket and she lay down and propped her head up on his knee, the fireflies swirling around them like restless stars. Laughter floated over the dune from Starlight Cottage behind them, both of them twisting around to see Uncle Hank and Aunt Clara in rocking chairs together on the porch.

"That will be us someday," Nate said, pushing a rogue piece of hair behind her ear adoringly.

Sydney rolled onto her belly and propped her chin on her

hands. "You sure you want to spend every single day of your life with me?" she asked.

His smile fell into a serious affection, his eyes devouring her. "Yes," he said with a quiet determination. "When you find the right person, it feels like you've found the rest of yourself. And that's how I feel about you. Without you, I'm not really me—just some half-empty version of myself."

He leaned down and kissed her, and even now, Sydney could still drum up the mix of fruity cocktails and the unique scent of him as his lips touched hers.

"I now pronounce you man and wife," the preacher announced.

Sydney blinked away the distraction, frustrated that Nate could still have that effect on her. She breathed in the briny air to steady her nerves.

"You may *now* kiss your bride."

Ben dipped Hallie, her arm dropping by her side, the bouquet dangling in her hand against the satin fabric of her vintage French couture wedding dress as the train fanned out along the boards of the gazebo. Their silhouettes were a picture of perfection in front of the glorious sunset that had materialized as if on cue over the water behind them. The crowd cheered. Beau barked. When Ben righted Hallie, the couple turned toward the onlookers, and Hallie was positively glowing.

The preacher stepped behind them, calling over the couple, "I now present to you Mr. and Mrs. Benjamin Murray."

Ben, a top Nashville music producer, had organized one of his new bands to play their jazzed-up version of a wedding march. He took Hallie's hand and gave her a spin, Hallie's train fluttering out around her ballet-slipper-style shoes. Then he dipped her one more time and kissed her again, the whole crowd whooping and clapping. While the music filled the air around them, mixing with the rustle of the palm trees in the ocean breeze and gentle lapping of the gulf, the wedding party made their way out of the gazebo and down the pier toward the reception.

Sydney took Robby's hand, grabbed Beau's leash, and walked in the procession, behind her sister and Ben. She kept her eyes straight ahead and tried to avoid the loaded look from Nate as she passed him. But walking across the lawn, her flats treading lightly down the path of rose petals, she knew just by his stare, that no matter how hard she tried, there would be no avoiding whatever it was that Nate had to say.

Chapter Two

"I just saw the food table," Hallie said to Sydney, swishing over to her in the incredible chiffon vintage gown with an open back and lace-edged empire waist that she'd picked out only a week after her engagement, when the two of them had gone out shopping.

Sydney smirked deviously.

Chewing on a grin, Hallie teasingly shook her sister by the shoulders. "Why do I have bowls of Doritos snack chips on the table between the dishes of lamb and rosemary appetizers and the prosciutto wrapped persimmons? Is this a football game?" Hallie broke her mock-seriousness and bent over laughing.

"That's what you said you wanted," Sydney said, unable to hide her own laughter. "There are also crystal dishes of pink bubble gum—did you see them? Dubble Bubble," she added as if that upped the status of the gum.

"Wait till your next wedding," Hallie said. "You're getting a Jell-O mold, a big, wiggly bride and groom in wild cherry."

Sydney burst into laughter.

When Sydney and Hallie were in elementary school,

they'd planned out their weddings. Sydney had wanted Jell-O for her reception, while Hallie had drawn a map of the table she'd wanted to see at her nuptials, which included Doritos and Dubble Bubble, both of which Sydney had managed to hide from her sister until this moment.

"You deserved the wedding of your dreams," Sydney said, still giggling. "Think of me as the magic maker."

Hallie rolled her eyes, still smiling from ear to ear before being pulled away to accept congratulations from a group of Ben's relatives.

Sydney waved at Robby from across the makeshift dance floor that had been built with old wood from original planks in the cottage. Aunt Clara had ripped them out in her previous renovation and saved pieces of them that were stored in the guesthouse basement. Hallie had decided they would be perfect at the reception. Together, Ben had sanded the edges, and Sydney and Hallie had oiled the boards, encasing the whole thing in an oak frame. It now sat in the center of the lush green grass, dotted by lanterns and hanging lights.

While couples filtered onto the dance floor, the band kicking up to a slightly more festive beat, Robby was at the dessert table, helping himself to the wedding-bell cookies and sneaking some to Beau. His light brown hair was disheveled, the sleeves of his tuxedo shirt were rolled to the elbow, and his jacket, shoes, and socks were long gone.

Robby was Sydney's whole world, the last remnant of the life she'd worked so hard for, which had come crashing down around her a few years ago when Robby's father Christian had left her for another woman. Sydney had known Christian since his family had moved down the road when he was fifteen but growing up, they'd never been anything more than friends. In her late twenties, he and Sydney reunited, falling in love quickly. They'd started dating seriously and soon after Sydney found herself swept up in a romantic whirlwind, everything moving in a flash. Not long after they started dating, they both admitted they had fallen head-over-heels. Christian rushed over one night, breathless, telling her he couldn't live without her, and before she knew it, she was planning her wedding. He'd ended up finding someone else, their relationship falling apart after only five years. She should've known it wouldn't last by the lackluster romance they had once they'd settled into their daily routine. It seemed he was more interested in the chase than the actual happily ever after.

As her sister began the wedding planning, Sydney feared he'd be invited, but Hallie had told her that even though they'd all known him forever, and he was Robby's father, she'd never put her sister in that position.

However Nate was a different story entirely. He most certainly got an invite.

A darling of the music industry, Nate Henderson had left Firefly Beach after college to pursue a career as a songwriter, and Sydney wasn't sure even *he* had been prepared back then for the future that lay ahead of him. In his career so far, he'd already achieved thirty-seven number one hits, and eleven movie soundtrack titles. His success, which earned him the title "King of the Ballad," and his unprecedented gorgeous good looks propelled him into the public eye and won him a spot on quite a few magazine covers. One of them had even titled his rise to fame as "extraordinary" and named him "Man of the Year." He and Ben, having grown up together, were easy collaborators in their line of work, and they'd teamed up on many major albums. A prominent Nashville news show had labeled them country music's dream team. So when Ben and Hallie began to make the guest list, Sydney knew that having Nate there would be inescapable.

Sydney allowed a little glance in Nate's direction, and it looked as though he was passing his business card to one of Ben's producer friends. *Ugh, figures*, she thought. She wondered if this was nothing but an opportunity to network for him.

She pushed her thoughts of Nate aside and swayed on the edge of the dance floor. The yard was full of candles and strings of lights in the trees, their branches hanging over masses of white tables adorned with magnolias and more hydrangea blooms bursting from centerpieces. It couldn't be a more perfect night. The weather was unusually cool for June, the evening temperature topping out at seventy-five degrees, without a cloud in the sky. With the sun now sinking low on the horizon, the fireflies had come out and were mingling with the crowd. Against the swells of champagne as the bottles were uncorked, and the live music, it was like a summer dream.

"Mom!" Robby said, running over to her with a handful of cookies. Beau chased him across the yard, both of them coming to a stop in front of Sydney. "Ben said later, when all the guests leave, if I'm still awake, he'll play football with me!"

With the wedding planning, Hallie and Ben had spent a ton of time around the cottage, playing with Robby to free up Sydney so she could plan with her sister. They were inseparable.

"It might be very late before everyone leaves, but perhaps you'll get a chance to play," she said, taking his free hand and swinging it back and forth to the music while he nibbled on the cookies in his other hand. Beau got tired of begging and trotted off. "Thank you for helping me hang the lanterns today," she said.

"You're welcome," Robby replied before popping the last cookie into his mouth. "It was fun!"

"You just liked sitting on my shoulders." Sydney reached over and tickled his sides, making him giggle. She wouldn't admit to him that he was getting so big that she'd had a pinched nerve from him being on her shoulders all day hanging the lanterns. She'd had to take ibuprofen to make the ache stop. But she would do it every day if he'd let her.

"Robby!" Hallie called from the dance floor. She twirled her train out of the way and beckoned for him to join her. "Come dance with me!"

Robby gave Sydney a bashful look. "She wants me to dance," he said. "Yuck."

Sydney stifled her laughter. "Aunt Hallie is only going to get married one time. This will be the only night you'll probably ever have to dance with her.... Unless you want to dance with her at your own wedding."

"I'm not getting married! Girls are double yuck!"

Hallie waved him over again.

"Go on. Ben dances with her." Sydney knew that Robby would do anything his new uncle did.

"Okaaay," Robby said, running over to the dance floor.

Hallie grabbed his hands and gave him a spin, introducing him to a few people around them.

Taking in the sight of him, Sydney thought about how wonderful he'd been while they'd restored the cottage and planned the wedding. He'd helped any chance he could get, sometimes sticking labels on the favors or folding the invitations, and when he couldn't help, like with the floral arrangements, he spent time drawing or playing outside. When she allowed the thought to filter in, she wished he had siblings and a better father. Robby only saw his father on the random holiday. Christian would call up out of nowhere, as if he'd remembered suddenly that he had a son. He'd offer to take Robby to a movie or some other location that didn't require a lot of parental supervision. Then he'd buy him something and bring him home.

If she were honest with herself, her life—and Robby's—wasn't what she'd hoped for the both of them. Growing up, she'd always envisioned that perfect little family, playing games together, reading stories at bedtime, taking summer vacations. That hadn't happened for the two of them....

Breaking through her reflections, Nate's voice sailed over Sydney's shoulder tentatively, and he was suddenly by her side, his hand outstretched to her. "May I have this dance?"

He had to be kidding.

"Shouldn't you be asking your date?" she asked, keeping her eyes on the crowd that had filled the floor around Hallie and Robby.

"Juliana didn't feel well...." he said, sounding shaky. "She went back to Malory's cottage..."

Sydney had been hoping to spend some time with Malory tonight. Malory and Sydney had spent their summers in Firefly Beach with one another, and the Hendersons and the Flynns were always together in those days. In fact, that was one of the things that had brought Sydney and Nate closer. He'd been that annoying big brother type, splashing her and Malory while they sunned themselves on the dock or chasing them around with the water hose when he was washing his truck. As they got older, he took on a more protective role and began to watch over them, walking with Sydney whenever she went home after dark to be sure she was okay.

Malory had been a driving force in getting Sydney and Nate together. She'd urged Sydney to spend time with Nate, telling her more than once that they were perfect for each other. She invited Nate to every activity the two of them did together. He was there for Sydney's softball games, he magically showed up at the ice cream shop when she and

Malory got mint chocolate chip ice cream cones. He found his way to the beach on the nights they made bonfires and roasted marshmallows...When they'd finally started dating, Malory teased them, telling them that if they ever got married, Hallie would have competition for maid of honor. "You're like a sister to me," she'd told Sydney.

When Nate left them all for LA, it was clear that Malory held on to a lot of guilt over Sydney's heartbreak. One night, as they'd sat together in near silence at the top of the lighthouse, the gulf, as big as Sydney's emotions, stretching out before them, Malory had apologized to Sydney for hurting her so badly by encouraging her brother's advances. And even though Sydney assured her that she'd done nothing wrong, the two of them drifted apart, the absence of the laughter that they used to have in Nate's presence settling heavily between them. About two months after he left, when Nate finally began making contact with his sister, calling her to catch her up on what he'd been doing out in Los Angeles, and Sydney had moved back to Nashville for the winter, Malory stopped calling Sydney altogether under the strain of the whole situation.

"I want to dance with *you*," Nate said.

Sydney forced herself to focus on the ruggedness that was still present on his face despite the years spent in the land of beauty and excess, and shook her head. His date had gone back to the house alone, and he'd wasted no time at all moving in on someone else. He was unbelievable.

"Sydney...." he said quietly. "Will you let me talk to you?"

He placed his hand on her arm, but she flinched, jerking it away instinctively. The reaction surprised even her. It had been a long time, and the wound was still very much there. She scanned the crowd, making sure they weren't drawing attention to themselves before she finally looked him in the eye, but she was at a loss for words. There was nothing more to say. She didn't like the man he'd become, and he'd made it pretty clear when he'd left that this was the lifestyle he'd wanted. Well, he'd gotten it.

"Look," he said under his breath, his voice tender, "we don't need to do this here. The last thing I want is to upset you—you deserve to be happy." There was a long pause, deliberation on his face. Finally, he said, "I won't bother you anymore tonight."

The disappointment and sadness in his eyes as he walked away made her second-guess her response to him, but she didn't trust it. All she had to do was remember how he'd left. The night before, they'd celebrated her huge accomplishment. Sydney had received a letter inviting her to travel around the U.S. for three months, documenting the work of Eugene Storer, a famous humanitarian who was collaborating with students from various universities.

One of her professors had asked her to apply, and she'd gotten accepted as a staff writer. Nate had brought over a bottle of champagne to commemorate the occasion.

"You're amazing!" he'd said that day, picking her up and giving her a squeeze, the champagne bottle in his grip, swinging with her as he turned her around.

"Do you think I should go?" she'd asked once he'd put her down, and she could still remember the complete bewilderment on his face.

"Why wouldn't you?" He leaned over and nibbled at her neck playfully, his arms finding her again.

"It means we'll be apart for a while," she said, earnestly. The thought bothered her more than she wanted to say.

When she said that, something registered on his face. "It's okay to be apart. We can make things work."

"I'd rather stay here with you, even if it means making

different choices in life. All these things pulling me away...
I feel like it would ruin us."

He stared at her, clearly working something out. "Is
that why you didn't transfer to Emerson College like you'd
wanted to? Because you were worried about being away
from me?"

"It's in Boston, Nate. We'd never see each other."

"It's *the* top journalism college in America, and you were
accepted," he countered. "You'd told me that living in the
north would be too cold and busy...."

"It all means nothing if I can't be with you. Relation-
ships are about compromise, right? Being with you is more
important than some fancy college. And the same holds true
for this trip."

"Syd, I *overwhelmingly* support you going on this trip.
I've never met anyone as talented as you are. You can't let
your feelings about us hold you back from what you were
born to do."

"I don't know...." she replied, unable to articulate how
much it would bother her to be away from him. She knew
this was a fantastic opportunity, but was now the right time?
"Let's celebrate that I got it," she said with a smile. "We can
decide if it's the right thing for me to do later."

As the evening went on, he'd seemed slightly withdrawn,
but it was late, and she figured he was tired. She remembered
how much love she felt for him that he was working so hard
to mark the occasion given how worn-out he clearly was,
and she hadn't thought a thing about it when he'd decided
to go home alone instead of staying over like he usually did.

She had no idea what awaited her the next morning, so
full of joy and anticipation.

She just couldn't understand it, the grief of losing him
stinging her like a pack of bees, swarming her for the longest

time. They'd dated exclusively throughout college—madly in love with one another—and they'd talked about "forever" as if it wasn't just a possibility but a reality. They'd been so in love that she just knew after graduation, he'd pop the question and they'd live happily ever after. But instead, out of nowhere, he'd broken her heart, moved to LA, and begun to build a larger-than-life persona that included dating actresses and supermodels and jet-setting across the world, leaving his old life—and her—behind.

She'd gone on that trip with Dr. Storer after Nate left, but she'd spent the entire time missing him, and she never really felt much like writing after that.

When the two of them had sprawled under the oak trees together with their pencils and notebooks, their aspirations floating around them like untouchable butterflies, she'd never considered that their lives would turn out so differently.

Now, he was a famous songwriter, and she'd ended up leaving Nashville unemployed and moving back to Firefly Beach for good, having quit her job as a paralegal on the advice of her Aunt Clara, who had told Sydney in the inheritance letter that the one regret she never wanted Sydney to have was to look back on her life and know that she hadn't used her talents.

Sydney took in a deep breath and tried to get her emotions under control, the music from the dance floor filtering into her mind again as she returned to the present.

"I heard Justin Timberlake is here somewhere," Uncle Hank said, walking up to Sydney.

Uncle Hank had really come a long way this past year. They hadn't been able to get him to see a counselor for his grief over the loss of Aunt Clara, but he'd made strides, and restoring the house back to its original condition had seemed to help.

"And did you see that woman Nate was with? She's famous too, you know." His bushy gray eyebrows danced animatedly. "She's a swimsuit model in that magazine." He waggled his finger in the air, clearly trying to remember the name of it.

"Yes," Sydney replied, his excitement making her feel a little better.

"And there are so many country music stars here that I can't keep track of them all," he carried on. "I've had my eye on the guestbook to make sure no one runs off with it. With all the signatures in it, someone could retire if they sold it on eBay."

Sydney laughed. "Uncle Hank, I'm so happy you came up just now. I needed that." She wrapped him in a warm hug, the tight squeeze of his arms around her taking her back to her childhood. He was in good spirits, and it was so wonderful to see.

For the last year, Sydney and her son Robby had lived at Starlight Cottage along with her mother and Hallie when they came for long stints as their work schedule allowed. They'd thrown themselves into restoring the cottage and helping Uncle Hank get back on his feet after the death of her beloved Aunt Clara. But now she was at one of those turning points in life where she knew change was about to take place; she just hadn't actually figured out how to make it happen.

Uncle Hank was doing incredibly well, and he'd even asked his brother Lewis who lived alone in his own cottage down the road to stay with him some of the time so her uncle needed her less and less. Sydney had been looking at jobs over the last year and none of them had hit the mark yet, but she had found a few new ones to look into. On a bet with Hallie, she'd sent her résumé and a significant writing sample to a major New York magazine called *NY Pulse* that was offering a remote content editor position in the world and humanities section, but with no formal writing experience, she knew nothing would come of it. The one thing she was certain about, however, was that Firefly Beach was where she wanted to be, and the right opportunity would come along.

Uncle Hank's expression sobered. "I saw Nate walking away," he said, his disappointment in Nate's choices made evident by his frown. Nate hadn't just left *her*; he'd left them all. Uncle Hank had checked the oil in Nate's truck and topped it off whenever it was low; he and Nate had gone fishing all the time together; and any evening that Nate was at Starlight Cottage after five o'clock, he was certain to get an invite to dinner, many nights staying over on the sofa. "I never liked that boy anyway," Uncle Hank said, but his smirk and the fondness in his eyes gave away his lie. "And he was a *terrible* football player."

Sydney burst into laughter then. Uncle Hank had managed to get away with the first fib, but that whopper was too difficult to let go. Nate's team had won the championship his senior year, and he'd been offered college football scholarships to a few small universities, but he'd turned them down to pursue songwriting and attend Belmont University in Nashville. She'd loved visiting him there. In the winters, he'd been right down the road from her mother's home in Nashville, and then, when the universities would let out for the summer, they'd travel to Firefly Beach together. She would stay at Starlight Cottage with Uncle Hank and Aunt Clara, and he'd stay with his parents down the road.

"You plan to talk to him?" Uncle Hank asked.

A server came by with a tray of champagne and Sydney grabbed one, tipping it up against her lips and swallowing a sip before answering, "Probably not."

"You gonna spend the night with that champagne instead? I know Nate's a headache for you, but I can guarantee the champagne packs a stronger punch."

She offered a half grin.

"You know he's moved back, right?"

"What?" She nearly spilled her champagne, her hand going limp and the glass tilting precariously to the side.

"He couldn't wait to get out of Firefly Beach all those years ago. Why would he want to come back here?" she said, nearly spitting the words at her uncle.

"You could ask him." Uncle Hank nodded toward a group of tables where Nate now sat, fiddling with the stem of a wine glass while he talked to a family member from Ben's side. The woman was getting up as they finished whatever it was they were chatting about, leaving him alone at the table.

"I'd rather not," she said, finishing her champagne and switching out the empty glass for a new one when the server came back by. But then, her fears subsided just a little when she remembered an article she'd read on him, highlighting all the homes he owned and noting how he'd barely lived in any of them. Every time, he spent a few months in a new place, immersed himself in renovations, and then he'd get bored, leaving it to sit vacant while he moved on to the next place.

Robby skipped across the grass, coming to a stop beside them. "They're almost ready to cut the cake, Mama! Ben told me!" he said, swiveling toward Uncle Hank at the same time. "Hi, Uncle Hank." He beamed up at him. "Are you gonna have cake?"

"Absolutely!" Uncle Hank nodded with vigor.

"I know *I* am," Sydney's mother said, joining in on the conversation. She straightened her white rose and baby's breath wrist corsage, the smile she'd had all day still plastered across her face.

"Hallie just has to throw her flowers at people first—that's what she said." Robby added, "What's that all about?"

Sydney laughed. "Not throw them *at* people; she probably said she was going to throw them *to* people. It's the bouquet toss—an old tradition."

"All the single guys are gathering for the garter now," Jacqueline said, pointing to the group of men huddling around Ben as he pulled out a chair for his bride. Hallie sat down, to the whoops of the crowd, her wedding dress puffing out around her. Sydney noticed Nate's seat at the table where he'd been sitting was now empty. She tried to locate him in the crowd but was unsuccessful. Maybe he'd gone. She could only hope.

Ben walked around the chair and kneeled down in front of Hallie, a playfully suggestive look on his face as his hands disappeared beneath her gown to a drum roll, not emerging again until he'd pulled the garter over her foot. He twirled the little slip of lacy elastic on his finger and the single men roared again. Ben turned his back to the group, waving it in the air. Then he tossed it behind him, the garter sailing over the heads of some of the men as they jumped to get it. An arm shot up from the center of them all, and Sydney recognized the suit sleeve immediately, her disappointment surfacing. It was definitely Nate's. The garter disappeared in his fist and the crowd parted.

Sydney's attention went straight to her sister. Hallie was already looking back at her, and Sydney subtly shook her head. Her sister nodded, telling her with that silent gesture that she wouldn't throw the bouquet in Sydney's direction. The last thing Sydney wanted was to allow Nate to push that garter up her leg. She wasn't superstitious, but she couldn't be too careful. She didn't need anything pointing toward her marrying Nate. No way.

"Are you going to try to catch the bouquet, Mama?" Robby asked.

She squatted down to eye level with her son. "Do you want me to?"

She knew, after her explanation to him that, as legend had it, the person who caught the bouquet would be the next to marry, Robby would be worried. Sydney would love Robby to have a solid father figure in his life, and to witness a happy marriage, but, over the years that his new uncle Ben had been with their family, Robby had bonded with him so strongly that he wouldn't give anyone else a chance. Sydney had introduced him once to someone she'd met at the coffee shop in town and he'd refused to even say hello. Later, Robby fretted that she was going to get married to the guy, and he didn't want her to. They'd spent so many years, just the two of them, that anyone moving in on that dynamic would be a major disruption.

"You don't need to catch it, do you?" he asked.

Sydney glanced over at Nate. "Definitely not."

Robby grinned.

"I'll tell you what: I'll go out there so I can be a part of Hallie's big night. There are lots of single girls who would love to catch it." Then she leaned toward him and whispered, "And I've already told her not to throw it to me." No sense in worrying Robby over a silly wedding tradition. "But I'd better hurry so we can get to the cake-cutting, right?"

"Yes, Mama!" Robby pushed her forward lightheartedly.

Sydney hustled out to the group of girls, waving her arms early to give Hallie her coordinates before her sister turned around. Hallie gave her a silent okay and, with her back to Sydney, she raised the flowers into the air. Nate was at the edge of the group, his eyes on Sydney, the garter dangling by his side from his pointer finger. She stared back at him and offered her best don't-even-think-about-it look while the girls counted down, "Three! Two! One!"

Hallie threw the bouquet, the heaviness of it creating an unforeseen arc. It sailed straight for Sydney. She quickly stepped to the side, the bundle of flowers landing with a thud onto the grass. One of Ben's cousins scooped it up, waving it in the air.

Sydney offered one more look at Nate before walking back toward Mama and Uncle Hank. On her way to them, a striking man about her age, with wavy blond hair and a friendly smile, whom she hadn't met before stepped into her path.

"Hello," he said with a kind smile and gentle eyes. He was strikingly handsome—probably one of Ben's new singer-songwriters. "Bride or groom?" he asked.

"Uh, bride—technically—but both, really. You?"

"Groom."

She knew it.

"I'm Logan." He held out his hand in greeting. "Logan Hayes. And you are?"

"Sydney Flynn." She returned his handshake. "It's nice to meet you, Logan."

"Likewise," he said, with a smile. "Having a good time?"

Sydney thought about her evening so far, wishing Nate would disappear. "Yes," she lied.

But there was a flicker in his eye and he tightened his focus on her.

She felt her cheeks flush at his observation. "What?" she said, caught off guard, her pulse rising.

"Your face just went all red."

"Oh, it's just my blush. Blame my sister. She did my make-up for the wedding. I had to stop her before she gave me eyelids that rivaled a Jackson Pollock."

"Mmm," he said with a chuckle. He looked out at the crowd. "It's a beautiful wedding. Probably one of the most perfect weddings I've ever been to."

"Yes," she said, looking over at Hallie who was positively glowing as she nearly floated across the grass from guest to guest in her exquisite gown, Ben on her arm. "I agree."

"It would be a pity not to enjoy it." He eyed the dance floor. "Want to go out there?"

Sydney considered Logan's request as she looked around for Robby. He was at the edge of the yard, playing games with a group of kids, so he wouldn't notice her. Then she caught sight of Nate. He was standing in a group of people, but his gaze was fixed on her. "I'd love to," she said, grabbing Logan's arm and hurrying to the dance floor.

As soon as they hit the dance floor, Logan took her by the hands and moved her arms to the music, spinning her around and pulling her into him. His grip on her was commanding but careful in a way that made her feel completely comfortable. Her satin dress slid up and down against her with the movement of his hands, and she allowed herself to enjoy the night, to relish the attention, and to shut off from everything except for this moment under the rising moon and twinkling string lights.

They danced until she'd forgotten all about her worries. Logan was an enjoyable partner, slipping in little funny comments as they moved to the music of the band. When they finally stepped off the dance floor, he turned to her. "We should get a cup of coffee sometime."

"That would be nice," she said, the reality of Robby's issues regarding men sliding into her consciousness now, making the idea of going on a date more difficult than giving a simple yes.

Logan leaned over to a nearby table and swiped a cocktail

napkin. With a pen from the inside of his jacket, he scribbled on it and handed it to her. "This is my cell. If you ever want that cup of coffee, give me a call."

"Thank you," she said, folding it and securing it in her fist.

"It was wonderful meeting you," Logan told her.

"Same." Sydney felt a lift in her spirit as he walked away.

The wedding guests had dwindled and Jacqueline had taken Robby up to bed. Ben was spinning a now barefoot Hallie on the dance floor while Sydney sat amidst a table full of empty glassware and leaned on her hand, her eyelids drooping from such a big day. She'd hit the ground running at about five thirty this morning, helping Hallie finalize the last few details. She'd organized the wedding party breakfast at Starlight Cottage, gotten five women through hair and make-up, and picked up Beau from the groomer's in town—all while trying to keep her own appearance wedding-ready, wearing one of Uncle Hank's button-down shirts and flowers in her up-do. The wedding couldn't have been better—she was so happy for Hallie. Her sister deserved this night.

Sydney contemplated heading in to the cottage, all the champagne and festivities making her feel like she hadn't slept in weeks.

"You could've caught the bouquet," a familiar voice settled over her, making her fatigued shoulders tense up.

Nate dropped down into the chair beside her. His jacket and tie were gone, the top button of his shirt undone, and his sleeves rolled. He looked as tired as she felt, but she sort of liked it, because when he relaxed, he seemed less like Nathan Carr and more like Nate Henderson. It gave her a rush of nostalgia, and for the first time in quite a while, she considered how much she missed him.

"Is your date still sitting alone at your sister's cottage?" she asked, ignoring his first statement.

"Malory's with her."

She'd have liked to have been a fly on the wall when Nate had faced his sister. It was no secret that Malory wasn't happy at all with the fact that Nate hadn't been back to see anyone since he'd left. While he'd called his sister fairly often, he hadn't bothered to come back for any length of time, until now.

When his parents passed away, they'd left him their cottage in Firefly Beach, and it held so many memories for Sydney. There were six mailboxes between Starlight Cottage and the tiny little house where Nate Henderson used to live. She'd counted them every day that she'd made the walk between the two homes. On those lazy summertime days when she'd traveled that route with Nate, their faces warmed from a day in the sun, both of them barefoot, her sandals swinging from her fingertips, she'd never have imagined this. Nate had returned once a few years ago, and everyone wondered if he'd finally come back to spruce up the cottage his parents had left to him and his sister, but instead, he'd leveled it and created two separate lots: one with Malory's new cottage and another that sat abandoned while the weeds got cut twice a month; nothing had been done with it. He'd left in less than twenty-four hours.

Sydney twisted toward Nate to figure out exactly what he wanted when he'd said himself that he wouldn't bother her any more tonight.

"Can we talk?" he asked, surrender in his eyes. In that light, he looked just like he had all those years ago. She could almost swear she saw that same love in his eyes now that she'd taken for granted when they were younger. She'd have never imagined that she'd have to go so long without it.

Sydney was completely drained. Her head ached, the pinch in her shoulder was back in full force, and she'd had too much alcohol to have any kind of major conversation. All she wanted to do was crawl under the crisp covers of her bed, up at the cottage, and sink into glorious sleep.

"It's a little too late for that," she whispered and to her complete surprise and panic, tears welled up in her eyes. She was clearly exhausted, and had definitely had too much to drink. She blinked away her emotion. It had been easy to be strong when his face was on a glossy magazine cover, but with him right there in front of her, it felt too much like old times, and her resolve was slipping. She cleared her throat to keep the lump from forming.

"I feel like we never really got any closure, and that was my fault," he said, the softness of his voice as warming for her as the morning sun under the crisp coastal breeze. He looked out over the yard, littered with party debris. The gulf shone like diamonds under a full moon as fireflies danced along the edge of its lapping waves. "I haven't been able to get any of this right," he admitted. He looked back at her.

"And I just want you to know I'm sorry, Syd. I'm so sorry."

It was surprising how much her heart ached still when she let him get close enough. She'd thought she was over it. And now he'd just apologized, which was the one thing she'd wanted in all this.

But there was a part of her that was cautious about his motives. Right before her wedding to Christian, Nate had called her out of the blue—it had been the first time they'd spoken since he'd left that day for California. Things had started with her being angry, just like they had today, but he had sweet-talked his way into an easy conversation, and she'd found herself wondering about what could've been. It had terrified her, since she was on her way to the altar with someone else whom she thought she loved, and she'd cut the call short.

Later, she'd heard from someone in town that he'd tried to buy his sister's cottage out from under her, asking her to move, and Sydney couldn't help but wonder if he'd wanted something that day, which only made her feel more terrible for allowing her feelings for him to bubble to the surface. He'd upped his game tonight with an apology. Did he want something now?

Nate stood up and held out his hand. "Take a walk with me?"

She stared at the slight pout that his lips made when he was asking a question; it was an expression that she knew so well. There wasn't a shred of arrogance in his eyes, and she wanted so badly to believe the honesty she saw.

But life was about forward movement, not getting stuck in something from the past that obviously wasn't going anywhere, judging by his wedding date who was still sitting back at Malory's. She knew what she had to do. Sydney picked up the shoes that she'd kicked off earlier and stood in front of him in her bare feet.

"I don't think so," she told him. Then she walked off toward Starlight Cottage, feeling a swell of pride but knowing that the minute she got to her room, she'd let the tears come.

Chapter Three

The old farm table in Uncle Hank's kitchen at Starlight Cottage was abuzz with family this morning. The coffee pot gurgled, filling the room with the heady, chocolaty aroma of ground coffee, while the small television on the kitchen counter chattered in the background, offering up a day of glorious weather ahead.

Hallie and Ben had wanted to stay for breakfast before leaving for their honeymoon—their suitcases were already packed and ready against the wall. Sydney tried unsuccessfully to ignore the reading material for the plane that Hallie had stacked with their bags. The magazine on top had a giant photo of Juliana with a thumbnail of Nate in the corner. The headline read, "The It Couple's Decision to Leave the Spotlight: Is It a Publicity Stunt?" Had they fled to Firefly Beach to drum up interest in some new project? She took in a gulp of air to clear her mind and turned back toward her family.

Uncle Hank and his brother Lewis were chatting about the local news while Robbie wriggled up next to Ben to find out when he'd be back from the honeymoon so they could play football in the yard. Beau sighed from his dog bed in the corner. The regularity of the scene was comforting to Sydney, given the events that were invading their normalcy.

Sydney and Jacqueline had been up cooking since the early hours like they did sometimes. Sydney had come downstairs to find all the kitchen windows open, allowing a picturesque view of the turquoise Gulf and a warm breeze to blow in intermittently. Sydney hadn't slept well last night, and she wondered if the alcohol from the wedding had made her restless. She certainly wasn't going to admit to herself that it had anything to do with Nate being right down the street. Her mother hadn't asked about Nate, which only made Sydney more uptight about him. When Jacqueline was quiet, she was thinking. Well, her mother shouldn't have *anything* to think about when it came to him.

Sydney took the serving bowl of potato casserole over to the table and sat down with the rest of the family, her mother following with a platter of eggs.

"So what's everyone else doing today?" Ben asked, grabbing a few pieces of bacon from one of the dishes with the serving tongs and placing them on his plate before passing the dish to Hallie.

"I'm starting my new job today," Sydney said, buttering a biscuit. Sydney had been hired to write a small column for a section in a national magazine called *You* where she answered letters that were sent in. "I've chosen my first week's letters," she said. "I'm hoping the writing might get my creative juices flowing again." It wasn't the job of her dreams or anything, but it was a step toward her goal of getting into the business of content writing. "And I'm seeing Mary Alice for lunch. She says she has a favor to ask."

"Oh, that's wonderful!" Jacqueline said. "I haven't seen Mary Alice in so long. Remember when you two used to do that lemonade stand together?"

"I do," Sydney said, remembering her friend.

Uncle Hank beamed at her. "You're going to be writing again?"

"Well, writing letters, yes, but it's a start."

"It certainly is," Uncle Hank said, clearly delighted.

Growing up, Sydney had wanted to write about world events, interviewing people and bringing light to humanitarian issues, dreaming of traveling to faraway lands and documenting all the splendor of the human race. Once she got in to college, her interests widened to more social topics, but her love of writing never left her. She'd consumed entire days climbing shelves in the local library and gathering all her information to help her understand culture and history, and then she'd meet Nate, spending evenings after he'd gotten off at the beachside bar and grill where he worked on his summer break from college, both of them scribbling in their notebooks for hours—Sydney writing her articles and Nate writing songs.

Nate had written her more love songs than she could count over the four years they were together; she'd cherished every one of them. Her favorite moments were the ones when he'd drop his pencil, roll onto his back and play with melodies, humming the words to different tunes. Then he'd turn back over and scratch down a few more notes. During creative lulls, he always wanted to read her pieces. He said it recharged him. He'd been so supportive of her writing, telling her that she was going to do great things one day, and to remember him when she shot up so high that she'd have to look down to see everyone. Funny how ironic life could be sometimes.

She'd heard some of those songs on the radio, but every time one came on, she turned it off as fast as she could. She didn't want Nathan Carr's version of them to taint those precious moments they'd had together.

"Local Firefly Beach residents are going to face the largest summer crowd on record for this small village...." the television said, pulling everyone's attention over to it. "The current public beach area downtown," the reporter continued, "is the busiest location in all of Firefly Beach. From May until September...." The video footage showed the steady stream of people as they filtered through the access point to the shoreline, leaving bottles of sun lotion, trash, and swim gear in their wake to litter the coast. "And it's getting worse," the reporter said. "Local contractor Colin Ferguson, builder of the new beachfront hotel Luxury in the neighboring village of White Sands, is hoping for the opportunity to build on Firefly Beach's unspoiled shores, which will send even more people to the village as they look for uncrowded beaches."

Jacqueline clicked off the TV.

Uncle Hank picked up his cup of coffee but didn't drink it. "Lewis and I will be attending the town meeting today to show our support for maintaining our coastline," he said, filling the quiet that had settled over the table.

With the wedding and everything on her mind, Sydney had totally forgotten about the potential problem facing Starlight Cottage. Some people on the town's board of supervisors wanted to lessen the foot traffic downtown, so they had proposed a public beach access down the road from Starlight Cottage. "What's the latest?"

"They're still pushing the public beach access that would run along the lots right next to Starlight Cottage, and the most recent development is the additional plan for expansive parking and retail. That's where Colin Ferguson is getting involved."

"From what I've heard, the shops are supposed to stretch the length of road between the old Henderson lot and us,"

Jacqueline said. "I'll be very interested in hearing the specifics after you attend the meeting today," she said to Uncle Hank.

With the growth of tourism in the surrounding villages, the number of visitors finding their way to Firefly Beach had increased, and it was only a matter of time before the town would be facing the same summer gridlock that its neighbors were already dealing with.

It had taken two crews to maintain the cleanliness and quality of the public beach last summer, so to alleviate the growing congestion, the local government was planning to open a second access point, bulldozing all the trees and small cottages that separated Starlight Cottage from the town.

Starlight Cottage had been in the family for generations, but her great Aunt Clara and Uncle Hank Eubanks were the first to give the home a name. They'd called the cottage Starlight because of the lighthouse that sat on its own private peninsula, jutting out into the sea, behind the main building on the Eubanks' sprawling property. For years, the lighthouse had illuminated the water over a distance of nearly twenty miles, assisting the usually dazzling stars when cloud-cover hid them. With the increased use of electronic navigational systems, it wasn't a working lighthouse anymore, but Aunt Clara had always maintained it, and on Christmas, she lit it. She said that, on that night in particular, she wanted just one more opportunity to get sailors home to their families where they belonged.

Earlier this year, Sydney and Hallie had organized the revitalization of the lighthouse along with the surrounding structures—everything had been painted a bright white, the gazebo widened, landscaping along the seashell paths leading to the shore, boat docks, spacious patios out back ... It was completely restored to the way it had been when Aunt Clara was alive—a little oasis, secluded just enough to make Sydney feel like she could escape the stress of real life for a while. But if the planning commission had anything to do with it, things wouldn't stay that way for long. As a girl, Sydney used to take in the sweeping coastal views from the top of the lighthouse, but now there was a possibility that she could be looking down at a mass of out-of-town cars instead of the palm trees and little southern cottages that she loved so much.

"There's no way that plan will ever get off the ground," she said. "The city would have to knock down all the houses between us and the corner lot. I can't imagine that the neighbors would give up their land," she added, holding out hope.

"Well," Lewis piped up. "Yesterday, I ran into Tom McCoy from down the road, and he told me he *would* sell if they made him an offer he couldn't refuse. The growth in the area recently is what made him finally decide he'd let it go. He wants to move down the coast. The sale of his land could give him enough to retire."

A wave of uncertainty washed over Sydney. "Then he wouldn't be running the fruit stand anymore. . . ." she considered aloud.

The McCoy fruit stand was anything but a simple stand. It was an enormous expanse that stretched the side of the McCoy home and across part of the front lawn. Tom hosted hayrides and face painting for the kids; he offered free dog biscuits for pets of anyone stopping by, and he always managed to have the sweetest peaches in Firefly Beach. On walks between their houses, Sydney and Nate would always stop there. Since they were kids back then, Tom would give them each a peach free of charge every time.

"When are you gonna let us pay?" Nate would tease him.

"When you bring your kids here," Tom told him.

If only they'd all known how things would turn out....

"Will you tell me anything new you find out today?" Sydney asked Uncle Hank and Lewis, not bothering to hide her concern.

"You know I will," Uncle Hank replied.

She wished she could go with them to offer her own opinions on the matter, but she knew that Uncle Hank wasn't shy about sharing what he thought. The future of Starlight Cottage was in good hands.

"Text me to let me know what happens," Hallie said, apprehension written on her face.

Sydney laughed. "I'm not texting you in Barbados! You and Ben deserve this time together."

Unable to have children, Hallie and Ben had decided to adopt, and they'd completed and passed the home study. They'd gotten everything filed at the agency they'd chosen, and they were currently awaiting selection as adoptive parents. Hallie and Ben were so excited, but Sydney knew, from raising Robby, how important their time as a couple was.

There were eight chairs at the table and seven family members at Starlight Cottage. They'd said, after Aunt Clara passed, that the empty one was for Aunt Clara, but Sydney was more than willing to bet that Aunt Clara wouldn't mind sharing her chair with the newest member of the family when he or she arrived. It was as if the spot were just waiting to be filled, and now the empty chair felt less like an old memory and more like Aunt Clara, with her arms open wide, poised like she used to be, ready to grab on to her loved ones as they rushed toward her.

After breakfast, Uncle Hank took his coffee and went out to his spot on the back porch overlooking the sea, where he'd been going every morning recently. Sydney joined him, lowering herself into one of the rocking chairs. Uncle Hank rocked back and forth, his eyes on the turquoise water as it caressed the white sand, ebbing and flowing in a hypnotic way, while the breeze turned the paddle fans that lined the porch ceiling above them.

"When your Aunt Clara died," he said, still gazing out to sea, "what struck me most at first was the silence. It was just me in this big house and the quiet was so loud that I couldn't stand it." He took a drink from his mug and tipped back in his chair, rocking. "I didn't have Clara's chatting about nothing." He grinned at the memory.

Uncle Hank had struggled with Aunt Clara's death for a long time, but having his family around, and Sydney and Robby living there with him, had helped him. He was back to himself again. And he enjoyed talking about Aunt Clara, often telling Sydney stories she'd never known about her great aunt.

"She was always buzzing around," he continued, "asking me questions about something she'd noticed in town, or deciding out loud whether she should make us new cushions for the outdoor porch swing, or she'd point out the change in color of the palm trees that I never could see...My whole life with her, I'd never prepared myself for what it would be like to be without that. But every morning since the whole family has been here for the wedding, I feel that buzzing again, as if Clara's spirit is in all of us."

"I thought about her this morning," Sydney said. "Her chair at the table...I miss her, but I feel like she's here."

"Me too."

"What do you think she'd say about the public beach access coming our way?" Sydney asked.

Uncle Hank laughed. "I think she'd have already been in their offices, driving them crazy. She'd have produced an entire alternative plan, and it would almost certainly be something they'd never thought of, *and* it would work better than one anyone else could've devised. 'Firefly Beach is in our soul,' she used to say. She wouldn't let them come near it."

"She was so creative and talented."

He nodded, content.

They both looked out at the tranquil gulf, its crystal waters rushing in and out all the way to the lighthouse and beyond. Something told Sydney to take it in. She couldn't help but feel like this was the calm before the storm.

Mary Alice Chambers looked exactly the same as she had as a girl. Her white-blond hair was swept up in a bun, accentuating her sky-blue eyes.

"Thank you for meeting me," she said to Sydney as she sat down at the little bistro table on the deck at her favorite restaurant. The red and blue bungalow known as Wes and Maggie's was surrounded by palm trees and sat right on the water in a strip of sand. Matching red and blue flags, fighting madly against the coastal wind, lined the outdoor seating, which was usually full of vacationers, but it was early afternoon and, as she looked out to the shoreline, the beaches were still crowded with visitors. She could remember when that beach was only dotted with a few residents, and now it was towel-to-towel, on the strip of sand.

Next to Wes and Maggie's was Cup of Sunshine, the coffee shop, where Sydney had spent many mornings reading and job-hunting since their WiFi was stronger than the connection out at Starlight Cottage. Locals and visitors alike couldn't get enough of their signature butter pecan latte or their homemade pumpkin pie breakfast bread, and the owner Melissa was a master at preparing delicious French toast served with a drizzle of cream cheese syrup. Every patron, no matter how small the purchase, went home with a complimentary dark chocolate truffle that had an icing-piped chocolate sunshine on the top. As Sydney had walked past this morning, on her way to Wes and Maggie's, Melissa caught her eye through the window of the shop and waved like she always did.

"Hey, pretty ladies," Wes said as he came over to Sydney and Mary Alice. He was an old family friend and owner of the restaurant. "What kind of day is it for the two of you—an iced tea day or try-my-new-Passion-Punch day?"

"Passion Punch?" Mary Alice replied, as she shifted her bag to get comfortable in her chair.

"It's got two kinds of rum, strawberry daiquiri puree, and a splash of pineapple and coconut. I've been selling 'em like hot cakes to the tourists. I even have new painted paper umbrellas with coconuts on them." Wes, an artist, was known for the hand-painted little umbrellas he placed in every drink he made at the bar.

"I'm up for one if you are," Mary Alice said, consulting Sydney.

"Two Passion Punches then," Sydney said to Wes.

"Comin' up! Anything else?"

"I'm fine for now," Sydney replied. "Mary Alice?"

"We'll start with drinks, but I'm not going to definitively say I won't be ordering your seafood sampler."

Wes laughed. "If we make one for someone, I'll have them throw a few extra bites onto a small plate for you, on the house." He gave her a wink and headed toward the bar.

Once Wes had left them alone, Mary Alice placed her forearms on the table, leaning closer. "Your mother told me at the wedding that you got a new writing job."

"Yeah, it's nothing too grand, but I'm hoping it will get me warmed up in case something bigger comes along. I'm writing a daily column called 'Dear Ms. Flynn' for the *Panhandle Gazette*."

"That sounds interesting."

"People write in with things that are weighing on them and I answer." She shrugged to convey that it wasn't the most glamorous of writing jobs but it was a start. "But enough about me! Tell me what you've got going on—it sounds huge."

Mary Alice beamed, pulling a glossy brochure from her bag. "I had these made this week," she said, her eyes shining with excitement as she pushed it across the table. "It's for my new wellness center."

"Oh wow," Sydney said, opening the brochure to view the services offered by the center. "This is great."

"Thank you." Mary Alice beamed. "It's a big leap, but I've decided to start my own center here in Firefly Beach so I can give back to the community that I love."

"That's amazing," Sydney told her, setting the brochure down. "I'm excited for you!"

"Thanks!" Mary Alice offered her a big smile. "I was wondering if I could ask a huge favor."

"Of course," Sydney said. "What is it?"

"I'm offering a free magazine for my patients . . . and I was wondering if I could ask for you to use your content editing skills? It needs a front cover, would you be able to help with the layout and photo shoot for that, and maybe offer me some quick ideas for the organization of the magazine? I can't afford a full staff and I know how good your attention to detail is."

It would be nice to be a part of something with such passion behind it, Sydney thought. She still had her inheritance and the money from the sale of her house back in Nashville, so she didn't mind taking this time to do a little something for herself. It had been a long time since she'd allowed herself to be solely in the creative field, and she still wasn't sure she could do it, but she'd never know until she tried—it was where she was always the happiest.

Mary Alice ran her hand over the brochure that had a photo of a family gathered on a picnic blanket with the title in block font:

SEASIDE FAMILY CALM AND WELLNESS CENTER
A complete approach to a healthier you.

"Absolutely." Sydney felt a thrill just looking at the pamphlet in front of her. This type of work was right up her alley. "I can see the title *A Better You* on the cover of the magazine. Just thinking out loud, you could have a range of sections that might go something like...'Find Yourself,' covering organic and cruelty-free products, vitamins, local spots to get outdoor exercise...Maybe a section on the latest in psychology, for example, a spot on meditation or mindfulness...You could call it 'Mind over Matter'?" She kept going, the ideas flooding her. "You could even do another piece with celebrity spotlights—people in the public eye who are making a difference in their environment and themselves, and then ways to help and get involved...."

When she looked up, Mary Alice had her hand over her mouth, covering a giddy smile, her eyes wide. "I *knew* you were the one to ask," she said. "I already love it all. Would you be free to come in to the office when we open tomorrow at nine? I have counseling clients already lined up first thing, but I'll show you some of the ideas I've got to get you started."

"Of course I would!"

"That's amazing. I'll set up a table for us in one of the spare rooms at the center so you and I can have a quiet place to talk."

"That sounds marvelous."

Wes brought their drinks to the table—tall narrow glasses filled to the brim with dark pink liquid, a slice of pineapple on the rim, and his signature umbrella, speared through mixed fruit, floating on top.

"I suppose these drinks are celebratory," Mary Alice said, her eyes dancing with enthusiasm for the project.

Sydney, nearly overflowing with hope, raised her glass. "Cheers to that."

Chapter Four

Sydney clicked on the lamp as she sat at the desk in the small office she'd converted from Aunt Clara's sewing room, leaning back in the chair she'd chosen during the renovation of the cottage because of the oatmeal color that matched so nicely with the linen drapes. She opened her computer to begin her first response for her column, under the banner of "Dear Ms. Flynn." She opened the first letter:

> Dear Ms. Flynn,
> I'm writing you with a heavy heart. I've taken a new job and had to move away from my entire family. Now I'm all alone in a new city....
> Best wishes,
> Rebecca

Sydney copied and pasted the letter into a new document and began her response, addressing the sender:

> Dear Rebecca,
> It must be terribly difficult to be without your family.

Her fingers stilled and she stared at her screen, thinking, but nothing was coming to her. What should she say to this woman that could make her feel better? Should she take the approach that this kind of thing happened sometimes and this too shall pass? Sydney tipped her head up and focused on the crystal light fixture in the ceiling, trying to think of just the right thing to say. What would it feel like if she moved away from everyone? Well, she wouldn't. But if she did... Sydney placed her fingers on the keys but they just hovered there. None of her ideas seemed heartfelt enough.

A wave of fear washed over her. She hadn't written in years. What if she didn't have the ability to do what she used to do? What if she was too jaded to be that open? Sydney closed her eyes, trying to force the creative energy, but she was coming up empty. How had Aunt Clara done it? She'd been a successful designer and no matter what was going on in her life, she could just create. Almost on command. "Tell me what to do," she said silently to her aunt, praying she'd hear her in the heavens and send some sort of magical answer down to her.

She leaned back, her eyes falling on the new drapes she'd hung and a memory of Aunt Clara came to mind, making Sydney smile. When Sydney was about fifteen, she'd gone in to the living room once when Aunt Clara was hanging a new pair of curtains. Her aunt was up on a ladder with a pencil in her mouth and a measuring tape stretched out between her fingers. "Why do you keep changing the curtains?" Sydney had asked her.

The measuring tape zipped back into its spool, and Aunt Clara took the pencil from her lips and tucked it behind her ear. "Well, darling, the first set of drapes were an idea I'd had years ago. But if you keep relying on the old ideas about what works, you may never actually let enough light in. There's always room for change." That had never made sense until right now.

A knock at the door pulled her attention away from the screen. She shut her computer. "Come in."

Uncle Hank peeked into the room. "What are you doing?" he asked, curious.

"Trying to let the light in," she said.

Uncle Hank frowned. "Isn't it already coming in?" he asked, peering over at the window.

"The creative light," she clarified.

"Ah," he said, sitting on a nearby chair.

Sydney scooted over to give him more legroom.

"The elusive creativity."

"It's just not flowing right now," she said, wondering again about Aunt Clara's advice.

"Not being the artistic type, it's difficult to know how to help you. What did you used to do to get into an imaginative mindset?"

Sydney chewed her lip. She didn't want to say that she used to talk to Nate. He could always help her. But just as Aunt Clara had said, if you rely on the old ideas about what works, you may never let enough light in. Nate definitely didn't let her see any light now. His star was so large that it overpowered everything in his path. No one else could even twinkle. "I can't remember what helped me," she lied. "Did you need me?" She set her laptop on the floor.

Uncle Hank looked around the room. "This house has grown with us," he said. "I just assumed it would continue to do so...." He took in a deep breath and let it out slowly. "They only sent one of the board members to the meeting today," he said. "And he was there simply to jot down our questions."

"Do you think they're listening at all?"

He shook his head. "No. Tom's the only one who's agreed

to sell his property, although he hasn't signed a contract yet. The others are all against the project, but I could see their interest when they heard what was being offered for their land. I don't know how the county is getting the kind of money they're proposing."

"It's not right," she said. The image of their quiet street crowded with cars and people filing onto the beach along their side yard flashed in her mind, causing a lurch of panic. Starlight Cottage had always been Sydney's safe place, away from the noise that life could bring. It was the place where she'd stayed in the years following Nate's leaving, the house she'd retreated to when her marriage dissolved, where she'd spent every childhood summer, and now it was her home. The calm of this estate had been her quiet getaway from life's stresses. She'd never have imagined that one day she might have to survive without it.

"We've asked for another meeting, and we want the full board there." He pursed his lips in disapproval. "But it's not looking good for our case. The impact on residents is small—the public beach would only affect five of us on this street, since the area isn't built up. I'm worried the other Firefly Beach residents will be in favor of the project, or at the very least not be opposed."

Jacqueline came in with a plate of leftover wedding cookies, setting it down on the side table next to the chair. "I thought you could use a pick-me-up," she said. "How's the writing going?"

"I haven't really gotten started," Sydney replied, the seed of fear sprouting in her gut. "I was just reading the first letter when Uncle Hank came in."

"Are you talking about the meeting?" she asked.

"Yes," Sydney said, the weight of the impending decision sitting heavily on her.

"There's nothing we can do about it right now. We've offered up our questions and concerns, and asked for another meeting." She grabbed a cookie. "Try not to dwell on this," she told Sydney. "Focus on your new working adventure."

Despite her worries about the cottage, with the support of her family, Sydney felt something moving within her, and she wondered if this would be the change she needed. It would certainly take her a while to get acclimated to a creative mindset again. But she couldn't wait to get started.

"It's strange without Ben and Hallie here," Jacqueline said as she fiddled with the petals of one of the geraniums in a pot on the back porch. She'd come out to enjoy the salty evening air before starting supper, and Sydney and Robby had joined her.

Sydney settled on the porch swing they'd installed just before Hallie and Ben's wedding. The couple had had their engagement portraits taken on it—Ben sitting with Hallie lying beside him, knees up, her head resting on his knee. They'd looked incredible. Even Sydney noticed the absence of the calm they both brought with them anywhere they went together.

"I miss Ben," Robby said.

Sydney's chest tightened. Ben had been with their family for years—Robby's entire life—and he was the only man who'd ever really connected with him. With Ben starting his own family, Sydney couldn't help but worry for Robby. When the adoption came through, Ben would be with Hallie, and where would that leave her son? Robby was too young to understand the demands of adulthood, and he was bound to feel left behind by both Christian and Ben.

Robby's father was barely around. He'd moved on with

his life, leaving them behind. He showed up at major holidays but only ever stayed a few hours. And now his new wife was expecting a baby, so he'd be wrapped up in his new family.

"I miss Ben and Hallie too," she said, keeping her thoughts to herself.

"Can we call Ben?" Robby asked, climbing up onto the swing with her.

"Sorry, honey. When two people are on their honeymoon, they're usually pretty busy sightseeing and spending time together," she said with a discreet wink to her mother. "We need to give Ben and Hallie their privacy."

Robby's face dropped, and Sydney already felt the disappointment that would unquestionably settle upon him as time went on. She wanted to give him more healthy role models, but she just didn't know what to do. She'd tried to take him to see Gavin Wilson, who owned the art gallery in town, thinking they could connect on a creative level this summer, but Robby refused to talk to him. Then he'd worried incessantly Sydney was going to date Gavin, which couldn't be further from the truth. He was only an acquaintance, a friend of Hallie's. It wasn't healthy, but she didn't know what to do. She figured she might run it by Mary Alice at some point to see if she had any suggestions from a counseling perspective.

The crunch of gravel on the walk leading around to the porch where they sat pulled her from her introspection. A lone, overlooked paper napkin, the last remnant from yesterday's wedding, blew like a tumbleweed across the lawn until a masculine hand stopped it, balling it up in his fist, and shoved it into the pockets of his jeans. Sydney followed the arm up to the face, her mouth drying out. She stood up.

"May I help you?" she asked Nate.

"Hi," he said, his hand raised in greeting. When she

didn't say anything, he lowered it slowly, his eyes full of silent messages to her that she couldn't decipher, and really didn't want to.

"Robby," Jacqueline said. "I need your help snapping the ends off the green beans for supper tonight. You're so good at it. Think you could help me inside?" She eyed Sydney. Her mother knew all about Nate, and she also knew exactly what Sydney thought of him.

"Okay," Robby replied, regarding Nate cautiously. He followed Mama inside.

Nate stepped onto the porch. "I thought I'd stop by," he said, moving toward her tentatively.

Sydney backed away, her heart racing.

"I didn't push you at the wedding because it wasn't the time nor place, but I was wondering if you'd hear me out." He took another step forward, and this time she allowed the proximity, her curiosity getting the better of her. "Let me get this off my chest and then you can tell me to leave. Because if I don't say anything, I'll regret it, and when it comes to us, I have enough regret already."

At least he wasn't entirely heartless. Although, judging by how quickly he'd moved on to better things in LA after leaving Firefly Beach, she doubted he'd spent long nights, his heart breaking until the tears were literally flooding him, the emptiness so raw that he didn't know how he'd pick up the pieces. Seeing him brought it all back for her, and she scolded herself for letting him affect her.

"Can we just be us for a little bit?" he asked. "Just you and me, Syd?"

She felt the swell in her chest at the thought of him and her, like old times. But the problem was that they'd been irrevocably changed by everything that had happened. "We've both moved on with our lives," she said. "You're not who you were anymore and neither am I. Dragging each other through our muddy past isn't healthy for either of us."

His gaze dropped to the floor, but it was clear that his thoughts were somewhere else. "I hadn't meant to change...." His voice trailed off.

Sydney wondered if he regretted leaving, and despite her anger about how he'd handled things, she felt an odd sort of guilt for making him question something that had led to his success. "Your life now is your destiny," she said. "I know that because you are an incredible songwriter. You deserve to be right where you are. You don't belong under the oaks at Firefly Beach anymore, Nate. *We* are a casualty of that success, no matter how rocky the journey was to get you there."

Sadness seemed to wash over him, and before she could act on it, his arms were around her, his familiar scent of fresh cotton and spice overwhelming her senses and making her lightheaded. The feel of his chest against her face took her right back to those years they'd spent curled up together all night after they'd stayed up writing and talking about their future, neither of them wanting to move as the sun broke on the horizon, the day inching between them and making them finally get up. She fought back the prick of tears.

"My heart will always be under those oaks with you," he whispered into her ear. Sydney worked to swallow the lump forming in her throat, the ache that had been long forgotten surging through her with a vengeance. In that moment, how he'd left wasn't what surfaced, but instead a deluge of memories from all the wonderful times they'd shared together, and she realized that even though she kept telling herself that she shouldn't, she loved him, and if she allowed herself to admit it, she was *still* in love with him.

Nate pulled away and looked down at her. "Even after all this time, it feels like yesterday," he said.

Sydney knew that telling him she felt the same way would do more harm than good. Keeping him at Firefly Beach because of her would be like caging a wild bird—his wings were too big for this town, and it was only a matter of time before he'd leave again.

She was still swimming around in her feelings when the reality of the whole situation set in: it wasn't fair to Juliana to have her boyfriend running around after an old flame. So why was he? That single question pulled Sydney back into the certainty that Nate Henderson was no longer the person standing in front of her. The very best Sydney could hope for was to have the strength to keep her emotions in check until Nate had his fill of Firefly Beach and pulled away from town and away from *her* for good.

"Mr. Carr," she said quietly, purposely using his pen name to drive home the point, "it isn't yesterday." Sydney had to literally push the words from her lips when all she wanted to do was to fall back into his arms as if the time that they'd lost had been just a bad dream. "If you're here to say you're sorry, then apology accepted. But I'd appreciate it if you would, *please*, let me move on with my life." Her heart slammed around in her chest, and she feared that he could see through her.

Nate stared at her questioningly. It seemed like she was hurting him, but what did he expect? He might be used to girls falling at his feet these days, but Sydney wouldn't be one of them.

"Mama?" Robby's voice tore through the moment.

Sydney whipped around to address him. "Hi, honey."

"I'm all done helping with dinner." His little eyes fluttered over to Nate.

"This is . . . an old friend," Sydney said. "His name is Nathan Carr." The name rolled heavily off her tongue.

Robby moved slightly behind her when Nate bent down to say hello.

"You can call me Nate," he said gently. When Robby refused to acknowledge him, Nate stood back up.

"Will you say hello to Nate?" Sydney asked him.

"Hello," Robby said bashfully. Then he turned to Sydney. "Will you come inside soon?"

"I'll be inside in just a minute," she told her son as he ran back into the cottage.

"Your son looks like you," Nate said. After that, he was quiet, unspoken words on his lips.

Sydney remembered the article she'd read where he'd said he couldn't see himself with children, so his comment seemed laden with the screaming reality that what they wanted in life was very different.

They both stood together—so many obstacles stacked between them—and then he spoke again. "I wish things could've been different. I thought I was doing the right thing at the time. . . ."

That call he'd made to her right before her wedding came to mind. Despite the way things were between them, he'd made her laugh, bringing up an old memory. And now, here he was, trying to tell her how he felt, when his girlfriend was down the road. In both instances, his timing was unbelievable, and absolutely selfish of him.

He shook his head as if he were jostling the emotions free, an exhale bursting from his lips. Sydney wondered if he, too, was thinking that he shouldn't be there. She felt guilty for the tiny bit of pleasure she got in his presence. It seemed as though there was unfinished business between them, as if something was still left unsaid and they had this minute to say it.

"I should probably get inside," she said, wishing all their

problems could be like helium balloons and they could both just let go, watching them float away until they were so small they didn't matter anymore.

"Well, look who the cat dragged in," Uncle Hank said, stepping outside. His expression was playful but also a little cautious. "I've missed ya."

Nate smiled. "Caught any redfish in the slot?" he asked Uncle Hank.

That was always their first conversation when they hadn't seen each other in a while. Nate would come home for the summer, sneak up behind Uncle Hank on the shore, throw his arm around him, and ask him that question. Sydney had grown up fishing at Firefly Beach with Uncle Hank so she knew that "in the slot" meant that he'd caught a fish that measured between seventeen and twenty-seven inches in length. Law only allowed fishermen to keep one redfish per day that was in the slot.

"Caught a bull in the Choctawhatchee Bay. Thing weighed twenty-nine pounds."

Nate raised his eyebrows in interest. "Did you keep it?"

"Nah. I threw him back."

Nate chuckled. Uncle Hank was never one to keep the fish. Nate had said once that he thought Uncle Hank actually enjoyed setting them free more than hooking them. He'd never harm a soul.

"I didn't get to talk to you at the wedding," Uncle Hank carried on, rotating toward the sun and closing his eyes briefly while the orange light washed over his face. "But I've got time now." He turned to Nate. "Wanna come inside and have dinner with us?"

"What about Juliana?" Sydney heard herself ask. Just saying her name out loud caused a torrent of remorse to pelt her insides. Sydney was letting old feelings for Nate seep

back in, and now Uncle Hank was asking him to dinner—
not a good idea.

"She's having a spa day with Malory. They aren't getting
back until tonight," he said. "They're going to a new beachfront restaurant down the road, in Rosemary Beach."

Juliana was getting to know Nate's sister, spending time
with her...People didn't do that unless things were serious.
But then Sydney's feelings turned to frustration. Why was
Nate even standing on her porch? Had he left for Starlight
Cottage the minute Juliana was out of his sight? Sydney
had seen the magazine headline: things were looking up
for them. Well, maybe Juliana would like to know that her
boyfriend had run off to his ex-girlfriend's house...It all
gave her a bitter taste in her mouth.

"I don't think he's hungry," she offered, sending an icy
glance in Nate's direction. The ease with which he could
pull her in unnerved her, and all she wanted was for him to
leave.

"I'm starving, actually," Nate said.

Uncle Hank threw his arm around Nate. "Well, come in
then. We've got an extra seat at the table."

Was this really happening? How would she hold a normal conversation with him there? What were they all going
to talk about anyway? She wouldn't be able to eat a single
bite; her stomach would be in knots. Suddenly, Sydney
wished she would have crawled into Hallie's suitcase and
shipped herself right off to Barbados because right now, as
he looked back at her with those unspoken words of his, she
wanted to be as far away from Nate Henderson—or should
she say Nathan Carr?—as she could be.

Chapter Five

Over the years, Sydney had allowed moments of affection for Nate, but the more she thought about it, the more she convinced herself it was simply a longing to have the old Nate back. Seeing him in Firefly Beach, those blue eyes on her in the same way they had looked at her so long ago—it was toying with her rational side. She'd gotten very good at building up the walls that could keep her safe from heartbreak, and until Nate went back to LA, she'd have to put that skill to the test. Because he *was* going back to LA, and back to his life and back to his girlfriend.

Judging by the sparkle in Uncle Hank's eyes when he talked to Nate, she wondered if he'd missed Nate as much as she had. Uncle Hank had asked him all about Malory and the cottage, how he was doing, and whether he was happy to be back in Firefly Beach again . . . Sydney had focused on bringing the food to the table and tried to have a regular conversation with her mother to drown him out. She barely even looked Nate's way.

Nate's phone went off at the table, the irritation scratching down her spine as he picked it up. "I'm so sorry," he said, "may I take this call?" Nate put the phone to his ear and stepped over toward the door. "Nathan Carr," he said into his phone in a business-like tone that she'd never heard before. "Hey . . . Yes . . . I was going to touch base when we're all in the same room for the Grammys . . ." He stepped outside for a second, an awkward lull hanging in the air as everyone tried to ease the disruption. Soon he was back inside, setting his phone on the table, and dropping into his chair.

It frustrated her to see him sitting in Aunt Clara's chair. In her mind, that place was reserved for family, and he didn't feel like family at all anymore.

"So Nate," Jacqueline said with an uneasy smile, "how's the songwriting business?" She passed him a plate and a handful of silverware.

"Busy," he said. "But in my business, busy is good." He took a roll from the platter and passed the plate to Lewis. "I thought coming home would give me a break from the madness, and it has, but I can't stop writing songs here. I've written three new ones in the last two days." He glanced over at Sydney.

Sydney remembered how he'd get stuck sometimes when writing. He was always in motion, telling her how move-ment helped him think, so she'd tacked little stories about their lives—memories—to the trees around the property to inspire him. As they walked together, talking and reminisc-ing, he'd stop and jot down a few lines. Before she knew it, he had notebooks full of them. "You're my muse," he said once, before pulling her in for a kiss and wrapping his arms around her. He'd always insisted she was a more talented writer than he was—now, judging by his success, it was clear he'd been so wrong.

"That's wonderful," Jacqueline said, dragging her from her thoughts. "Sometimes we just need to have a new perspective for the ideas to come. Would you share one of your songs with us?"

Nate buttered his roll, his mind clearly heavy with something. "Okay," he said, and his gaze landed on Sydney. "I've got one in particular that I'm writing and I haven't gotten the beginning yet, but I have the chorus. Here it goes. . . ." He started to sing.

"If only I had that moment back
That day, that hour, that minute
Would life have carved out something more—
A life with you in it?"

Sydney dropped her fork, the utensil clanging to the ground, stopping Nate. The lyrics were too close to her own heart to bear, but that was what he was great at, right? He used to take her feelings and turn them into songs, but this was too much. He was a master at storytelling. He could spin fiction until it was difficult to know what was real and what wasn't. Sydney stood up to get the fork, bumping the table and jostling everyone's glasses. Nate's juice sloshed over the rim of his glass, spilling onto the table. "Sorry," she said, picking up her fork. She sat down and handed Nate her napkin.

"It's okay," he replied with a look of questioning interest.

"That sounds like the start of another hit," Uncle Hank said, once everyone had settled again.

"I truly think my creativity has spiked because I'm getting back to my roots. It feels good to be home."

"Too bad Ben's not here," Uncle Hank said. "We could all go fishing like old times. Have you been since you've been back in Firefly Beach?"

"I haven't." Nate took a drink of his iced tea and swallowed. "I don't have a fishing pole anymore."

"Good grief, son! What kind of life are you livin' out

there in that big city?" Uncle Hank teased, making Nate laugh.

"I'd love to go fishing," Nate replied.

"Just say the word." Uncle Hank leaned over to Robby and whispered, "You could come too," he said. "We can show him how it's done."

Robby grinned up at Uncle Hank, but all Sydney could think about was the fact that she didn't want Nate at dinner or fishing with Robby . . . She just wanted him to leave.

"I'm free all evening," Nate said, his expression serious and intentional.

Uncle Hank's face lit up. "I've got bait and rods out back if you're looking to shore fish tonight."

Nooooo. Sydney did not need Nate hanging around Starlight Cottage any longer than he was already. Why was Uncle Hank being so accommodating when he knew how she felt? Her uncle had been there the day Nate had left her. He'd seen her moping around for weeks, for months, unable to get her head around the fact that the future she'd been building in her head for years had come shattering down around her. Uncle Hank knew how much Nate had hurt her. What was he doing?

"I'd love to."

Robby sat up on his knees. "May I fish with you, Uncle Hank?"

"Of course you can!"

Was Sydney on some kind of hidden camera show? Didn't anyone realize that Nate hadn't bothered to contact a single one of them in years, but now they couldn't seem to get rid of him—wasn't that a little too weird?

"Uncle Hank, after dinner, can I speak with you?" Sydney asked to the hush of the table.

"Of course you can." Uncle Hank seemed unfazed by her

request. "But you'll have to make it fast, unless you'd like to fish with us...."

"I think we need to show him how great life is here at Firefly Beach," Uncle Hank explained when Sydney had pulled him aside to find out why in the world he'd asked Nate to dinner and then to stay this evening.

"Why, when he's moved on from us and from here?"

"When you're young, it's only natural to move beyond where you came from, to see the world and push yourself to find your own limits. I watched your Aunt Clara do that with her design business—it took her all over the world. But once a person has that perspective, if they're lucky enough to get the chance to look back, they'll see what's most important: the people they love. That's why your Aunt Clara always came back to this home and to her friends here. These people are more important than any *place* in the world. Nate has experienced success; he's been away. We've been blessed to have him return. Let's show him what he's missing in that big city of his."

Uncle Hank had good intentions. He wanted to fill that silence he'd spoken about earlier, and he truly enjoyed having all his loved ones around him. But Sydney wasn't so sure he'd want *this* Nate back. She worried that Nathan Carr would disappoint him. After the year she'd spent helping Uncle Hank deal with his grief and get back onto his feet, she felt extremely protective of him.

"I'm fishing too," she said, the tension in her chest rising at just the thought.

Uncle Hank, obviously misinterpreting her decision, beamed. "Excellent. I'll need help with the supplies."

When they all got down to the shore, Nate cast his line

into the gulf as the salty tide rippled around their ankles. Sydney reeled hers in just a bit and waited, the way Uncle Hank had always taught her to do. Robby and Uncle Hank were down the beach from her—Robby wouldn't speak to Nate, so they'd fallen into an odd pairing because Robby still needed quite a bit of instruction and Uncle Hank was the one who did that best.

"I know Ben was happy you came to the wedding," she said, trying her best to make small talk.

Nate nodded, reeling in when he got a tug on the line, but then evidently deciding it was a false alarm, so he let it be.

"What does Juliana think of Firefly Beach?" she ventured.

Sydney had read that Juliana Vargas, a swimsuit model, had traveled the globe and lived in luxury at various sought-after beach locations like Fiji and Belize. She was the third highest paid model in the industry and her Instagram feed looked like an advertisement for the diversions of the rich and famous. The quaint little village of Firefly Beach was probably quite a different experience for her.

"She likes the quiet," he said, not taking his focus off his line. The breeze coming off the gulf rustled his hair like it used to do when they were young. "And the seclusion."

His answer was surprising. "I just assumed, by what I'd read about her, that she preferred things that were more—I don't know—fast-paced."

Nate finally looked her way. "She grew up in a little village in Argentina. Her grandfather owned a small winery. She said that her only companionship there was the breadth of the grape vines on their fencings and the mountainous rock that jutted into the sky. She showed me a photo of it once."

Sydney gave him her full attention.

"The red-rock hills around the town have these incredible stripes on them; they're beautiful." He reeled in, checked his bait, and then recast his line. "All that to say that she's not used to the craziness she's been immersed in lately. It doesn't come naturally for her, and while it's exciting, she feels like she can breathe when she's here."

Hearing such personal information about Juliana made the situation more real, which only caused Sydney to feel more uncomfortable about being with Nate. While they weren't doing anything wrong, she felt the pull of their past whenever she was with him, and there was the fact that he'd come over today at all. The whole situation was unsettling.

Sydney got a tug on her line, jerking her attention to the rod in her hand. The line began to pull harder, her rod bending with the force of whatever was on the other end. She started to reel, gripping the handle with all her might.

"You got something?" Nate reeled his line in quickly and set his rod onto the powdery sand behind them, ready to help her like he used to do so long ago.

The line was taut between the end of her rod and the lapping water as she reeled, barely able to get the spool to rotate an entire turn fast enough. Her breath caught when Nate was behind her, his arms around her and his breath at her cheek. His hand was on top of hers, reeling faster now. Panic shot through her and she felt woozy from the sheer proximity. She ducked out of his grasp, leaving him to reel the fish in on his own.

"You don't want to claim the catch?" he asked with a sideways grin.

"Nope," she said. "You can have it."

Nate reeled it in, grabbing the line just above the fish's mouth. "It's a redfish," he said proudly. "Hey, Hank! Syd caught a redfish!" His use of the nickname he used to call her crawled under her skin like a swarm of fire ants.

Uncle Hank and Robby both looked over from their spots down the beach. "In the slot?" Uncle Hank asked.

"Looks like it could be a keeper!" Nate called to them. "Got a measuring tape in your fishing gear?" With the rod in one hand and the line in the other, the fish dangling from his fist, he jogged over to Uncle Hank and Robby. Sydney followed.

"You can throw him back," Uncle Hank said, predictably.

Nate held the fish lower. "Robby, want to see what your mom caught?"

Robby set his rod in the sand but didn't step toward Nate.

Nate held the fish a careful distance. "Has your Uncle Hank told you about the spot here on his tail?"

"No," he said, looking away.

"It's said," Nate nearly whispered, his voice dramatic, despite Robby's quiet protest, "that they grow spots on their tails so other fish will think it's their eye." Carefully, he moved closer to Robby.

Robby took a step backwards, but his interest was undeniable. "Why?"

Nate continued, "They can heal a lot more easily if the other fish takes a bite out of their tail instead of their head."

Robby leaned in just a tiny bit and peered closer at the tail of the fish, fascinated. "That's cool," he said.

"Syd, can you grab those pliers for me?" Nate asked.

"I've got 'em," Robby said, running over to the plastic box of supplies, most likely to get away from Nate. He grabbed the tool and carried it over to his mother, handing it to her.

Sydney walked the tool to Nate.

"I'm going to cut him loose. Want to watch him swim away?" he said to Robby.

Robby kept quite a distance but followed Nate into the water until it was up to his knees. With swift, fluid actions, Nate used the pliers to release the fish. It dropped from the hook and shot through the surf, disappearing. Robby smiled, a genuine sparkle in his eye as he looked up at Nate, taking Sydney's breath away. There, in the setting sun, Nate and Robby were side-by-side grinning at each other like some sort of family postcard. But then Robby quickly moved away from Nate, running back up onto the shore.

"Robby, it's probably time to go inside and get your bath," Sydney suggested, the look they'd shared a little too close for comfort.

"Ah, let him stay up," Uncle Hank called over, holding his fishing rod, his line still sunk in the waves.

There was no way Sydney was allowing Robby to warm up to Nate. Yes, she wanted him to have a male role model in his life, but Nate was *not* the one to serve that purpose. And there was no way this would end well, because Nate would undoubtedly leave and Sydney knew she couldn't count on him to keep in touch. Nor did she really want him to anyway.

Nate took the pliers over to the box and stopped by the bag of fishing line and lures. "Oh, look what's in here," he said, pulling out the football that they'd used for family games in the yard. He backed away from them. "Hey, Robby! Can you catch?" He held up the ball. "Go long!"

Robby seemed torn between the game he loved so much and the fear of allowing Nate to interact with him. But he started to run, hands in the air, his eye on the ball as Nate let it go. The ball fell perfectly into Robby's arms and he cradled it as he ran through the yard toward the house. Sydney couldn't deny the similarities in interests between Robby and Nate. Her mind moved to Robby and his newly found love of drawing, the image of him on his belly in the grass with his notebook open, scribbling away, and a pang of trepidation shot through her.

"Nate's a heck of a football player," Uncle Hank called up to Robby as the little boy headed to the house.

Robby stopped and turned around to listen to Uncle Hank.

"He was a famous receiver in his time." Uncle Hank reeled something in on his line. When he realized he'd pulled up a clump of seaweed, he dislodged it and threw it back into the water.

"Can you catch this then?" Robby called to him. He threw a pass to Nate, who caught it, the ball coming to a silent stop in his hand.

"Good throw!" he said, looking over at Sydney in surprise.

"I think Nate should come over and play a football game with us tomorrow," Uncle Hank offered.

"Okay!" Sydney butted in, putting a hasty stop to the conversation. "Bath time. Ask Nana if she'll get your water to a good temperature. I'll be up in just a bit."

"Okay...." Robby replied.

"I'll go up and make sure he gets his bath," Uncle Hank said, setting his rod down next to his tackle box, "if you two would bring these things up to the house for me when you're done."

"Thanks," Sydney said.

"I'd love to play tomorrow, Robby!" Nate called up to the house.

Sydney's pulse was throbbing in her ears. Nate had been awfully chatty with Robby despite what she knew about him never planning to have children. If he was using Robby to get Sydney to change her mind... He wouldn't dare do that... She began to question even his hug earlier. As soon as her son was out of earshot, she stomped over to Nate. "What do you think you're doing?" she snapped through gritted teeth.

"What do you mean?"

Nate's look of innocence was infuriating. "Listen, you can come waltzing back here, throwing out lines about how sorry you are, trying to make amends for leaving everyone who loved you with barely a goodbye, and we're all adults; we can handle it. But don't you dare pull my son's fragile emotions into this."

"I...." Nate shook his head, stunned and obviously at a loss for words, but Sydney was so terrified at the possibility of her son getting hurt that she didn't bother to decipher Nate's feelings on the matter. "I just got caught up in the nostalgia and excitement of fishing here at Starlight Cottage again. I found that football and I wasn't even thinking.... I was just playing around. I miss this...."

"Well, Robby isn't someone to play around with. And neither am I." She grabbed the rods, collecting them all into her arms, her hands shaking as she shut the tackle box and secured the latch, picking it up. Then she snatched the football and shoved it into one of the bags, her arms full.

"Here, let me help you—"

"I've got it!" she barked, jerking away from him, all the fishing gear in her small arms. To her frustration, tears were surfacing again in her eyes, and she didn't want him to see them. He'd crossed the line tonight.

"Syd...." He came up beside her, trying to take something off her hands.

She pulled away again, his efforts only making the tears worse. "Go home," she said, her voice breaking as she attempted to swallow her emotion.

"Talk to me." His hand brushed her arm softly, sending a shiver down her spine.

"I'm done talking," she said, refusing to make eye contact with him for fear that her resolve would crumble into a million pieces when she looked into his eyes. This was the last straw. She lugged the fishing gear through the yard, dumping it at the edge of the back porch, and she went inside without looking back. She had to be strong. For herself and for Robby.

Chapter Six

Sydney held her mug of coffee in both hands, the caffeine a welcome sight this morning when she'd come downstairs to a full pot still warming. Her mother had made it for her, with a note that said, "Have a great day!" Sydney was heading in to the wellness center to chat with Mary Alice about the magazine.

The house was still quiet as she sat in the crisp morning air—that slip of time before the sun brought the intense heat of the day—the French doors ajar, the porch open to allow the breeze to come inside. She walked over to the open living area that was adjacent to the kitchen and ran her fingers along the whitewashed chest Aunt Clara had bought because she thought it resembled the color of a sand dollar. Everything in this room was hers, down to the creamy textured walls and the carved driftwood moldings along the doorframes and windows. Sydney could still remember Aunt Clara's excitement as she'd shown them all once they were installed. "Feast your eyes on this!" she'd said, delighting in customizing this cottage to make it feel uniquely theirs.

Beau got off his cushion and greeted her. She reached

down and patted his head and his tail wagged weakly. It was clear that he missed Ben.

"I know, boy," she said to him. "Ben won't be gone too long."

Beau's ears perked up at the mention of his master's name.

Sydney took a long drink from her mug, savoring the nutty, smooth flavor of it and stared out of the bay window at the gulf. It was another perfectly clear early summer day, the palms dancing in the breeze, the bleached sand nearly glowing like a winding strip of white paint out at the shoreline. One of the groundskeepers was up early, cleaning the glass of the lighthouse. She'd had to hire a brand new staff to take care of the Starlight Cottage estate after Aunt Clara had passed away. Uncle Hank wasn't great at managing the property himself, and in his grief of losing Aunt Clara, he'd let the place fall into disrepair, but now Starlight Cottage was just as it had been growing up, and Sydney couldn't imagine being anywhere else.

She was glad for the comfort of the cottage this morning. She'd been up a lot of the night, thinking about what had happened yesterday, wondering if she'd overreacted. Nate had no right to offer to spend time with Robby without discussing it with her first. But she kept thinking that if it had been anyone else, she would have been overjoyed to have an opportunity for Robby to warm up to someone.

"You look nice," Jacqueline said, coming into the kitchen. She walked over to the window and put her arm around her daughter.

"Thanks," Sydney replied, giving her mama a side-squeeze.

Sydney had curled her hair and put on make-up. She'd even decided to wear the pink summer dress she'd found on sale at the beginning of the season that matched her flats almost perfectly. After helping Mary Alice, she was heading to the coffee shop to make some headway on her first Ms. Flynn response. Today was the start of something great—she could feel it—and she wanted to step into this day believing change was coming. Mary Alice had texted yesterday to confirm with Sydney that she had a therapy session at nine o'clock, but she'd be ready to meet with Sydney a few minutes before, and she would have some ideas laid out. Just the idea of working on something new filled her with a buzzing excitement.

"I heard you tossing and turning in your room last night," her mother said. "You were restless. Was something on your mind?"

"Nate being back has been hard." She hadn't wanted to bring it up before she left for work for fear that it would own her thoughts all day.

"I know," her mother said, consoling her with another little squeeze. "Do you think he regrets leaving?"

Sydney shrugged, still unable to process her own feelings on the matter. There was a side of her that reverted to the twenty-two-year-old who still struggled to cope with the grief of losing her best friend. But the woman she'd become knew better and wanted to put up the protective shield that she'd worked so hard to erect over the years.

"I think he misses you," her mother ventured.

"He made his choice," Sydney said.

"You're right," her mom replied, clearly being agreeable so as not to upset her before her day got started. "I'll go make some more coffee. Uncle Hank and Lewis will want some when they get up and you'll have enough to fill a travel mug for the road."

Sydney sat down at the kitchen table and let her eyes

fall on Aunt Clara's seat that always remained empty. She wished her great aunt could be there to help her. Aunt Clara would lean over her steaming mug with an intense stare and tell Sydney exactly how to handle the situation. That was how she was. And now that they'd all come through the initial blur of grief from her death, the whole family was scrambling to find their own direction. Sydney's mother didn't have the answers for her any more than she had them herself because they were all trying to get their footing without Aunt Clara's wisdom to fall back on.

Sydney wasn't really sure how Aunt Clara had done it. She'd been a world-renowned designer, running her company Morgan and Flynn while simultaneously being there for every single one of them. She'd been a wife, mother, nurturer, friend, neighbor—everything to everyone. She'd made it look so easy that none of them had considered how to navigate their own hardships by themselves.

Sydney was a thinker. She didn't often share her feelings with people. Instead, she kept them inside, protecting them from judgment. But Aunt Clara could always tell when something was bothering her. She never had to say anything. She could hear Aunt Clara's sensible voice in the back of her mind, saying, "The minute you stop thinking so hard about it is the minute the answer will come to you." That was exactly what she would do: Sydney decided right then and there to put all her focus on what made her happy. If she did that, she couldn't go wrong.

Sydney walked up to the white clapboard storefront that Mary Alice had converted into her practice. The old display window had been renovated into a window-seat with coordinating patterned pillows in calming shades of green and cream. An oval sign that read "Seaside Calm and Family Wellness Center" hung by the door. Sydney straightened her dress and squared her shoulders, the anticipation of the day humming within her. But when she opened the door and stepped into the main room, she had to keep her mouth from dropping open.

Nate and Juliana were sitting together on the sofa in the waiting area. They both looked at Sydney just as Mary Alice walked in from the back.

"Oh, hi!" she said to Sydney. "I'll just show you to the back room." Then she turned to Nate. "I'll be with you two in just a second."

Nate's gaze was on Sydney but she ignored it completely, her mind whirring.

"Nate is your first client?" Sydney said in a whisper as they reached the spare room where they'd be meeting. The room was a crisp white with a small desk in the center and a window view of the strip of grass that ran along the back of the building outside.

Sydney wondered if Nate and Juliana were there for couple's therapy but she didn't need to confirm it. She'd read that Nate and Juliana had had a rocky relationship—on-again-off-again—but they were working things out. And now, here was Juliana, with him, in Firefly Beach. Surely it would be easier to get therapy here, without the glare of the media spotlight.

Then the thought occurred to Sydney that there was a slight possibility that Nate might actually not tire of Firefly Beach and leave the way she'd hoped. He'd said himself that Juliana liked it here, that it was remote like her childhood home. And now he was moving back, getting therapy. They were clearly settling in. Sydney's breakfast sat like a cinder block in her stomach.

*   *   *

"Hey there, Miss Sydney," Melissa said with a giant grin. The owner of the local coffee shop Cup of Sunshine greeted everyone with Mr. or Miss and then their first name. Her chocolate-colored hair was piled on top of her head in a messy bun, and her reading glasses were perched on the end of her nose.

"Hi, Melissa." Sydney slid her laptop onto the counter so she could fiddle around in her handbag for her wallet. She pulled out a crumpled napkin and two receipts, and set them aside.

"No Robby today?" Melissa asked.

"No, I'm going to try to get a little work done."

"Ah," she said, grabbing a square of parchment and taking a small button cookie out of the glass display case, handing it to Sydney. Whenever Robby went in with her, Melissa always gave him a button cookie. "You'll have to eat this for him then," she said with a wink. "What'll it be?"

"Definitely the Butter Pecan Latte. What else is there in this world?"

Melissa's large bosom heaved with her light laughter. "Absolutely nothing," she said, ringing up the drink.

Sydney handed over her credit card.

"I'll bring it out to you," Melissa said, swiping the card and handing it back. "Want me to throw this stuff away?" She took the receipts and napkin and held them up.

Sydney thanked her for taking care of her trash.

Then something caught Melissa's eye. "Hang on," she said, holding out her hand. "Do you want to keep this one?" She held out the napkin. "It's got something on it."

"Definitely not. Why would I want to use a napkin that's

got something on it?" she teased, looking down at the writing that was scratched onto the napkin.

Melissa laughed, handing it over.

"The rest is trash, thanks." Sydney peered down at Logan's name and number. She remembered at the end of the wedding, taking the napkin inside and stuffing it into her handbag. Logan had been so nice. He'd made her laugh on the dance floor... She headed to an open table while nibbling on her cookie, thinking. She'd made some good headway on the magazine cover with Mary Alice, and she was feeling excited about starting her response for Ms. Flynn. Perhaps it was her good mood, but after she set her things down, she picked up her phone and texted Logan:

This is Sydney Flynn from the wedding. Just wanted to say hello. Thanks for a fun evening at the wedding.

Then she put her phone away and opened her laptop.

What should she say to Rebecca who'd moved away from her family? She considered her own life....

Sydney began to type.

Hi Rebecca,

It must be difficult to be alone. But perhaps you were meant to be on your own so that you could think through your circumstances properly. Consider the people around you—those are the people who have been put in your path. If you could pick one person you'd like to impact—a coworker? A neighbor?—who would it be? And now, if one person could impact you, who do you think has the best chance of being that person? Seek the person out, and find ways to spend time with him or her. At the end of the day, life is about the

connections we make, and starting over with a fresh slate for
making those connections could be an exciting adventure.
Good luck with the new job!
    Best wishes,
    Ms. Flynn

Sydney sat back, happy with her first response. She'd
done it. The words had rolled off her fingers effortlessly as
she typed.

"Your coffee," Melissa said, gingerly setting down her
mug.

Sydney admired the heart that Melissa had drawn in
the foam. "Thank you," she said, feeling accomplished.
The answer to Rebecca's dilemma had come easily to her
today, and she remembered Aunt Clara's advice: "The
minute you stop thinking so hard about it is the minute the
answer will come to you." There was something to be said
about that.

Her phone lit up on the table with a text.

I'm delighted to hear from you. Let's get coffee soon.
Logan

Maybe she could apply Aunt Clara's idea to the harder
things in life....

Sydney arrived back home at Starlight Cottage with a note-
pad full of ideas. She'd spent the rest of the day jotting down
ideas for the magazine cover and choosing the next few Ms.
Flynn letters. The creative outlet had been good to get her
emotions into a calmer state and to push away thoughts of
Nate. But when she saw who was out in the yard, she felt like

the wind had been knocked out of her. She got out of her car and shut the door.

Robby ran around one end of the grassy area with a football tucked under his arm while Nate jogged over to him.

"That was a good move you made," Nate said, laughing, slightly out of breath before he caught sight of Sydney and offered that eerily familiar smile that made her feel like she was twenty again. Nate and Robby together was an unnerving collision of past and present that made her want to shrink in on herself, unable to face her emotions. But she forced herself to be strong, marching across the yard.

"Hi, honey!" she said, giving Robby a bear hug, lifting him up. She offered a half smile at Nate before turning her attention back to her son. "How was your day with Nana?"

"Good." He twirled the football in the palm of his hand, the oblong shape of it causing it to wobble. He tossed it into the air.

Nate reached out and caught it above Robby's head. "Ha! Got it," he said.

Robby smiled uneasily at Nate, not attempting to get the football back. Clearly reading him, Nate offered him the ball.

Sydney's blood was beginning to boil. "Robby, do you mind if Nate and I go for a little walk?" she asked.

"May I come?" he asked.

"Not this time. But I'll come inside in a minute, and we can talk all about your day, okay? Why don't you see if Beau needs to be let out?"

"Okay," he said.

"Thanks, buddy."

Shyly, Robby turned to Nate. "Can we play again?"

Nate kneeled down to get on Robby's level. "That's up to your mom. But I'll try to convince her on our walk."

After Robby had run off, Sydney whirled around to Nate. "How dare you put me in that position? If I don't allow you to see him anymore, it will make *me* look like the bad guy," she snapped.

"Why wouldn't you want me to see him?" he asked.

"You don't even like kids, do you?"

"What?" His face crumpled in confusion. "What ever gave you that idea?"

"It doesn't matter," she said, frustrated that she was spending time with him instead of being inside with Robby.

"Syd, why wouldn't you want me to see Robby?" he repeated.

She gritted her teeth, trying to keep her emotions in check, but it was a losing battle. "Because he doesn't warm up to just anyone. And he doesn't need someone who will walk out of his life without notice."

Nate stared at her. "I won't do that to you again," he said, his face full of remorse.

"What do you want, Nate?" she asked, her tone now resigned.

He walked over to the pier and sat on the edge of it, his forearms on his knees, his hands clasped, and his head lowered as if he needed a moment to decide what he wanted to say. "That's not an easy question," he finally said.

So he *did* want something. She knew it. "Well, just come out with it."

"I knew coming back would be hard. . . ." He looked up at her. "I've ruined everything, and I don't know how to make things right." He stood up to face her. "I'm trying, Syd. But you won't let me in. I miss you so much it hurts."

"Why did you come back?" she asked, not replying to his admission—she didn't know how to respond. She just wanted him to leave her in peace so she could get on with her life.

It seemed as though the answer were on the tip of his tongue, yet something was holding him back. Finally, he spoke. "Because this is home for me."

Sydney knew exactly what he meant; she felt the same about Firefly Beach. But she wished he didn't feel that way. Why couldn't he have just stayed in LA or Nashville and left her and her family alone?

"Where will you live?" she asked, the idea that she'd have to face Nate and Juliana for the rest of her days settling hard in her gut. She remembered how, all those years ago, they'd talked about finding an old farmhouse right on the water and restoring it. How naïve they'd been....

"Right now I'm staying with Malory but I bought a lot on the other side of town and I'm building there."

"And what's wrong with the lot you already have?"

He didn't answer.

Without even knowing it, he'd just betrayed her again. It made sense, though, that he wouldn't want to wake up with Juliana down the road from his ex. The ex he'd run away from, the one he'd planned on marrying at one time.

He'd put a quarter in the bubblegum machine in town and gotten Sydney a ring with a plastic purple stone. He'd said she could wear it until he could afford to get her the best ring money could buy. One day, Robby had found it in her jewelry box and asked to play with it. She couldn't bring herself to let him. She wasn't sure why she kept it, but to this day it was still in the same spot in her jewelry box. She'd taken it off the day he'd left and initially, she hadn't had the strength to take it out of the little velvet cushion where she'd placed it

that day. Then the days turned to weeks and weeks turned to
months and...that was it.

He caught her looking down at her empty ring finger.
"Whatever happened to...." he began before evidently
deciding not to bring it up.

"I don't have it anymore," she lied, and their eyes met.
She looked away for fear that he'd be able to see through her
answer.

When she turned back to him, Nate nodded, but the disappointment was clear.

"Look," she said. "This is difficult for both of us. There's
too much between us to keep going on like this. I don't think
we can see each other without bringing our history back
up, and it's not something I want to keep reliving. If there's
something you want from me, then ask me now. But then I'd
appreciate it if you would give me my space."

"Something I want from you?" he asked, his brows
furrowing.

"Is there?"

He took a step toward her, reaching for her arm, his finger trailing down it. She let him, although she could feel the
tears welling up. She blinked them away. "Somehow...I just
want to make you happy," he said.

"You can't do that anymore," Sydney told him honestly.

His hand found hers and he caressed her empty ring
finger the same way he used to do when she was wearing
the ring. The hollow feeling that she'd thought she'd gotten over came rushing back. She pulled her hand away
gently, wishing things could be different. "I have to go
inside," she said, unable to keep her emotions at bay. She
needed to get a handle on herself so she could spend time
with Robby.

"Wait," he said, stopping her.

"Wait for what, Nate? Why aren't you putting this much effort into making Juliana happy right now?"

"Because I'm not in love with Juliana," he said, matter-of-factly. Then it was as if he'd wanted to suck the words back in, and she realized what he was implying: that he was spending his effort on the person he *was* in love with. That didn't make any sense, given the way he'd left without a care in the world. Then she wondered if his reaction was simply due to the guilt he felt by betraying his girlfriend with his words just now.

"That's a pretty big admission," Sydney said. "You'd better let Juliana in on that bit of information." The whole situation made her feel uneasy. This was definitely not how she'd wanted a reconciliation to happen with Nate if he ever came back. Early on after their break-up, she'd fantasized about what it would be like to have him run into her arms and tell her how it had all been such a terrible mistake. Lost and confused, she'd prayed for it, but now she wished he'd have never returned to Firefly Beach; not like this.

"Juliana knows," he said. "She's known for a while."

Juliana knew that Nate felt something for Sydney? And she was still with him? Sydney wasn't even going to get into their off-again status. Who knows what they'd talked about in therapy today, and it was none of her business anyway.

"If you had some kind of change of heart, why didn't you come find me years ago?" she asked.

He took in a deep breath and blew it out loudly, tipping his head back. "I tried, but we were never in the same place emotionally at the same time. You were getting married...."

She didn't dare tell him that had he actually been honest about why he'd called that day, it would've shaken her so badly that she probably would've called off her wedding.

And she'd have never had the love of her life—her son. That was proof that all of this happened for a reason and they were trying to hold on to something that was never meant to be theirs. Sydney shook the thought free from her mind. She was letting Nate get to her. He was simply on the rebound from whatever falling-out he'd had with Juliana. If Sydney allowed him to continue to make these little appearances, she would undoubtedly let him in, only to have him break her heart when he realized that he was better suited for someone like Juliana. They'd run back to LA together, leaving Sydney shattered, and she didn't think her fragile heart could take Nate leaving a second time.

"I don't know any other way to tell you that I'm not interested, Nate. How can I make you understand?" She didn't bother to clarify that it was Nathan Carr that didn't interest her. Nate Henderson would always have her heart.

Nate pursed his lips, clearly unable to find the words to convince her. She'd made it pretty clear. "I'll just give you this," he said, pulling a card from his pocket and handing it to her. She opened the envelope. "It's Malory's birthday tomorrow. I'm inviting a few friends over to her house after work tomorrow night. She'd love to see you—she told me herself. Bring Robby. I'm sure he'd like to get a piece of cake."

"I don't know, Nate. I love Malory, but it's too difficult...."

"I won't make it weird, I promise." He held up his hands in surrender. "Just friends. No pressure." When she didn't answer him, he gave her that crooked grin she loved so much. "Come on," he urged. "It won't be much fun with no one to say, 'Happy birthday.' I need you." His smile widened. "And I've already invited your mom and Uncle Hank, and they're coming."

Sydney really would like to see Malory..."Fine," she said.

"Ah!" He picked her up and twirled her around, making her laugh despite herself. "I *knew* you'd cave! It'll be fun." He set her back down.

Sydney shook her head.

"It's a party! What's the worst that could happen?"

Chapter Seven

"Is Nate coming again tomorrow?" Robby asked as he climbed under his covers, his eyes sleepy from a busy day.

"I'm not sure," Sydney said.

Sydney wasn't lying to him. She had a feeling that Nate was going to do what he wanted to do regardless of her wishes. Protectiveness over Robby surged through her. Nate's commitment to them and to Firefly Beach was just too uncertain for her to allow anything to develop between him and Robby. Ben would be back from his honeymoon in a few weeks, which would buy her some time to figure out what she could do, if anything, for Robby. But allowing him to see Nate certainly wasn't the answer.

Out of nowhere, he asked, "Do you like him, Mama?"

Unexpectedly—perhaps out of worry for her son or wistfulness over what was lost with Nate, she felt tears surface. She must have been just as tired as Robby. To keep her mind from wandering any further, she busied herself with tucking the covers around his little body while clearing her throat to keep the lump from forming. Despite her best efforts, she couldn't avoid one sniffle.

Robby was paying close attention to her, which made her

anxious. She smoothed out his covers and tugged on the end of them to make sure he was snuggled in.

"You love him?" Robby asked.

An icy sensation spread over her. "What?"

"You're crying."

"I'm fine," she lied.

But Robby shook his head. "No. You're crying. You used to cry about Daddy when he left too, and when I asked you why once, you said, 'Sometimes we cry over people we love—that's how you know you really love them.'"

Her little boy was so perceptive.

This was different. When she and Christian divorced, Robby was only four years old—too young to understand what was happening, but too old to be oblivious to it. "Why isn't daddy coming home tonight?" he'd ask, literally tearing her heart out. One day she'd found him in the closet, staring up at the empty hangers on Christian's side, and she could see the confusion on his face. While she was managing her own loss of love, she also had the burden of what Christian's leaving had caused for her son.

And now, how would she explain to him that she missed the person Nate used to be, terribly, and her tears were because she could never have him back? "Nate used to be my best friend," she said, stumbling over the words because "friend" just didn't even begin to cover what they'd been. "And he had to go away. I missed him so much that it still makes me sad."

Robby seemed to understand. "I miss Ben like that," he said. "But when I play football with Nate, I don't feel as sad." He sat up. "Will he come over again?"

"We'll see," she said, unable to provide the answer he wanted. "I'm glad you had fun with Nate." Sydney kissed her son's forehead. "Now, let's get a good night's sleep, okay?"

"Okay, Mama. I love you."

"Love you too."

Sydney settled onto the porch swing outside, next to Uncle Hank. They sat in silence together, watching the fireflies dancing through the trees at the edge of the property. The sun had already disappeared below the horizon, and the night sky had just begun to emerge, the first few stars making an appearance.

"You look tired," Uncle Hank said, pushing them back and then lifting his feet so the swing could rock them. "Something on your mind?"

She let the air out that she only just realized she'd been holding in. "Nate has me in a tizzy," she said.

"What's new?" Uncle Hank smiled knowingly at her, lightening her mood.

"I think Robby might *like* him," she confessed, still totally baffled that Robby was warming to Nate at all.

"He's a likeable guy."

"If I let him come around, I'm afraid Robby will get hurt when he decides to leave again. He'll get his heart broken."

"Is it only Robby's heart you're worried about?"

She dared not say, so she turned her head toward the wind, a warm gust blowing across her face.

"Have you ever talked with him about the day he left?" Uncle Hank asked.

She shook her head.

"I wonder what went through his mind." Uncle Hank pushed them again on the swing, the movement having a lulling affect on Sydney, and she could feel the heaviness in her eyes. "He's a good man. We all make mistakes, Sydney."

"But he isn't the same person anymore," she challenged.

"Even if he regrets that day, he's not the same boy who pulled out of our driveway in his old truck. Time just keeps moving us all forward and we can't go back."

"That it does," Uncle Hank agreed. He turned his head to look down the beach, the lapping waves nearly invisible against the night's sky. "You two used to walk all the way to his house at the end of the shore," he said, pointing to the strip of sand that ran along the coast past the lighthouse. He fell silent just long enough to get Sydney's full attention, something washing over him. Then, his mournful eyes met hers.

"What's on your mind?" she asked.

"There are so many memories here… Are we going to have to sell Starlight Cottage?"

"What?" The question seemed to come out of nowhere.

"Clara and I bought this house because of the serenity of this view. But soon it will be gone, the trees leveled, and the coastline full of out-of-towners…."

"So you're thinking about selling?" Just the idea sent an ache through her temples.

"It's a lot of house for just me."

"Robby and I are here too."

"Eventually, you'll want your own space, I can imagine."

"Not necessarily. I love living here with you."

"At some point, Sydney, you're going to move forward with your life, settle down with someone wonderful, and you'll want somewhere that you can be a family."

She let that comment register. "Are you saying that I'm not moving forward with my life right now?"

"I am incredibly grateful to you for helping me get back on my feet, but you can't spend the rest of your life taking care of an old man. You've made a good start by taking a job that's using your gift of writing. Keep going! Get out there.

Take risks. Let Robby play a few football games if he wants to...Stop worrying so much about getting hurt. You have to live like there's no such thing as heartbreak. If you tiptoe around, trying to keep yourself safe from it, you'll miss all the moments that will make you who you are."

They rocked together, Sydney contemplating Uncle Hank's advice. Sydney always took the predictable route, the path with the least amount of resistance. She considered herself to be the levelheaded one of the family—stable, reliable. But had she missed out by not taking chances? Had Nate felt like she was holding him back—was that why he'd left her behind? She tried to conjure up what her perfect future would be, but she came up empty, not knowing what she really wanted for herself and Robby. She'd had such a clear picture when she and Nate were dating, but when he left, he took all her dreams with him.

"I don't know what I want my future to look like," she worried aloud.

"You don't have to have all the answers right now, Sydney. You just have to want to find them. The minute you let that desire take over, your future will show up right in front of your eyes."

Sydney had spent the last decade focusing on being a wife and a mother. At the time, she felt that that was what she was meant to do. But now, it was time to concentrate on what would make her the happiest and also the best role model for Robby. He deserved the world, and she decided right then and there that she was the one who could give it to him.

Chapter Eight

Not a cloud in the sky, the gulf sparkled like diamonds. A lone sunbeam made its way past the thickly painted white windowsill and onto the rustic plank wood of the kitchen floor.

Sydney sat at the kitchen table, opened her work email the next morning, and found a new Ms. Flynn letter, the subject line catching her eye: Heartbreak. She could definitely relate to that...Mama must have opened the window to let the morning breeze in, and it brought with it a swirling scent of briny air mixed with the coconut aroma from the candle that was burning on the table next to a note that said she and Robby had taken Beau for a walk. Sydney made herself a cup of coffee, opened the message on her computer, and read.

Dear Ms. Flynn,

I have a problem. I'm in love with someone who isn't in love with me. I can't live without her and I feel like my heart is breaking every time I see her. What do I do?

Best,

Mel

She stared at the letter, trying to find the right words. This wasn't a simple issue. She copied and pasted the email into a new document and sipped her coffee, savoring the nutty, bitter flavor, as she began to try to construct her response.

> Dear Mel,
>   There's no easy answer for this. It's something that only time can fix....

But then Sydney deleted the line she'd typed. Because it wasn't true. Time hadn't repaired her heart after Nate had left her, so it was insensitive of her to believe time could fix Mel's life. She imagined what she'd say to herself, and started again.

> There are things in this life that aren't meant to be fixed. They will always hurt. But the human heart is resilient in that it can beat again after even the toughest blow. I'd like to say we're stronger because of it. We can't know true joy until we've experienced absolute heartbreak. My hope for you is that one day you'll be able to see that person and be happy for her because you loved her enough to let her go and find whatever it was that made her complete. That is love.

This would be her next submission. She signed the letter, checked the piece for errors, and emailed it to her editor. Once she got the okay from the *Gazette*, she'd email mel4221 and let him know his letter would be published.

Then she headed over to the wellness center to get to work on Mary Alice's magazine. It was going to get her full attention today, and she was planning to knock everyone's socks off with her ideas.

* * *

Mary Alice had a concept that people could relate to: finding balance for the whole self. It had been done before, but how could Sydney spin the idea to make it something everyone was dying to find out more about? She started brainstorming: What about people who had never been to a wellness center? What could they begin to do at home that would start them on the path to better health? She started typing slogans, her mind buzzing: *Reinvent Your Life*, *Discover the Real You*, *Reclaim Your Destiny.* . . .

Sydney grabbed her pad of paper and scratched down a note to talk to Hallie when she got back. With Hallie now running Morgan and Flynn, Aunt Clara's worldwide design company, her sister had media contacts across the globe that would gladly do her favors, like giving a quote for a little Firefly Beach magazine, for an exclusive peek at Hallie's upcoming designs. Perhaps Hallie would be interested in collaborating on a new holistic décor line, and Sydney could write the press release copy, including Mary Alice's philosophies. It could be their first feature in the magazine.

But today was about the cover. She needed photography—a big, glossy image to draw in the consumer. She'd call local photographer Gavin Wilson, who owned the gallery in town, to see if he'd be interested in doing a photo shoot for her. Gavin had only moved to Firefly Beach last year, but he'd done some painting for Uncle Hank, and he'd taken her uncle fishing when he was at his lowest over Aunt Clara's death. Sydney had had coffee with him a few times, and he was always willing to lend a helping hand.

If Gavin agreed to let her hire him, she'd need a design concept as soon as possible. She imagined a couple on a cover with all the calming colors: blue, violet, light pink,

green, grey . . . Easy. She needed a couple on the beach at
sunset. The woman in a white dress. Holding hands with
someone. Hair blowing in the wind as they faced away from
her . . . Sydney sketched the image onto her pad of paper.

The bells at the front door jingled, pulling Sydney out of
her creative cloud. She leaned over and peered through the
open door to find Juliana taking a seat on the sofa. She had
on the same big sunglasses from the wedding, her rounded
lips set seriously. It seemed to be just her for this visit, and
Sydney couldn't help but wonder if Nate had said anything
to her about the talk he and Sydney had had at Starlight
Cottage yesterday. Juliana took off her glasses and Sydney
swore the rims of her eyes were red. Regardless of Nate and
Juliana's relationship issues, Sydney wasn't in the business
of breaking up couples, and the guilt from her own thoughts
about Nate was enough to make her get up to shut the office
door before Juliana saw the flush of crimson that had certainly taken hold on Sydney's cheeks.

She walked over to the door to close it but stopped cold
when, to her surprise, Juliana's perfect lips turned upward,
her face lifting cordially from under the flowing waves of
hair she'd been hiding behind, and she offered a dainty wave
in Sydney's direction. So obviously Nate hadn't said a thing.
Typical. No matter how sorry he told Sydney he was, she
couldn't change that truth about him: he was a selfish person.
Judging by Juliana's expression and the defeat in her eyes, she
was in a fragile state, which only made Sydney feel worse.
She smiled weakly and waved back, then shut the door.

Despite forcing herself to turn her attention back to her
work, Sydney was unsuccessful at shutting out the image
of Juliana's meek smile. The photos of her in the magazines
and on television made her seem so self-confident, so sure
of herself. But even in her delicate state now her beauty was

undeniable. Sydney tried to refocus, sending Gavin an email through his website and telling him she'd call him later.

Photography locations were key to grabbing the readers' interest; she needed buy-in. Serene, casual, happy... There was only one place that came to mind: Starlight Cottage, down by the lighthouse, the couple standing together on the sand, the gazebo out of focus in the background. That would be perfect.

There was a knock at the door and Mary Alice poked her head in. "I was just checking in before I begin with my first client. Everything going okay?"

"Yes," Sydney said with a smile. "I'm organizing my thoughts at the moment." She turned her pad of paper around to show Mary Alice a quick look at her sketch. "I emailed Gavin to see if he'd do a photo shoot. I want to put a couple on the beach at Starlight Cottage. I can tell you more about it when you have time."

"I'm excited! It sounds fantastic."

When Sydney and Mary Alice left the wellness center together, headed for their cars, Sydney told her she'd gotten confirmation from Gavin to do the photo shoot, and he'd said he had everything for the lighting and staging at Starlight Cottage. Mary Alice had been thrilled with the idea as well as the articles Sydney had come up with so far.

"We just need to find a couple for the shoot," Sydney said as they reached the parking lot.

"I thought about that when I saw your sketch," Mary Alice told her.

"Any ideas?"

"Well—confidentially—even though I promised to keep it a secret," she leaned in and whispered, "Nathan and

Juliana didn't want a paper trail of any kind that the press could get a hold of, so they aren't technically on my books, and, because of that, I wouldn't let them pay me, so Nathan said he owes me one. I'm sort of counseling them as a favor and I'm only seeing them here at the center because it's easier than making Malory leave the house to keep things confidential if I made a house-call. If I asked for a favor in return, they'd most likely do it for me. They'd be a gorgeous couple for the magazine and the photo would be from the back, right? So no one would recognize them anyway."

Of all people.

"Juliana told me earlier that you're going to Malory's birthday party tonight," Mary Alice continued. "I hate to suggest this...." she said, making a face. "Maybe you could find a quiet moment to ask Nathan then?"

Why had Juliana mentioned Sydney at all? While Sydney hated the idea of putting herself in Nate's path again, she knew that they'd be the perfect couple for the cover. Perhaps she could avoid asking Nate altogether and approach his girlfriend—as a business venture. After all, this was what Juliana did for a living, so she would probably welcome it. And she felt like she needed to be friendly with Juliana to assure her that there was absolutely nothing going on between her and Nate.

Maybe the project would be helpful for all of them. They could see each other in a different light and move on from whatever moment it was that Nate was having. Perhaps he'd realize he was trying to relive the past and he'd finally leave Firefly Beach for good.

The thought crept in that Sydney should face this, put Juliana right in the line of her vision to drive home the point to herself that the old Nate wasn't coming back, no matter what she wished for.

* * *

Sydney's phone pinged with an email, but she ignored it. She stood in the yard after work, her hand on her forehead as if in salute, to shield her eyes from the glare of the sun, just enough to make out the enormous boat that was sitting on the shore out back of Starlight Cottage. The massive shiny white vessel looked out of place next to the rustic pier. Its front was pressed against the shoreline, its back end bobbing in the lapping water.

"Mama!" Robby said, running through the front door of Starlight Cottage and bounding down the porch steps toward her. "Can I take a boat ride?" he called to her, excited and out of breath, pointing to the yacht.

"Whose—?" She was about to finish her thought when Nate appeared in the doorway with his hands raised in surrender, his cell phone pressed against his ear with his shoulder.

"Go ahead and pitch it to the label," he said into his phone, his eyes on Sydney. "I'll call you back with the idea for Timberlake." He ended the call and gave Sydney all his attention. "Don't yell at me," he teased. "It isn't my fault I'm here this time. I was minding my own business working, but Uncle Hank invited me over."

"And you came in that?" she asked, jutting a finger toward the boat.

"It's my first purchase since moving back," he said. "I can't be by the water and not have a boat."

Sydney didn't want to consider the fact that buying that boat would make it more difficult for him to just pick up and leave. She'd hoped he'd get tired of his old small-town life sooner rather than later.

"Take a ride with me," he said, walking toward her. "Just

friends, I promise; no pressure. I brought Juliana," he offered
when he reached her, as if that would make the situation any
better. "She's on the boat."

"Can we go, Mama?" Robby pleaded.

"I just got off of work...." she said, knowing her excuse
was flimsy at best.

Robby clasped his hands together, begging her with his
eyes to say yes. The boat ride was so enticing that it was
overpowering his reluctance to be with Nate.

"Why did Uncle Hank ask you over?" Sydney asked, still
trying to make up her mind.

"He said he wanted to talk about Starlight Cottage, but
then Lewis asked him if he'd take a walk, and he said he'd
catch up with me later."

Sydney wondered what in the world Uncle Hank would
want to discuss with Nate regarding Starlight Cottage. She
was definitely going to ask when he and Lewis got home.
But right now, Robby was tugging on her arm, giving her
puppy-dog eyes.

"I've got food on the boat," Nate said. "Why don't you
put your swimsuit on and come with us? Robby wants to
jump off the back so I'm going to take him out in the gulf."

She opened her mouth to protest but he cut her off.

"I've got a life vest for him. And an inner tube. And
goggles."

Sydney tried to come up with some reason to say no.

"...And peanut butter sandwiches," he added. "Syd,
come on. Have a little fun."

Was he implying that she didn't have fun? She might be
having a blast right now and not need his fancy boat to give
her a good time.

"I'll go get my towel!" Robby said, running off toward
the cottage, clearly trying a different persuasion tactic.

Nate took a step closer to Sydney. "I remember when you were a fearless dreamer who could outthink me in a second. You wowed me at every turn. You'd have been the first one on the boat, probably even driving it yourself. You're so cautious now."

She didn't dare tell him that he'd broken her when he'd left. His leaving had caused her to grow up quickly, to get her head out of the clouds. All those dreams and possibilities that she'd pondered—he'd taken them with him when he'd left.

"Things change," she said, her tone less harsh than it had been before. They couldn't change how he left, so all they could do was move on from this.

"They definitely do," he replied, his mind clearly heavy with thoughts. He cleared his throat. "Juliana wants to meet you," he said, changing the subject.

Sydney's heart pounded. Talking with Juliana would give Sydney closure on the whole thing; meeting her would solidify the idea that Nate Henderson was in her past and Nathan Carr was the person standing opposite her now. And Sydney had wanted to talk to her about the photo shoot anyway....

"Come on," he urged. "I need you to guide me back into the water."

That made her smile. Years ago, whenever he'd bring the boat down from his house, Nate had always gotten it stuck on the sand, and the two of them had to push and pull until it floated free.

"I won't be able to move that monstrosity," she teased.

"I just bought it. You don't like it?" There was a twinkle in his eye when he asked, which made Sydney take another look at the boat.

"Is that a bridge boat?" she asked.

He nodded. "A Sea Ray."

A distant memory floated into her consciousness. "When

we're both old, I still want to sit together just like this," he'd said as they rocked in two chairs on the porch at Starlight Cottage, both of them looking out at the glistening water that seemed to stretch forever, just like the years ahead of them.

"Nah," Sydney told him. "We'll be too famous. No one will ever leave us alone if we sit out here on these chairs. We'll have to float way out to sea on our yacht if we want to be alone."

Nate had laughed. "Yes, we'll definitely need a yacht. How about a Sea Ray?" he said, naming one of the boats he'd pointed out to her once in his fishing magazine.

"Yes!" she replied happily. "A Sea Ray will do. A nice big yacht."

"Which one of us is going to buy that big yacht first?"

"You will," she'd told him without hesitation, and it was at that moment that she'd noticed something shift in his expression, almost as if he didn't trust her suggestion. Or maybe he'd already considered leaving her by then... She remembered thinking that she'd only been kidding with the whole idea anyway, so why had he become so serious? His look and the fact that she couldn't decipher it had scared her, and she'd let the conversation die on the wind. Well, he might have doubted it at the time, but her guess had been dead-on. She hoped he hadn't purchased the boat just to prove a point—that would be a very expensive way to tell her she was right.

"What are you thinking about?" Nate asked, pulling her from her memory.

"I've got my towel!" Robby came running toward them, ripping through the moment. When he got to Sydney, he asked, "You coming?"

There was nothing left to do but grab her swimsuit and climb aboard.

Chapter Nine

When Sydney stepped aboard the yacht, Juliana was in a string bikini and sunglasses, lying on a towel at the back of the vessel. As she neared her, Sydney took in her perfect red pedicure that matched her swimsuit, the rounded softness of her knee on her flawless leg that was bent, her foot flat on the towel, her long dark hair fanned out around her, puddling at the nape of her neck in picture-perfect waves. She looked so different than she had at the wellness center and even at the wedding. Her body was made for this, and her star power was undeniable, making Sydney suddenly nervous as she realized for the first time that she was in the presence of a superstar. Juliana's stillness and relaxed appearance were hypnotizing.

She turned her head slowly and then popped up, pulling small wireless headphones out of her ears. "Sorry," she said, a slight accent still present even after so many years living in California. "I didn't hear you walk up."

She swung her legs around and scooted to the edge of the platform, hopping off of it, every part of her body in impeccable form as she moved about the boat. She placed a large hat over her hair—the brim of it covered her face down to her sunglasses—and sat on the bench to pick up a cocktail that had been resting in one of the cup holders. She stirred around the melted ice before evidently reconsidering and placing the drink back into its spot.

"I'm Sydney." She tried to keep her nerves down as she held out her hand to Juliana, willing it to remain steady.

"Yes," Juliana said, her dainty fingers gripping Sydney's hand briefly but warmly. "It's so nice to finally meet you. Nathan speaks very highly of you."

"Oh?" Sydney sat down beside Juliana. "That's ... interesting." What had he told Juliana?

"He was so happy to get back to Firefly Beach to see you."

"Is that so?"

"He adores you," Juliana said with a smile that showed off her bright white teeth.

Clearly, he hadn't divulged his true feelings. He couldn't have, given Juliana's reaction.

"Are you all right?" Juliana asked.

This was ridiculous. She couldn't just sit there next to Juliana, knowing all the things Nate had told her, and act like everything was just peachy. "Sort of," she said, unsure of how to answer the question.

"Are you sure you're okay?" Juliana tilted her head, her eyes curious.

Besides not understanding this odd relationship you have with my ex? Her heart pattered fiercely in her chest—a mix of nerves and awkwardness.

Juliana seemed as befuddled as Sydney was with this conversation.

It was time to get some answers once and for all. "This is a weird question, but are you and Nate ... dating?" she asked.

Juliana broke eye contact, her gaze moving to the floor of

the boat nervously. "Uh...." She looked over at Nate through her lashes. "No." The answer came out quickly and quietly as if she didn't want anyone to hear.

Juliana's response surprised Sydney. What was going on?

"Mama!" Robby said, running down the boat. "Nate has his fishing rod and he said that we could fish once we anchor out in the water!" Despite his excitement, she noticed his slight trepidation when his eyes moved to Nate, and she guessed that their shared interests were driving her son to accept the fact that Nate could fill something for him that hadn't been there since Ben left. It made Sydney queasier than a day at sea.

"That's exciting!" she said, ignoring her own baggage, genuinely happy to see her son so enthusiastic.

"I'll let you drive the boat, if you want, Robby," Nate said to him, as he took a seat at the wheel. "Your mom just has to help me out of the sand."

Sydney looked over at Nate and they shared a moment of reminiscence, making her smile despite everything. His face lit up at the sight of her, and for an instant, the fondness in his eyes, the heat of the sun, and the salty air, made her feel like she was in her twenties again. Robby climbed up onto Nate's lap, breaking the spell, but she couldn't pull her gaze from the two of them together. The rush of emotions made her need a minute.

"You're going to just hold the wheel like this," Nate told Robby. Robby gripped the silver wheel of the yacht. "Yep, just like that. I'm going down onto the sand to help your mom. I'll be right back up."

"Okay," Robby said, his face serious.

"Think you can drive it, Captain?" Nate said, tussling Robby's hair.

"Yes, sir!" Robby said.

"Hold it with the same strength as you hold the football when someone's about to come in for a tackle."

Nate turned to Sydney and gestured toward the ladder on the side of the boat. "After you."

Sydney climbed down onto the sand and went straight to the front of the boat to push it. The whole time, she was taking in slow, steady, deep breaths and trying to erase the image of Nate and Robby from her mind. She had to, or her heart would break all over again. When she and Nate were together, she'd imagined a family with him—they'd talked about it. He'd wanted lots of land so they could play outside, fish by the water, build sand castles... All the things Robby liked to do. The "if only" of it all was already eating away at her, and they hadn't even left the shore. She pressed her hands against the warm fiberglass of the boat and channeled her emotions into her strength, pushing with all her might.

Nate's phone began to ring on the boat.

"Nate!" Robby called. "Want me to bring you your phone?"

"That's okay, buddy. You just hold the wheel," he replied, ignoring the call.

"Whoa," Nate said, placing his hands beside hers. "You don't give yourself enough credit. You can probably move this boat all by yourself."

"Are you jealous of my biceps?" she said.

He smiled, and positioned his hands next to hers, his scent intoxicating. "On the count of three, ready? One, two, three."

They both heaved, the boat grinding against the powder white sand as it shifted.

"One more time and I think we've got it," she said, glad for the diversion. "Then you jump in the boat and I'll guide you around the pier."

"All right," he said, his arm brushing against hers.

He seemed to notice their proximity, giving her a little glance out of the corner of his eye. Given what Juliana had said, all of the attention he'd been offering Sydney was some sort of rebound for sure. And why was Juliana still in Firefly Beach if they weren't together? They'd been getting therapy…It didn't add up. Well, Sydney wasn't going to play his games. He and Juliana could do their little back-and-forth romance, but Sydney didn't want to have any part in it. Her heart wouldn't be able to survive when he decided that Juliana was the better fit for him, because she knew it was true. Nathan Carr would take nothing less.

Nate started counting again, "One, two, three."

The boat suddenly became light against Sydney's hands, its body bobbing in the gulf waves that splashed around them. Nate jumped onto the ladder, climbing it quickly, and moving over to Robby. He lifted Robby, and placed him back into his lap. Sydney looked away, focusing on the pier.

"Give it a hard right!" she called up to them.

The nose of the boat gently glided around in an arc.

"Straighten it up slowly and I'll jump on." She guided the boat, pushing against it, until it was completely clear of the pier and grabbed the ladder, pulling herself out of the water. Once she was on deck, Nate cranked the engine and began moving the boat out to sea, causing the wind to pick up and blow her hair behind her shoulders. It was the best feeling in the world. Only then did she grasp how long it had been since she'd been on a boat, her feet wet like they used to stay all summer.

Sydney took a seat next to Juliana just before the boat picked up speed, slicing through the cobalt blue water, the spray dancing on her skin. The wind rushed through her ears, nearly drowning the constant buzzing of the engine. Nate and Robby were in her peripheral vision as the coastline zipped past them in a blur. The total assault on her senses made her feel alive for the first time in a very long time. Being out on the gulf gave her so much joy. She needed to do more of this, stir up that old creativity that used to come so easily for her. Now she knew why her ideas had come so effortlessly when she was younger: she had to feed her imagination with sunshine and happiness.

When the boat began to slow, Nate lifted Robby off his lap and stood up. "You know how to do it now, Captain," he told Robby. Nate cut the engine. "Just keep her straight ahead for me while I drop the anchor."

"Yes sir," Robby said with authority.

With Robby and Nate both busy anchoring the boat in place, Sydney turned to Juliana. "So," she said, "are you enjoying Firefly Beach?"

Juliana spread her slender arm along the back of the bench seat where they were both sitting and nodded. "It's very beautiful and quiet here," she said. "It is the kind of place where I could live."

"Are you planning to stay?"

"For right now, yes."

By staying, was Juliana hoping for some sort of reconciliation with Nate? Probably. According to the tabloids, they didn't dare move their things out of each other's apartments because they'd be back together before they could get it all unloaded. "Will you be staying with Nate?"

"If he says it's okay. We haven't really discussed all that just yet."

With the boat anchored down, Nate grabbed a fishing pole and walked over to Robby. "Want to see what we can catch out here?" he asked.

Robby's head bounced up and down, his face beaming with delight.

"Perfect. Okay, here's how you work this rod. Put your thumb against the line here...." He showed him where to place his thumb on the spool to keep it from unwinding too quickly—a trick Nate had learned from Uncle Hank on one of the countless fishing trips when Sydney had tagged along.

Sydney turned her attention back to Juliana. "So will you be doing any work while you're here?"

"No, I'm taking some time off from modeling," Juliana said. "The schedule is hectic...Things became so crazy. My soul was suffering."

"Your soul?"

"I was so busy trying to...manage things...I lost who I was."

Juliana showed an intense sadness just then, the emotion surfacing even through those big sunglasses of hers. Her honesty seemed brave, given the fact that she looked like she wanted to close in on herself. And now she was dealing with relationship issues with Nate. Poor girl. Looking at her, it was clear that the Juliana in all those glossy magazines wasn't necessarily representative of who Juliana was. She was hurting and uncertain—a far cry from the self-assured bikini model who seemed to have the world at her fingertips.

"What will you do now?" Sydney asked.

Juliana grabbed her sarong and draped it over her lap, smoothing it out on her legs. "I'm not totally sure. I have been modeling since I was fifteen. I have no experience doing anything else." She dragged her manicured finger under her glasses and sniffled before she turned toward the wind, her dark tresses cascading down her back.

Nate let Robby hold the rod by himself and came to join them. "That's why you're here," he said, his voice gentle and calming. "Take your time; don't rush it. You are one of the most resilient and passionate people I know. Breathe in this air and let it soak down to your bones. I find inspiration everywhere here. I'm hoping it'll do the same for you."

Nate's fondness for Juliana was clear, which only left Sydney feeling more confused, and hurt.

"I got one, Nate!" Robby called, reeling as fast as his little fingers would allow him to, the rod bending at the tip, giving him quite a struggle.

Nate rushed over to him to help pull in the fish.

"I wish I had your talent," Juliana said with a sigh, still clearly immersed in their prior conversation. "Nathan said you are an amazing writer."

Her comment surprised Sydney. "I don't know about that."

"One thing I can say about Nathan is that he tells the truth. If he tells me you're a great writer, I believe him." She took off her dark glasses, revealing her tired but beautiful almond-colored eyes. "He says you're a better writer than he is."

Completely baffled, she turned to look at Nate, only to find his eyes already on her, those unsaid words crashing upon her like the roll of a stormy tide. He quickly moved his attention back to Robby and the fish that was dangling from his line.

"Do *you* like to write?" she asked Juliana.

"I don't think so. I would like to design things. I really love choosing the layout for my photos. Sometimes I was able to collaborate with the photographers on the photo shoots, and tell them my ideas. The ones who would listen usually liked them."

"So perhaps you'd like to be a layout editor for a magazine?"

Juliana smiled. "That is exactly what Nathan suggested. But we searched online and for most of the jobs, I need a graphic design degree. I do not have a degree or any formal experience."

If someone had told her even a day ago that she would be suggesting this to Nate's on-and-off girlfriend, Sydney might have died laughing at the absurdity of the idea, but Juliana seemed genuinely kind, and it only made sense, given what she'd shared. "I'll tell you what. If you enjoy that sort of thing, maybe you can show me some of your ideas for the magazine I'm working on as a favor for Mary Alice for the wellness center. I'm designing the cover."

Juliana sat up straighter, her interest clear.

"I wanted to talk to you about the cover anyway. I was going to ask you... Would you and Nate pose for the cover image?"

"Oh, I am sorry," she said, "I am no longer modeling." Tears swelled suddenly in her eyes. She slipped her glasses back on.

Sydney thought she said she was taking a break from it, but Juliana's reaction just now told her something totally different. Then, as though Juliana could read her mind, it was as if she realized her blunder and wanted to take her words back. Sydney's question had put her on the spot and caused her just enough anxiety that she clearly couldn't hide her feelings anymore. Had Juliana Vargas, one of the world's top supermodels, literally at the height of fame, left modeling for good? And was Sydney the first to know of this decision?

Nate quickly got Robby's line baited and talked him through casting it before rushing over to Juliana. "You okay?" he asked quietly in her ear but Sydney heard. Juliana nodded, wiping a tear from her cheek. The exchange made Sydney feel like she was eavesdropping, so she got up and walked over to Robby.

"What did you catch?" she asked him, turning all her

attention to the rocking sea surrounding them to give her calm.

"Nate said it was a snapper," he told her, reeling in, checking his line, and casting back out. He was becoming quite skillful, and she had to wonder if Nate had taught him a thing or two in their short time together.

"Hey, what do you say we pull up the anchor and do a little tubing?" Nate said to Robby, appearing next to him. "I can pull you and your mom behind the boat."

Juliana had taken her spot again, sunning herself on the towel at the back of the boat, her headphones in her ears. Sydney considered the fact that it might be an effort to shut everything out. A tear escaped from under Juliana's sunglasses, and she wiped it away. What had happened to her? Nate was right about one thing: if there was anywhere on earth that could make her feel better about whatever it was she was going through, Firefly Beach was the place.

Chapter Ten

Sydney clicked on the radio in the kitchen, the sun from the day still on her skin, and pulled out Aunt Clara's lemon bar recipe. She was going to make some for Malory's party tonight. Aunt Clara had said, "You never know when life will give you lemons, so it's best to have all the ingredients for lemon bars on hand. That way you can make something sweet out of the whole thing." With a nod in the direction of Aunt Clara's chair at the table, Sydney lumped an armful of lemons onto the counter. They all began rolling in different directions as she scrambled to get control of them.

Out of nowhere, Nate caught one before it tumbled to the ground and set it on the table. "Hi," he said, helping her roll them into a pile. He'd showered, his hair still wet, and his cheeks pink from all afternoon on the boat. He surveyed the kitchen, the counter filled with sugar, flour, a bowl of eggs, and the utensils she'd need for baking. "You're trying to drum up good luck for something," he said, the idea causing a sparkle in his eye.

Sydney took one of the lemons and ran it under the water at the sink, drying it off. "What gives you that idea?"

A tiny smirk formed on his lips. "When you want

something to go well, you bake and, by the look of that pile of lemons, you're making Aunt Clara's lemon bars. Something big must be on your mind."

"The lemons were already here," she said. "Mama had them in the center of the table to look nice."

"Whatcha making, Mom?" Robby said, coming in to the room and crawling up on the barstool to see better. "Hi, Nate," he said a little more bashfully than he had on the boat earlier.

"Lemon bars," Nate told him, clearly not needing confirmation.

"Oh, I love those!" Robby wriggled on the barstool. "She always makes them before I have big tests in school."

Nate eyed her and raised an eyebrow, and Sydney's cheeks burned with the memory that she knew had been conjured up with Robby's comment.

Sydney ignored his look and started shaving the zest off of the lemons. "I wanted to bring something summery for Malory's birthday," she said. "That's why I'm baking them." She tried to hide the fact that she was hoping things went well with Malory tonight. She missed her.

"Do you remember when we made these together?" Nate asked. But before she could answer, he turned to Robby. "Your mom and I both grew up here in Firefly Beach, and we used to make these before our big tests in college like she does for you." He grabbed two lemons, cradling them in one hand, and then took a third. "Your mom and I can juggle these lemons, each of us only using one hand."

Robby lit up. "You can?" He looked over at Sydney for confirmation.

She smiled, unable to deny the fondness she had at the memory. It had started as a bet.

"You should ask him out," Nate told Malory, all those

years ago, when the subject of his sister's crush had come up, as they all stood together in the Hendersons' kitchen baking. "Put the moves on...." His eyebrows bounced up and down. "I can give you some pointers if you need them."

"Absolutely not," Malory said, rolling her eyes playfully.

"Oh, come on," Nate teased his sister. "You know I've got all the moves," he said, grabbing Sydney and tickling her, making her squirm and wriggle away with laughter. He grabbed two lemons from the counter and juggled them high in the air.

"Gross," Malory said with playful disgust. "I do *not* want to know about my brother's moves."

"I'll tell you what," he said, grabbing a third lemon and adding it to the two already circling in the air. "If I can juggle these for one minute straight, you have to ask him out."

Malory laughed. "Too easy," she said. "You have to juggle them with one hand."

"Of course!" he said, the lemons coming to a stop one by one in his hand. Start your timer." But before he began, he walked around the kitchen island and stood next to Sydney. "I can't juggle with one hand," he whispered to her and then nuzzled her ear, making her giggle. "Remember how I taught you to juggle?" he asked.

Nate had taught Sydney how to juggle using Aunt Clara's scarves. When she'd gotten good enough at it, he had her try tennis balls, and she'd gotten to be a pretty smooth juggler. She nodded, wondering what he had up his sleeve.

"I'm going to be your right hand, and you be my left. Think we can juggle together?"

Malory piped up, "That's totally cheating, but I can't wait to see if you can pull this off, so I'll let it go." She leaned on the counter with her elbows and put her chin in her hands.

"Can we have a practice round?" he asked.

"Nope." Malory's chin remained in her hands, amusement on her face.

"Fine," he said. "But if we can do this for one minute, you have to ask Brian out."

"Okay," Malory said, getting up and setting the kitchen timer. "On your mark, get set, go!"

Quickly, Nate faced Sydney, putting his arm out and tossing a lemon in the air. To Sydney's surprise, she was able to manage, keeping the lemon in the air.

"Here comes number two," he said, tossing it into the mix with his free hand.

The lemon sailed up in the air and came down in her hand as if she'd tossed it up herself. She kept it going. He threw the third one up, and there they were: both of them working together like they'd done it all their lives. She kept her concentration, not wanting to break for a second, but wondering how long they'd been going.

When the timer finally went off, Malory moaned a loud, annoyed groan. "I cannot *believe* you two pulled that off!"

Aunt Clara had burst into the room and asked, "What in the world is going on in here? You all sound like you're having too much fun." She winked at them.

"*They* certainly are," Malory said.

She'd asked her crush Brian out, and they'd ended up dating for about six months before they finally decided they were better off as friends.

"Show me!" Robby said.

Sydney swam out of her memory.

"We might be a little rusty," Nate said, positioning himself up next to her, making her pulse rise. He handed her a lemon. "We had gotten pretty good at it—we used to do it at parties."

"Why did you come over again?" she asked, recognizing

the incredible distraction he'd caused. She was running out of time to make the lemon bars.

"Stop trying to change the subject. Let's show Robby," he said, already tossing a lemon in the air.

Just like they'd never stopped practicing, she caught it, sending it back into the air. The lemon went around a few times before Nate sent the second one up. Pretty soon, they were juggling all three to Robby's cheers.

Nate caught them one at a time, stopping and setting them back on the pile where Sydney had originally put them. "We make a good team," he said, but when he said it, there was more to his observation than what was on the surface. "And by the way," he added, "I just came by to say hi. Malory and Juliana have the whole cottage full of hairspray fumes while they get ready for the party, and I had to escape." He gave Robby a wink, making Robby giggle. "Looks like we'd better get a move on with making these lemon bars. Wanna help, little guy?"

"Sure," Robby said. Sydney couldn't deny the curiosity in her son's eyes when he looked at Nate right then, giving her two juxtaposed reactions: the first was the flutter in her chest at this little moment they were having together and the second was the utter fear that Robby could fall for Nate's charm as easily as she could.

The last of the lemon bars had come out of the oven, filling the air with the sugary sweet nectar of lemon and butter, and Nate had gone home to help get things ready for the party tonight. While Jacqueline ironed the shirt Uncle Hank was wearing to the party, Sydney grabbed her phone to check the time, and only then did she remember the push notification of the email she'd gotten. It had been from someone she didn't recognize, but seeing the subject line now, it made her pause: *NY Pulse Magazine Content Editor Position.* Quickly, she set down the strappy sandals she was holding, opened up the email, and scanned the message.

> *Thank you for reaching out... The team has reviewed your submission and we'd like to set up a call... Could you send us available times and days...*

Sydney clasped her hand over her mouth in complete shock. "Oh, my gosh," she said from behind her fingers.

Jacqueline stopped and set the iron upright, turning down the radio that was playing beach tunes and fixing her eyes on Sydney. "What is it?"

"Uh... It could be nothing," she said, the insecurity about her ability to compete with the applicants for that level of a writing position surfacing. "Hallie and I were messing around a few weeks ago and we sent my résumé to this big magazine in New York... They want me to call them."

"Oh, Sydney, that's amazing!"

"Well, let's not get too excited," she warned. It was more directed to herself than her mother.

Robby wandered into the room, wearing the new shorts Sydney had gotten a few weeks ago for church and a two-button Polo shirt. "How do I look?" he said, holding out his arms and tapping his feet in the loafers she'd asked him to wear tonight.

"If I was eight, I'd date ya," Sydney teased.

Robby squeezed his eyes shut with embarrassment. "Mo-om."

"What?" She dropped her phone onto the bed and took his hands, dancing with him. "You're a chick-magnet," she teased again.

"Mom!" he said, shaking his head. "That's gross."

Sydney laughed. "One day, you won't think so."

"I will always think so." He made a face.

"One day, when you grow up, you might get married," she said.

"No way. I want to live with you forever." He wrapped his arms around her and squeezed her tightly, making her glow with adoration for him.

"You're welcome to," she said, kissing the top of his head.

"I'll live with you...." He pulled back. "As long as you don't make me wear these shoes very much. Yuck."

"It's good to dress up every now and again," Sydney told him.

"Your mother's right," Sydney's mom said. "How else will you appreciate the comfort of your sneakers?"

"I already had to wear fancy clothes at the wedding," Robby said, tugging on the collar of his shirt.

"You'll be a pro at dressing up then," Sydney said. "Your *girlfriend* will be impressed!"

"I don't have a girlfriend," he said, giving her the side-eye.

"What about Susie Jones at school?"

"She's not my girlfriend! She just talks real weird around me. *Like this*." He said the last two words in a sultry voice, making Sydney and Jacqueline laugh out loud.

"Watch out," Jacqueline said. "With that kind of talk, she'll be your girlfriend before you know it."

Robby rolled his eyes. "What time are we going to the party?"

"We'll leave in about twenty minutes," Sydney replied.

"Okay! I'll go get my football!"

"Try to stay clean!" she called after him as he ran down the hallway.

*　*　*

Sydney walked along the road toward Malory's house with the rest of the family, the birthday-themed bag containing an expensive bottle of wine and the gift card they'd all pitched in to buy swinging by her side, while Jacqueline carried the tin of lemon bars.

Robby strolled along next to her, tossing his football into the air and catching it. "Think Nate will play a game or two with me tonight?" he asked.

"It's his sister's birthday, so I'm not sure, but probably," Sydney said. She'd started to get her mind around the idea of Nate and Robby spending time together, although she still wasn't certain if it was the right thing to do or not. Robby just seemed so relaxed around him. Even after all his fame, Nate had that effect on people.

"I heard that Nate managed to get his hands on one of Sally Ann's peach cobblers for tonight," Uncle Hank said, pacing up beside them. "Between that and the cake, you'll need to play some football to burn off all that sugar."

"How did he get one of Sally Ann's cobblers?" Sydney's mother asked. "The bakery's been sold out of them for a week now, since the tourists have started arriving."

Sally Ann, the town baker, was famous for her home-made peach cobbler. The whole village knew how good they were, and in the summer months they had to be ordered specially, because they sold out faster than one could say "pie."

"I asked her when I saw her in town this morning," Uncle Hank said. "She was so star-struck by Nathan Carr entering the bakery that she gave him one from her personal stash in the back that she reserves for special occasions. She took a photo of him holding it, and then ran straight to her phone and posted the picture on all the bakery's social media outlets."

"Why does Nate have two last names?" Robby asked.

Unaware that he even knew that fact, Sydney tried to hide her discomfort while she tried to figure out the most concise way to explain a pen name. "When he's writing, he uses the last name Carr."

"Why doesn't he just use his regular name?" Robby asked.

"I think it's easier to remember a short name like Carr than a long one like Henderson, and it isn't as common, so people will remember it." She didn't want to mention her own opinion about it: that she'd felt Nate wanted to get as far away from who he was as possible—as far away from *her*—and that he wanted to reinvent himself as a superstar with no connections to his past.

"Oh, that makes sense," Robby said. "When he's with us, his last name is Henderson, right? That's what I heard Hallie say at the wedding. But someone else called him Mr. Carr. *I* think it's because he's like Superman." Robby grinned. "Superman has two names."

"I doubt Nate would consider himself a hero. . . ." she replied. She certainly didn't.

"You certainly have taken a liking to Nate," Uncle Hank said, moving over and walking beside Robby. "You like him?"

"Yeah." Robby tossed his ball into the air and caught it with both hands. "He's as much fun as Ben."

"It's good to have those kinds of people in our lives, isn't it?" Uncle Hank said. He winked at Sydney, but she didn't find the humor in this conversation. It terrified her. Nate clearly had too much going on in that head of his to be what Robby needed.

Sydney's mother waved at Nate, who was headed toward them. Speak of the devil.

"Robby! Go long!" he called down the road, his hands in the air.

Robby's face lit up like the sunrise on a clear day and he cocked back and then let the ball go. It landed right into Nate's hands.

"You've got a good arm on you," Nate said to Robby when they reached each other. He tossed Robby the ball. "I've got a big spot in the back yard cleared out for us to play."

As they reached Malory's cottage, Robby ran ahead. "Show me, Nate!" he called, not stopping as he got to the grass.

"Guess I'd better follow him around back," Nate said, running off before Sydney had even had a chance to redirect her son.

"Here, let me take that." Sydney's mother hooked her fingers through the handles of the gift bag. "You need to go inside and relax. It's been ages since you've spent an evening with Malory. I'm sure she'll be delighted that you've come tonight."

"I should probably go find Robby," Sydney said, but her mother caught her arm.

"He'll be okay," she replied, unspoken words in her eyes. "He's just playing football. Let's go in, say hello to the birthday girl, and get a drink."

When they got inside, Malory rushed over to them happily. "Hi!" she said, giving Sydney and her mother a big squeeze of a hug. She seemed genuinely delighted to see them, despite the undercurrent of unease that had slithered between Malory and Sydney because of Nate. "Uncle Hank! I'm so glad you could come too."

"Glad to see you," Uncle Hank said. Everyone in town who was Sydney's age had referred to Hank and Clara as if they were family, and Malory was no different.

"I was hoping to get to talk to you at the wedding. I had to take Juliana home," Malory said, linking her arm with Sydney's like they used to do. Her actions contrasted with the lingering questions in her gaze.

Sydney missed the days when they'd skipped along the side of the road between their houses without a care in the world.

"I know; Nate told me," she said, wishing Malory could've spent more time at the wedding, too. Sydney longed for the lighthearted atmosphere that used to follow them wherever they went.

Clearly sensing the dynamic, Uncle Hank said, "Malory, I'm so happy to see you invited the Fergusons. Jacqueline and I should say hello." Sydney's mother lit up at the sight of their long-time friends and followed Uncle Hank over to the owners of the bait and tackle shop in town.

"Can I show you something?" Malory asked the moment they were alone, noticeably taking advantage of the short lull in conversation with her guests. She took Sydney to a bedroom in the back.

The room was tidy, the bed made; the only evidence that anyone was even staying in the room was the lump of Nate's clothes that were draped on a side chair beside a pair of stilettos. Sydney sat down on the bed, trying not to imagine the two people who had slept in it last night.

Malory opened a drawer, and Sydney immediately recognized the old notebook she pulled from it. "That's mine," Sydney said, the surprise over seeing it again after all these years making her breathless. "I wondered where it went."

Malory sat down beside her and handed Sydney the
tattered leather-bound book. Gingerly, Sydney opened the
cover and ran her fingers down the words. "I couldn't think
of anything to say...." She looked up, swallowing to alleviate the lump that was forming. "Nate got me this notebook because mine was full, and it was so clean and perfect
that I remember I had trouble knowing what to write first
because I didn't want to ruin the beauty of it." She looked
back down at that first entry. "Nate told me to harness that
emotion and write the first thing that came to my mind. All
I could think about was how, one day, I wanted my writing
to be worthy of such a gorgeous gift as this book and a sort
of manifest destiny rushed through me. I wrote this." She
turned the notebook around and showed Malory what she'd
written:

I am destined for great things.

What had happened to that drive? Sydney knew exactly
what had happened to it. Nate had been that voice in her
head, cheering her on, telling her how talented she was,
and when he left her behind, it had made her feel like all
his words had meant nothing. She'd suddenly felt like she'd
been weighing him down. Looking back on her adult life so
far, she hadn't lived up to such a colossal statement as the
one glaring back at her from the open page in her hand—in
fact, just the sight of it made her feel like she'd been nothing but a silly child when she'd written that. Yet Nate had
actually done so many great things. Perhaps he really had
known back then how ridiculous that declaration was for
her to write, he'd been wise enough to see that she wouldn't
be able to achieve her dreams. Maybe leaving them all had
actually been the best decision he could've made....

"Nate had this book in his suitcase," Malory said, tapping the notebook, grabbing hold of Sydney's attention once more.

Sydney looked up at her friend, losing her breath for a second.

"I don't know what's going on," Malory told her. "He's secretive, and he's never like that with me. He's overly protective of Juliana, but then I see him reading that journal of yours at night by the lamp in the living room, completely consumed by it, tears in his eyes... You and I both know that he wouldn't be unfaithful to his girlfriend—I don't care what kind of celebrity he's become; he wouldn't do that. But you're all he talks about whenever it's just the two of us. I think he's come back here for you, Syd."

"That's ridiculous," Sydney said with an incredulous laugh.

"Is it?" There wasn't a shred of amusement on Malory's face. "You two dated for four years—that's longer than he's ever dated anyone else. He told me back then that you were the only person he could ever imagine spending his life with."

"People change," she countered. "And it doesn't make any sense." Sydney shook her head, completely baffled. Where had all this come from after so many years?

"I know he's my big brother, so I probably give him the benefit of the doubt above and beyond what I should, but something tells me that there's more in that head of his than what we're seeing on the outside." She leaned forward into Sydney's view. "Think about it: nothing has brought him home for any length of time in all these years. He told me he called you before your wedding, but he wouldn't elaborate as to why. All he said was that you shot him down and made him realize that you'd moved on with your life and he needed to do the same. Then you move back to Starlight Cottage—single—and within the year, he's staying at my house, buying property, getting involved with local events—he's even been working on his old truck."

"He still has that thing?"

"It's what he pulled up in. I've never seen Juliana Vargas so out of place in my life!" Malory said, giggling. "That's why I jumped at the chance to take Juliana back to the house during the wedding. I was hoping he'd open up and tell you what all of this is about."

Suddenly, those thoughts Sydney had seen in his stare at the wedding began to match up with this revelation of Malory's. She considered how he kept coming back to the cottage to see her, pouring out his heart. Was there more to his gesture than just making things right between them?

"He might have tried to tell me . . . But the whole situation rubs me the wrong way. I don't want him coming back here for me. Not like this."

"It's been a long time, and after he hurt you the way he did, I thought long and hard about whether I should tell you my opinions on the matter, but it would eat me up to not say anything. Talk to him, Sydney. Ask him your questions. Let him get whatever this is off his chest completely and then make a decision. You owe it to the both of you. Maybe, now that you two have grown up, this will be your chance for happiness."

"He lost his chance the day he decided I wasn't good enough for him." Sydney closed the journal and handed it back to Malory. There was a part of her that still held on to that magic of the past, that wanted to run into his arms, but the other side of her wouldn't allow it. She just couldn't, given the way things had ended between them. She had her pride and self-worth to think about, not to mention Robby.

A knock sent them both jumping, the notebook slamming down onto the floor.

Nate was in the doorway, his eyes on the notebook, looking as white as a ghost. "I was just checking on Juliana, but then I wondered why the birthday girl was tucked away in a back room," he said, coming in and picking up the book. He handled it gently as if it were fragile and then held it out to Sydney. "This belongs to you."

"You can keep it," she told him, her tone laced with the pain of what was written on the pages: all her dreams that had never happened.

"Is everything all right?" Juliana said from behind Nate in her Argentinean accent that sounded as comforting as home cooking.

Nate tossed the book gently onto the chair with his clothes, and turned to Juliana, a new sense of purpose overtaking him. "Don't go outside." There was warning in his words.

"Why not?" Juliana stepped up in front of him, concern written on her face.

"There's a photographer out there taking pictures of the yard from the tree line."

Juliana's eyes glistened. "Do you think he got any photos of me when I went out to bring you a drink earlier?"

"I don't know. I was playing football with Robby. I only just noticed him. I have no idea how long he's been there."

"How did they find us?" Juliana asked, her voice shaking.

Nate shook his head and ran his fingers through his hair. "I let Sally Ann post photos of me online." His jaw clenched, and he was noticeably remorseful about his error.

"I should've been more careful." He balled his hands into fists by his side. "Damn it."

"It's okay," Juliana said, rubbing his arm. "It was only a matter of time anyway. I can't hide from them forever."

That familiar unease Sydney felt when Juliana and Nate shared intimate moments like this came rushing back.

"I know. But I feel like it's my fault. I wanted to give you more of an opportunity to work through things before you had to deal with all that."

"Would someone like to fill us in?" Malory asked, standing up from the bed and walking over to Nate.

"It's just our daily struggle with the press. They connect their own dots about our lives, and they couldn't be further from the truth. And right now, we don't need any speculation about Juliana's life or what she's doing here." Just as the words came out of his mouth, the intensity melted as he looked at his sister. "I'm sorry. It's your birthday. Let's not let that one guy ruin your party. Juliana and I will stay inside for the night, and we'll close the blinds on the east side of the house so they won't get even a glimpse of what's going on."

"That's no way to live," Malory said.

"We're used to it." Juliana blew a frustrated breath through her red lips. "My aunt owned a restaurant in New York and my mother thought it would expand my horizons if I went abroad, so she let me visit. I was only sixteen when my first modeling agent saw me through the window of the restaurant and contracted me right there on the spot. All of the glitter in her talk and the promise of so many things— how could I say no? But she never told me about this." Juliana waved her hand at the window. "She never taught me how to live as a prisoner. And Nathan has it worse than I do—they hound him like crazy. I only hope that now that I have stopped modeling, after a while, people will tire of me and leave me alone."

"So that's why you're leaving modeling...." Sydney said.

"Part of the reason, yes."

"What's the other part?" Sydney asked.

Juliana paused. "I'd rather not say." There was a definite shift in her demeanor, and it was evident that whatever it was had certainly affected her. That was when Sydney noticed Juliana's hands shaking like a leaf.

Nate must have seen it at the same time, because he rushed over to her and put his arms around her. Feeling awkward and suddenly stifled in that tiny room while Nate consoled Juliana, Sydney took Malory's arm, and they slipped past the couple.

As they entered the living room, Malory got pulled into a conversation with some friends of hers and Robby ran up to Sydney.

"Where's Nate?" he asked.

"He's helping Juliana with something. He'll be back in just a minute," she said, her mind in such a muddle. She needed to refocus. "I see a table full of snacks. We better get over there before Uncle Hank finishes all the cheese." She pointed past a bunch of balloons to a table against the wall where her uncle was helping himself to a cracker with cheese. "Should we go over and see what's on it?"

"Yes!" Robby moved through the now crowded cottage to where Uncle Hank was still standing and Sydney followed.

"Hey, bud!" Uncle Hank said, ruffling his hair.

Robby wrapped his arms around his uncle. "This is a fun party, isn't it?" Robby said, pulling away and snagging a brownie from a platter of confections.

But before they'd been able to start any sort of

conversation, Robby left them, running off toward Nate as he came into the room. Juliana settled in a chair and started making small talk with a couple that was nearby, still noticeably shaken but doing well at hiding it. The woman speaking to her clearly hadn't noticed. Nate squatted down, saying something to Robby, and with the noise in the room, Sydney couldn't make out what it was.

"Those two get along famously," Uncle Hank noted, something clearly on his mind as he pointed it out. "... You know, I called Nate today."

Sydney nodded, her head still clouded with everything she'd just taken in, remembering what Nate had said when she'd gotten home from work. "Why did you call him?" Sydney asked Uncle Hank.

"I wanted to find out which realtor he used to buy his land."

"You mean the lot he bought?" Sydney asked.

Uncle Hank laughed. "I suppose you could call it a 'lot.' That is, if you think fifty-seven acres of beachfront property is a 'lot.'"

"Fifty-seven acres?" She looked over at Nate, processing this. "That's *millions* of dollars."

"He has it, Sydney."

With that kind of investment, Nate was most certainly planting roots here. A future with him in it was solidified in her mind now, and she scrambled for what to do. Could she handle that? Should she move back to Nashville? She didn't want to leave—she loved it in Firefly Beach. But all his back and forth was too difficult to handle, and she just wanted to escape it. Was it so wrong to want to run away? After all, that was what he'd done.

Suddenly, the question occurred to her: "Why did you need to know his realtor?" she asked Uncle Hank.

"I have to have the best, and I knew that he'd have chosen a top agent to help him find his property." Uncle Hank looked down at the balled napkin in his hands from his cookie. "I'm seriously considering selling Starlight Cottage."

Aunt Clara's smile as she waved to Sydney at the front door of the cottage flashed in Sydney's mind, all the memories flooding her like some sort of movie reel gone haywire. Starlight Cottage was part of the Flynn family. It had seen them through thick and thin. It had seen Flynn weddings over the years, the birth of babies, and it had seen Aunt Clara through her last days; it had been her great aunt's solace and sense of peace her entire adult life...

"I didn't think you were serious about selling," she said, her temples beginning to ache. She wished she could get Aunt Clara's opinion, at the very least, see her face—her expression would speak volumes about whether or not selling was a good idea. "There's no dilemma too great to conquer," Aunt Clara explained to Sydney once. "The hard part is knowing what it means exactly to 'conquer' it. The answer isn't always what you want or even think should happen, but it's what was in the cards all along. The 'conquering' occurs within sometimes, but everything can be conquered."

"It won't be the same once the public beach access is built," Uncle Hank said, drawing Sydney out of her memory. "The Starlight Cottage that we love will be forever changed the moment the clearing begins." He straightened his shoulders and grabbed another cookie. "Let's talk about it later. We need to enjoy the birthday party."

"You know what? You're absolutely right," she said, needing a break from everything.

On her way into the kitchen, she spotted Nate. She grabbed a cracker for herself and decided to head to the kitchen in search of a glass of wine. She couldn't conquer the issues facing Starlight Cottage tonight or the problems surrounding her and Nate, but she could completely conquer the rift that had formed between her and Malory. It was Malory's birthday, and she was going to celebrate with her friend.

Chapter Eleven

Sydney tipped her glass toward Malory as her friend topped it off with the last of the wine. They'd finally opened up about their feelings surrounding the break-up.

"I felt like it was all my fault for getting you two together," Malory told her, shaking her head. "It seemed like you two were perfect for each other. You were so perfect that it never even occurred to me that you'd ever break up. After, I felt naïve, like I had my head in the clouds, when maybe I could've focused more on your lives and at least warned you."

"Malory, it was my choice to date Nate. You couldn't have foreseen this, nor was it in any way your fault," Sydney told her. "I'm just glad I came over tonight. I should've come to find you sooner."

Malory smiled. "I missed you."

"Same." Sydney held up her glass to toast her friend. "To us," she said, clinking Malory's glass.

It had been just the two of them for a while. She had no idea where Nate was and everyone else had gone home. The two women sat together on the sofa, their feet kicked up on the coffee table that was littered with streamers and scraps of wrapping paper. Uncle Hank and her mother had refused to let her leave, telling her she needed to unwind, taking Robby home and putting him in bed for her. After everyone else had gone, she and Malory had stayed up talking, neither of them worried about the fact that they both had to work the next day.

"I'm calling in sick," Malory declared, giggling.

"I might sleep in late." Sydney forced the words to come out evenly through the buzz of the alcohol. "I need to get home soon though, or I'm going to end up falling asleep right here."

They both laughed. Malory snorted, only making them giggle harder.

"I've missed you," Malory said. She put her arm around Sydney and offered a slow smile under her drooping eyelids. "I'm getting sappy from all the wine." She took another drink from her glass.

"I've had so much wine," Sydney said, "that I caught myself considering whether Tommy Simpson from down the road might have actually been attractive and we just hadn't noticed it..."

Malory fell over laughing in fits of loud inhalations and cackling. Tommy Simpson had had a crush on them when they were younger. He was just a regular guy, nothing flashy, kind of quiet, bad haircut...

"But seriously," Sydney said, sobering, "I've missed you too." She sat up. "Happy birthday."

"Thank you. It was the best birthday ever with you here."

"Let's get a coffee tomorrow. I think we'll both need one..."

They both laughed again, but their merriment was interrupted when Nate came into the room. "Did I hear you say you need to go home?" he asked Sydney in a whisper that she could only assume was to avoid waking his girlfriend. "I'll walk you."

Sydney looked past him down the hall. "You should really stay with Juliana," she said, the wine giving an edge to her usual sadness. She cut her eyes at him.

Nate followed the track of her earlier gaze to his bedroom. "Juliana is sleeping across the hall," he said. "The one you were in earlier is *my* room."

"But you both had your things in there..." She was struggling to make sense of what was going on, given the buzz in her head from the drinks and a long day.

"Her room is too small for her bags, so she keeps them in my room." With a playfully annoyed look, he walked over to her and grabbed her hands, pulling her up from the sofa. "Stop being stubborn. I'm walking you home. You've had too much wine to go alone."

Sydney stood, the alcohol giving her courage. She wasn't drunk. She was just relaxed enough to give him a piece of her mind. She got onto her tiptoes and looked him in the eye. "I'm a big girl. I've done it alone for many, many years now, thank you very much," she said, glaring at him.

The corner of his mouth twitched upward and he gently pushed a strand of hair out of her face with his forefinger. With that one touch, her knees felt like soft butter and she wobbled. Nate caught her.

"I've got the key. Lock up after we leave," he said to Malory, his arm still around Sydney.

The street was dark and quiet, as the two of them walked toward Starlight Cottage. Neither of them said a word. The only sound between them was the soft caress of the gulf against the shore. She'd walked beside him so many times, but this time was different. She was aware of every breath he took, every stride he made, the way his shoulders tensed just a little when he slipped his hands into his pockets. A tiny subconscious part of her wanted the moment to stretch into the night, and with every mailbox they passed, she found herself willing him to keep walking with her past her house so he wouldn't have to say goodnight.

When the long drive to Starlight Cottage came into view, Nate took her arm to stop her. He looked around at the black of night and then leaned in to her ear.

"I don't know if we're being photographed," he said quietly, "so I'm going to whisper this to you." He put his lips right by her ear, his breath on her skin sending a chill down her spine. "Juliana isn't my girlfriend. But the press doesn't know that. There's a lot going on, and I hadn't really prepared for it all." He pulled back and looked her in the eye. "Can we talk tomorrow?"

Sydney wanted to be relieved by his admission, but the truth of the matter was that it didn't change the way he'd made her feel about herself. And even if she could get over that, there was that tiny voice in the back of her mind that whispered, "What if he left again?" This time, it wasn't just her he'd be abandoning; she had Robby too.

"Please meet me tomorrow," he said, interrupting her inner battle.

"I have to work tomorrow," she replied, knowing how feeble the excuse seemed. Sydney's head was starting to pound. She needed to get inside where she could clear her mind.

Nate reached out and caressed her arm. Just when she was about to take a step, a white-hot flash, like a lightning strike, burned her eyes. She blinked to try to clear it, but all she could see was a gray haze, her vision affected by the intensity of the light. Unexpectedly, Nate's hand was at her back, moving her forward, startling her and burning through the alcohol in her system. She stumbled alongside him blindly as the images in front of her slowly came back into focus.

"If I try to run from them, it will give them more ammo to make up stories about you and me," he said in her ear as another flash went off. "We have to look like we have nothing to hide." Then, he spoke urgently, "And I still don't know if they've realized Juliana is here in Firefly Beach. She doesn't sleep well, and she gets up in the night. I'm not even sure if the press is aware that I'm *staying* at Malory's; they could just think I was at the party there tonight. If I go back there, they might camp out until the morning to get a good shot. Once they know where I'm living, they'll be back every day. I'm coming inside."

"They got my picture?" Sydney didn't know how to feel about the possibility of being in Nathan Carr's circus of a world.

"It's dark. The photo's probably too grainy to use," he said as they neared the cottage. "I'm just being proactive."

There was something very unsettling about learning she'd been watched. Had the photographer been with them the entire walk home? She and Nate climbed the few stairs leading to the front porch together, and she noticed how calm he was in all this. His movements were deliberate and well practiced. This was his reality all the time. When she used to fantasize as a girl about being famous, this idea of it had never entered her mind. She suddenly felt glad that she hadn't become the famous one. This was not something she wanted to deal with every day.

"So you mean they might camp out at Starlight Cottage now?" she asked, slipping her key into the front door lock as she sent darting glances over her shoulder.

Nate ushered her inside and shut the door quickly behind them.

"It's possible," he said, regret filling his face. "I'm so sorry. I really didn't think that letting Sally Ann post a photo would cause this. They hound me at public events, but at home, they usually leave me alone." He stopped cold. "Unless..." He pulled out his phone and fired off a text. After staring at the screen for a long pause, he dialed a number and put the phone to his ear.

"Malory, I'm at Sydney's. Is Juliana awake, by chance?...Go check." He began to pace in front of the doorway. Sydney stepped aside, trying to make sense of the call. "Hey," he said, his whole body straightening up. "Juliana, don't go outside until I'm back. The photographer followed me here. But I started thinking...What if he isn't with the press? You have three months left in your modeling deal, right?" Nate walked over and shut the window blinds. "Are you in breach of contract being here right now?" He went over to one of the two matching dark blue bergère-style chairs that Aunt Clara had delighted in when she'd redesigned the living room and sat down. "What if it isn't a reporter? What if the camera man is an investigator?"

Investigator? Sydney took a seat on the floor next to Nate's chair.

"I'll be back the minute I think this guy's left, all right?" Then he listened quietly for quite a while before telling Juliana it would be okay.

"What's going on, Nate?" Sydney asked when he'd gotten off the phone.

He blew out a frustrated puff of air and rubbed his eyes. "I'm not sure. At first I thought it was just a rogue photographer, trying to make a buck on a quick story—and it could be. But then it hit me that Juliana's four-year contract will expire in three months, and her lawyer will be presenting her thirty-day notice to the agency to terminate the contract. She has about two working months left before the lawyer gives notice. I wondered if the agency has sent someone to find her because contractually she's under obligation to work, no matter what her mental health is like."

"Would they do something like that?"

"They would do a whole lot of things to get what they want..." He gritted his teeth and stood up.

"So why would the photographer follow *us*?" she asked, pressing her fingers against her temples that felt as if they would throb right out of her head.

"Hopefully, if they didn't see her earlier at Malory's, it was to document the fact that Juliana isn't here. That's our best hope. Maybe the photographer will assume she's somewhere else, and he'll go back to wherever he came from."

"And if it's the press? Would that be any better?"

"Not really." He leaned on his knees and put his head in his hands. "I wasn't even thinking about the agency when I posed with Sally Ann for that photo—if that's even what it was that caused this." He looked up at her with tired eyes. "I just...I feel more like myself here, instead of this celebrity figure that people have built me up to be. I guess I forgot who I'd become for a second." There was a tremble in his voice that made him seem more vulnerable than Sydney had ever seen him before.

"It's okay," she said in an attempt to console him. "It was just one tiny sidestep, but it will pass."

He shook his head. "I feel like I can't ever get anything right."

"What?" Sydney asked, nearly breathless by his confession. When it came to getting what he'd wanted, he'd achieved an incredible amount.

"I'm not happy," he admitted. "I've made a complete mess of my life, trying to do the right thing."

She looked into his eyes, and it was as if time stood still. She missed him so much. He stared at her, so many unsaid words between them, and she could've sworn by his look that he was trying to tell her how much he missed her too. Her forearm prickled, every nerve ending on high alert as he trailed his finger along it lightly, and she knew right then that she was still completely in love with him. In an instant, she wanted to put her arms around him and kiss his lips. They shared that space together, just the two of them, locked in that moment with one another. With the flutters going on in her belly the way they were, she considered whether she'd forgiven him for leaving her the way he had. Before she could contemplate her answer, however, he hastily broke his gaze and paced across the room.

"I feel like I'm having some kind of breakdown," he said. "I don't know what I'm doing."

The insecurity she'd felt all those years ago came slithering back in. Why had he pulled away just now? Had he realized that he was staring into the same future he'd left so many years ago?

"I . . . uh . . . I'm going to go up to bed," she said, trying not to let her hurt show. "Lock up when you leave."

He grabbed onto her with his stare, urgency in his eyes, but she turned away.

Then something came over her: she felt sorry for him. He was only a shadow now of the boy she'd known. That life he'd chased, gambling everything he loved and rolling the dice, was eating him alive. She went over to him and kissed his cheek. "Good night, Nate," she said, her tone telling him that they were done here.

"Good night," he said, barely audible under the confusion

and defeat in his voice. And as she left his sight and walked up the stairs, she stopped, sharpening her hearing. But all she heard was silence. Her mind must have been playing tricks on her because she could've sworn she heard him whisper, "I love you, Syd." But perhaps that was simply wishful thinking.

Chapter Twelve

The first sound that entered Sydney's consciousness was the tinkling of the wind chime on the porch outside, signaling a gentle breeze, but she couldn't quite swim out of her sleep enough to move. The morning sun streaming in through her window didn't even help. But then Nate's laugh sailed into her room from downstairs and her eyes flew open. Robby's giggle followed. It was seven a.m. What was he still doing here? Sydney grabbed her bathrobe and threw it on.

When she got downstairs, Nate and Robby were side-by-side on the floor in the living room, notebooks open, drawing together. A folded blanket sat on the sofa with a toothbrush on top from the packs that her mother had gathered for guests when they'd redone the bathroom. Nate was still in his clothes from yesterday, a shadow of stubble on his face. Ben's dog Beau greeted Sydney before retreating back to the sunspot on his dog bed in the corner of the room.

"Nate showed me how to draw a dinosaur," Robby said to her when she neared them.

Nate looked up at her, a fond grin spreading across his face. "Sleep well?" he asked.

It was only then that she realized she hadn't even looked

in the mirror yet. Her hair was still disheveled from sleep, and she had no recollection of taking off her mascara last night, which made for an amusing appearance, she was certain. She ignored his question.

"I'm just going to get a cup of coffee. And a glass of water."

Judging by the sandpaper feel of her tongue, she started to wonder if maybe she'd had more wine than she should've last night.

Nate twisted his notebook toward Robby. "Here's how to do the tail. Give it a try while I get a cup of coffee with your mom." Nate stood up and walked over to her. Once they were facing each other, she thought she saw a tiny bit of hesitation, as if he didn't know what to do around her anymore.

"What's wrong?" she asked.

He nodded toward the kitchen, so she led them down the hallway.

She could see her mother and Uncle Hank through the window. They were out on the porch like they often were before the heat of the day settled in. A full pot of coffee was waiting for Sydney, a familiar gesture by her mother. She slid the milk and sugar over before pouring two steaming coffees, but then abandoned the mugs and faced Nate, waiting for any kind of explanation as to his tentativeness a minute ago.

He swallowed, a gentle smile surfacing. "I miss seeing you like this," he said. "Remember when we'd get so tired writing that we'd fall asleep at one another's houses and we'd wake up the next morning and look at each other like that night's sleep together had been some sort of secret prize we'd both won? You'd always raise your eyebrows at me, your face looking like Christmas morning. Remember that feeling?"

"Like it was yesterday," she replied, allowing her emotion to show. His obvious adoration for her this morning was confusing her, and she could barely keep her mind straight, answering truthfully.

He stared at her, his face full of thoughts. Out of nowhere, it looked as though he were going to kiss her, a move she wasn't sure how to navigate, the two sides of her brain in stark conflict over it, causing her pulse to rise. He'd hit a nerve with that memory—waking up beside him had been her most favorite thing...

Nate leaned in, the warmth of his breath at her ear as he said, "I miss you."

Every nerve was on high alert, her mind totally clouded and unable to create a single thought other than the fact that she missed him too. In fact, if she wanted to be totally honest with herself, she'd never stopped missing him. She'd just pushed it down where it would stop hurting so much.

Just then, Uncle Hank came in and the two of them flew apart. "Ah, Robby let you have a break from the drawing lessons?" he asked, seemingly not noticing their proximity.

"Yes," Nate said, still clearly recovering from the moment. He cleared his throat. "I don't mind, though. I enjoy being with Robby. He's very creative."

"That, he is. Just like his mama," Uncle Hank replied, getting himself a coffee. He threaded his large fingers through the handles of all three mugs and brought them to the table. "Have a seat with me. I want to pick your brain."

Nate pulled out the chair.

Last night's conversation with Uncle Hank came rushing back to Sydney, and she knew that she wanted to be a voice of reason in this little chat. She sat next to Nate and stirred her coffee.

"I need a good real estate agent, and I was hoping you

could give me a reference," Uncle Hank said over his mug. "I'm considering the possibility of selling Starlight Cottage."

"Really?" Nate asked, his expression oddly unreadable.

"Yeah." Uncle Hank shook his head.

"Are you downsizing or something?" Nate's gaze flickered over to Sydney and then back to Uncle Hank. He was clearly trying to get a read on the conversation. It seemed to be making him uncomfortable, but he also didn't appear to be against the idea of selling.

"Everything is changing in Firefly Beach, and if the new shopping area they're proposing creates an environment anything like the massive influx of tourists that downtown has been facing every year, I'm not so sure I want to be this close to all the development." Uncle Hank looked down into his coffee.

Nate tapped his fingers against the table, clearly buying time before he responded. "If it's seclusion you want, you could build something by me. I've been talking it over with Malory. She's planning to sell as well, and I'm giving her ten acres of the parcel of land that I bought. I could definitely make room for you and the family."

Uncle Hank pressed his fingers to his lips in thought, clearly wrestling with the kindness of Nate's gesture and the anguish of losing the last tangible piece of Aunt Clara's legacy.

Sydney's opinion wasn't as diplomatic. Was Nate serious? He'd spent quite enough time here to know how much Starlight Cottage meant to Aunt Clara and to the family. And Uncle Hank was actually giving this ridiculous idea thought?

"You two can't be considering this," Sydney said, her heart rate quickening. None of it had seemed real until this moment.

"I'll bet we can even have the lighthouse moved," Nate carried on.

"Starlight Cottage is a lot to take care of…" Uncle Hank said, but she could see the sadness under his casual expression. He was stuck and deciding to settle.

"That has never bothered you before," she said. "That stupid public beach access—it's ruining everything. We need to fight it!"

"I will," Uncle Hank said. "In fact, they've scheduled an emergency meeting on Friday, and Lewis and I will definitely be there. I think we should all go to show our disagreement."

"Absolutely. I'm with you," Sydney said.

"I'll call around and see if I can drum up some more support. We need numbers at this point."

"Yes," she agreed, determined.

"But sometimes, Sydney, despite everything we do, things just change, and, while I'll do what I can, I'm too old to fight unnecessary battles." He leaned across the table and took her hand. "Would it be so bad to call another four walls home?" The uncertainty in his voice gave away the fact that he needed her to convince him. And that, she could never do.

Sydney looked over at the chair that had been empty since Aunt Clara had passed, wondering what her aunt would say. She tried to tell herself that Starlight Cottage was Aunt Clara's vision, and that maybe now it was time for them to all move forward, but just the thought of it brought her to tears. It had been hard enough to face being here without her favorite aunt. But losing Starlight Cottage would be losing the last shred of Aunt Clara, and something inside her screamed out how wrong it was to let it go.

"Do you know what Aunt Clara told me once?" she asked, trying to keep the wobble out of her voice. She had the attention of both Nate and Uncle Hank. "She told me that the name Starlight reminded her that even in the darkness that life could sometimes bring, this place shined—just like a star in the black of night. It brought her into the present, and she swore that she was her truest self when she simply existed in that single moment. She said that the past had already been and the future had yet to be dreamt. The present—this—" Sydney waved her hand around. "This is what matters most. This place was what made her whole again when the world made her feel less than that."

"She was a wise woman," Nate said, his knowing eyes on Sydney. "I like the idea of existing in the present moment. It makes everything else fade away."

"What if we're all still trying to live in *her* reality," Uncle Hank said. "What if I might miss her less when I didn't have so many reminders?"

The pain Sydney had dealt with over the last year as she tried to help Uncle Hank manage his grief while she coped with her own sadness came rushing back to her, so much so that she almost didn't register the ringing of Nate's cell phone.

"Sorry," he said, waving his phone at them. "Juliana's calling." He hit the speaker and held it in front of him. "Hey, Juliana. You're on speaker with Sydney and Hank."

"Okay . . ." Her voice sounded small through the phone. "They are outside the house and I can't leave."

"The photographers?" he asked.

"Yes. I don't know what to do. I'm supposed to go to my counseling appointment right now."

Sydney jumped up and looked at the clock. It was seven forty-five. She needed to get ready; she'd told Mary Alice she'd meet her at the wellness center to look over some ideas she had for the magazine. The thought was jarring, since she had so much on her mind already this morning, but she tried to focus on the issues she could solve right now. "I can pick her up and she can ride with me," Sydney offered. "She could wear one of Mama's big sun hats to hide her face."

"Hang on," Nate said. "Juliana, call your agent and explain what's going on. We need to know if it's just paparazzi or if you need to be in LA for a few more months to finish your contract."

"I cannot go back to LA," Juliana said, her voice breaking on the last word, panic in her voice.

"We can make sure you won't even have to see Seth. We'll file a restraining order." Nate spoke as if he were the only person in the room.

"No," Juliana said quickly. "That will make him unhappy and I don't know what he will do."

Nate took in a long breath. "Okay. Call your agent and feel out the situation. Once we know who's out there, we can figure out how to handle it. I'll make sure Mary Alice knows you can't get to her, and I'll reschedule. I'll work from here today."

Juliana said her goodbyes and Nate ended the call. He turned to Sydney. "If they're outside Malory's still, they're probably outside here too. Is it all right if I ask Mary Alice if she can come to you today? Otherwise, the photographers might follow you, and I don't want them to connect anything to the wellness center. If it *is* the press, then even the tiniest inkling that Juliana or I might be getting therapy could be terrible. They'll blow it out of proportion. The next thing we know, they'll say we're unstable."

Uncle Hank stood up before Sydney could respond, and retrieved a pair of keys from the cupboard. He walked back over to them and set them down in front of Nate. "Take my boat," he said. "No one will see you if you leave from the back of the cottage. Pack what you need for the day and the two of you can work out on the water."

Nate took the keys and his phone and gave Uncle Hank a squeeze around the shoulders with one arm. "You are the best, Uncle Hank," he said. "I'll call Mary Alice now so she knows what's going on."

"We won't have any Wi-Fi...Give me a second so I can pull up a few emails for my column." Sydney was trying to get her head around the fact that she was going to spend the day secluded on a boat with Nate.

"Of course," Nate said. In the midst of the drama, a small smile formed at the corners of his mouth. "You're writing again," he said. It hadn't been a question but more of an observation.

She nodded.

"I'm so happy to hear that." He turned to Uncle Hank. "Great idea," he said. "We'll take the boat."

"Excellent," Uncle Hank said as he opened the large bag of dog food and scooped up a cup of it, dumping it in Beau's bowl. The dog ran over and sniffed his new meal. "Then when you get home, perhaps you can fill me in on what in the world is going on."

Sydney patted his shoulder.

Nate, who'd stepped outside to make the call, came back in and dangled the keys in front of Sydney. "Mary Alice is completely fine with it. Get your swimsuit. It might get hot out there."

Jacqueline came in from outside. "I heard you two are taking a little boat ride today," she said with a cautious smile. "I'll make y'all some lunch and put it in the cooler."

Sydney's day was suddenly turning out a whole lot differently. And she wasn't quite sure about it at all.

Chapter Thirteen

Sydney stretched her bare legs out on the bench seat of Uncle Hank's center-console fishing boat, scooting back so that her laptop was under the shade of the overhang above the captain's chair and opened the few emails she'd quickly copied and pasted, praying she'd gotten something with substance. She'd been in such a rush that she hadn't read a single one before now, and she noticed that one of the emails was a response from Mel4221. She read that one first.

> *Dear Ms. Flynn,*
>
> *I definitely hear you that there are things in this life that aren't meant to be fixed, and I question whether this is one of those things all the time. She isn't coming back to me, and I can hardly manage, knowing that she was the one person in this life who completed me. I haven't found anyone who can fill her shoes since. What if I've ruined everything by letting her go?*
>
> *Lost,*
> *Mel*

Sydney's mouth dried out, her heart pattering. Mel's experience was exactly how she felt about Nate, but she couldn't help but let him go. He hadn't given her any other choice. What could she say to this man other than the simple fact that she totally understood. Her heart ached for him because there was no easy answer to heartbreak. She didn't dare tell him that a decade later, his pain might still linger in his chest and that the dreams he'd had of their life together would hang in front of him as lost opportunities for the rest of his life.

"What are you working on?" Nate asked, making her jump. He walked over with his notebook under his arm, drying his hands on a towel after dropping anchor.

They'd made it out of the house and down to the dock without incident, and now they were secluded out in the middle of the gulf, rocking in the endless expanse of the turquoise waters, nothing around them but the bobbing markers telling local fishermen where they'd placed their crab pots. Nate picked her legs up, plopped down, and put her legs in his lap, resting his notebook on them as if they were twenty again. Juliana floated into her mind like a strong wind. What would she think of Nate's actions just now? Was she okay with this, or would it break her heart to see it? She tried to suppress the butterflies that swarmed her stomach, telling herself it was only old feelings surfacing.

When she realized he was waiting for an answer, she wriggled upright a bit and said, "I'm writing a response to an email for my column."

Nate's hand rested on her knee. "I can't wait to read it."

"How do you know I'll let you," she said before she'd thought it through. That was what she'd always used to tell him when he'd said he was going to read the pieces she'd written. But this had been a knee-jerk reaction to hide her feelings for him. She didn't want to get into a conversation with Nate, and possibly compare their opinions regarding Mel's experience.

He didn't answer her, but his thumb moved affectionately on her knee, his gaze on her, making her jittery.

She pulled her legs free and twisted around to a sitting position. "We need to work," she said.

Nate sighed dramatically and opened his notebook.

Sydney stared at her screen, rereading the same sentence a couple of times before it finally sank in. This was going to be more difficult than she thought. She needed to focus. With her fingers poised on the keyboard, she forced herself to recall the memory of the taillights of Nate's truck as he left Firefly Beach that day. He'd made her feel so insignificant... That was all she needed to regain concentration on her work. She pulled up another email and started to read about a woman considering a full-time nanny for her only child, the ideas beginning to flow as seamlessly as the lapping waves under the boat.

The heat of the sun bore down on her skin, the salt settling on her lips as her fingers moved on the keys, and she started to get into the groove of writing. The energy of her thoughts as they moved down her arms and through her fingers was like finding a long-lost friend after years apart.

But as she worked, she was increasingly aware of the fact that Nate was staring at her. "What?" she asked, pulling herself from her screen to address him.

He was leaned back, his notebook open with quite a few lines scratched down, the pen in his hand hovering over the paper, his total attention on her.

"Will you please work?" she asked.

"I am," he said, looking into her eyes. "You inspire me." He smiled, giving her a flutter against her will. "It's been a long time since I've had this much to say at once. The ideas have flooded me since the moment I came back. Check this out. I can just hear the island beat in the background and the steel guitars..." He turned his notebook around, showing her the lyrics he'd written:

Sunny days
How I'd like to be castaways
Sailing out on the ocean blue
Spending all my time with you

"Why did you come back?" She could hear the defensiveness in her tone; it came out as irritated and short, when she was only trying to protect herself from getting hurt. It was time to answer the question once and for all.

Nate opened his mouth to say something but his pause gave away the fact that he'd reconsidered whatever it was he'd wanted to tell her. "Juliana needed to get away from someone awful in her life, and she called me to help her."

Disappointment swelled in her stomach as she realized that she'd been hoping for a different answer. But what did she expect?

"The most secluded, restful, comforting place I know is right here in Firefly Beach." He looked out over the gulf, squinting in the sunlight, those familiar creases forming at the corners of his eyes. He took in a deep breath as if the briny air were giving him life, and it made her wonder why he hadn't come back before.

"If it's so inspiring," she said, "then why didn't you come back sooner?"

"I didn't want to...disrupt everyone's lives. I'd made a mess of things and I felt like it might be better to stay away and let everyone enjoy their own happiness."

What did he mean by that?

"When Ben sent me the invite," he continued, "I knew it was the perfect time to bring Juliana here. What a wonderful way to spend a day in a new place: a wedding, where everyone is celebrating love."

How ironic, she thought. She and Nate certainly weren't celebrating...

"Did you bring her here because of that Seth person you mentioned on the phone?" she asked, pushing herself back into the conversation.

"Yeah. His name is Seth Fortini. He's the CEO of the modeling agency where Juliana works, and he's her ex-boyfriend, if you want to call it that." Nate closed his notebook and set it on the bench beside him. "He hurt her..."

Sydney's eyes grew round. "Physically?"

"Yes."

"Oh, my goodness." She put her hand over her mouth to stifle the complete shock of this revelation. Juliana's images in magazines and on social media feeds were alight with glamor and good times. The press had reported that Nate and Juliana were a couple, only having the odd on-again-off-again moments. They were pictured together: grainy street shots of Nate with his arm around her while she nestled into his chest, with dark sunglasses, a cup of coffee.

"Was it during one of your break-ups?" Sydney closed her laptop, placing it in the little spot of shade on the bench beside her.

"We only had a two-week relationship," he said. "We realized pretty early on that we were better as friends and we've been strictly platonic for years...It was a little like kissing my sister." He smirked. "Every time she took a trip or had a date, the press played into the rumors that we'd had some sort of huge fight. And when she started seeing Seth, Juliana didn't want the press to know she was dating him because it wouldn't reflect well on her, since he was her boss. Seth suggested that they keep it quiet, so we didn't let on that we weren't a couple."

"It seemed so believable that you two were an item..."

"We're great friends. After her break-ups, sometimes we'd go out for coffee together. I'm like her big brother, so I was the one she'd call, and I'd run right out to console her."

Sydney knew all too well about Nate's big-brother instinct; she'd felt protected by him her entire life.

"One shot of us walking together and the press can make up whatever they want, to sell magazines. I'm worried that's what's going on right now. Juliana hasn't told Seth where she is, so we don't want anyone taking photos, although I think it's probably too late for that."

"What will happen if Seth finds her?"

"I think he's pretty angry that she disappeared without warning. He left his marriage for her, falling in love with her while they were working. Although Juliana had nothing to do with the marriage breaking up. By the time she knew he was interested, the divorce was only weeks from being finalized."

"Wouldn't he just get the picture, given that she's gone?"

"He doesn't like to lose. When he gets angry, he snaps on her. She's terrified."

"Can Juliana report him?"

"I tried to encourage her to file charges. She doesn't want to. If anyone got wind of their affair, her reputation would be ruined; she's worried she'd never work a day at a reputable agency. She says she doesn't want to model anymore, but she also believes that she has to keep her options open and maintain her clean-cut appeal. At the end of the day, that's how she makes her money, and she may have to go back to that if she needs to."

"She doesn't want to model because of Seth?"

"He was hard on her. He pushed perfection in every shoot, and if she didn't fit that image, he told her to lose weight or to work out. He'd often assign trainers to focus on a specific part of her body, when I could never see what the heck he was even talking about. He told her that by pointing out her flaws, he was only trying to better her career, but no one should have to deal with what she endured. He pushed her through insane workouts that would have her so sore she'd have to take painkillers to move the next day. He only allowed her to eat food prepared by his personal chef, but I counted the calories and, given the workouts she was doing, she was way under. She felt lightheaded all the time, passing out at the end of a long day's shooting. Seth told her she was just frail, and it was a hurdle she'd have to manage if she wanted to survive at the top. For a while, she believed him. She trusted him. He was the person who'd gotten her where she was today. But once things became romantic, she started to notice the cracks. When she began to question him, he'd lash out at her, telling her she was nothing without him."

"My God." Sydney shook her head, trying to process it all. "I wish I could do something to help her." Her shoulders were tense, just thinking about it. "I asked her to model for my magazine. I hope it didn't upset her too badly."

"It's what she does. She wouldn't think a thing of it. But Seth ruined the allure for her. He stole the joy she used to find in it—that's why she doesn't want to do it anymore. It just brings back all those feelings of insecurity and pain."

She looked Nate in the eye and reached for his hand. "You're so good. I'll bet she's incredibly thankful for you."

Sydney couldn't help but draw upon her memories of how Nate had protected her in her younger days. It made her feelings for him surface, and she worried about her resolve with just the two of them out on that boat. But she had to remind herself that he hadn't come back to Firefly Beach for any length of time for her, but that he'd dropped everything and moved his entire life there for someone else.

"I'm hungry," Nate said, causing Sydney to look up from her computer.

She'd written her next two weeks' worth of email responses for the column, the inspiration coming easily to her out on the water, next to Nate. After their heavy exchange regarding Juliana, they'd settled into their work, both of them quietly creating, absorbed by their own energy, but inspired by the depth of conversation and being next to one another. Sydney hadn't felt that in so long; it was like finally getting her breath after being under water.

"Want me to get our lunches?" he asked.

She closed the various screens full of research she'd pulled up using Nate's hotspot, and saved her document, only realizing then that her stomach was growling.

"I wonder what Mama packed us," she said.

"Sandwiches," Nate said with a grin, walking over to the cooler. "I know because I caught a peek when I threw a bottle of wine and two cups into the cooler before loading it onto the boat."

She wondered why he'd gone to so much trouble to pack wine when it was just the two of them on the boat. She wasn't ready for this to get anywhere near romantic...

"I did ask Uncle Hank if I could swipe it." He popped open the lid of the cooler and dipped his hand into the ice, retrieving the bottle of white. With the bottle in his hand, he fished around in one of the bags, grabbing a corkscrew.

"I'm glad you asked Uncle Hank this time," she said with a smile.

He became still as he absorbed her statement, and then the memory passed across his face. Nate threw his head back and laughed. "We took all three of his bottles on that hike through the mountains!" He chuckled again. "How were we to know that he'd ordered them especially for Aunt Clara's business meeting and they were two hundred dollars apiece?"

The cork made a hollow pop when Nate freed it from the bottle.

"I had to clean his boat for three weeks to pay for it—one week for every bottle." He poured the wine into two plastic cups and handed her one.

Sydney took a sip, the icy cold bite of alcohol sliding down easily in the humid air outside. She grasped the cup, cooling the skin on her fingers.

"You're getting red," Nate said. "I think you should probably reapply your sun lotion."

"I'm not used to spending my workday in a bikini," she teased, getting up and digging out the lotion from her bag. She took another big drink of her wine and set it on the bench before squirting a line down her arm and rubbing it in. She followed with her legs and stomach, rubbing the excess on her towel.

Nate handed her a plastic bag with a chicken sandwich. "Let me get your back," he said. "No wonder you're so red. Have you put any on your back at all?"

"I put some spray on this morning but I can't reach it."

Nate squirted lotion into his hands and rubbed them together as she turned away from him, pulling her hair to the side. She felt his cool touch against her lower back and she had to force herself to breathe. His fingers moved up her spine and found her shoulders, kneading them softly, causing her eyes to close. His thumbs went up her neck, and it was the most amazing thing she'd felt in a long time. Nate had always been great with his hands.

"You're tense," he said, rubbing her shoulders more.

The motion and pressure of it robbed her of coherent thought.

He pressed against the muscles of her shoulders, knowing her exact pressure points. Under his touch, it was as if he were releasing the stiffness that had been there all the years she'd been without him. She opened her eyes as she felt him take the sandwich from her and then the wine and set them down, before returning his hands to her shoulders. She tried to turn to protest, but he gently turned her back around and continued working his fingers, under the tie on her swimsuit and along the large muscles on her back. She let her head drop, her shoulders slumping under the complete relaxation of it.

As he moved back to her neck, she was aware of his body closing in behind her, his breath near her ear, and the lightening of his touch to a soft caress, making her breathing become shallow. He nuzzled against her neck, his hands dropping to her waist, his fingers moving around her until he was embracing her from behind.

"I miss you, Syd," he said into her ear in a whisper. "I miss you so much it hurts."

He turned her around to face him and he put his hands on her face. She hadn't even accessed her rational brain before his lips were on hers and everything else faded away except the fireworks going off inside her. In that kiss, she felt Nate Henderson again—the sweet, loving, protective Nate that had stolen her heart all those years ago. It was like coming home. His lips moved on hers urgently, the salty taste of them making her lightheaded. She put her arms around him as if she were holding on for dear life, praying that all the things she'd known about the person he'd become over the last decade had been some sort of bad dream. The boat, writing, kissing him—it was all more her than she'd ever been.

But slowly her brain started working again. She remembered that he hadn't come back to Firefly Beach for her, and that he was no longer the boy who'd driven out of town all those years ago. He was the man who'd come back to Firefly Beach, in essence, to hide; he was the man being chased by photographers; he was the man who'd only called her once in all those years. The truth of the matter was that he felt their old chemistry being back here, and she was an easy escape for his problems. She'd let her guard down, but if she kept going on like this, it would eventually rip her heart out. She needed to find herself, to decide what exactly she wanted in life, and then she had to go get it. And if she let him, he'd pull her right back down where she was when he'd walked out on her.

She gently pushed him away. "I don't want this," she said. It was the truth. She didn't want the heartbreak anymore, the ache that she felt whenever he wasn't with her, the tears that surfaced every time she recalled how wrong she'd gotten it when she thought they'd spend forever together.

He stared at her, pain in his eyes, and she'd never seen him so exposed. Then he tipped his head back and gazed up at the clouds as if some sort of answer were hidden in them. He swallowed, blinking rapidly, and cleared his throat. "Let's pack up our stuff," he said quietly. He went over to the side and started to pull up the anchor. "I'll get you home."

"What about the photographers?"

"It's my problem, not yours." He dropped the anchor onto

the boat floor and sat down in the captain's chair, leaving her still catching her breath and trying not to still feel the lingering buzz on her lips from his kiss.

With a rev of the engine, the boat was moving, making its way back to Starlight Cottage.

Chapter Fourteen

"Guess what, Mom!" Robby said, running up to Sydney when she came in. The entryway was aglow with lamplight and the smell of peppers and onions from her mother's cooking filled the air.

Nate had been unusually quiet on the boat ride home, and she was still trying to shake the pain in her chest at the thought of not seeing him anymore. He certainly wouldn't be coming by the cottage now—she could tell by the finality she'd felt between them when he'd started the engine to head home. Their last exchange seemed to have been his final effort to make amends and she'd shot him down. Nate wasn't the type to continue on pursuing things if he knew she wasn't reciprocating his feelings, and she hadn't given him even the slightest hint that she still felt anything for him. It was for her own good, she told herself.

She dropped her bags inside the front door at Starlight Cottage and squatted down to address her son. "What?" she said, trying to allow his innocence to alter her mood.

"The informational night for football is tonight."

"Tonight?

"Remember you'd asked me to sign up Robby for little

league football this fall—we'd talked about it before the wedding?" Jacqueline said from the other side of the room as she came in to join the conversation. But then she seemed to catch up with Sydney's disposition, despite her daughter's attempt to hide it. She looked around. "Where's Nate?"

"He went back to Malory's." Just the mention of his name gave her a rush of guilt and confusion.

"So the photographers are gone?"

Sydney shrugged. "I have no idea."

"We get to find out our coaches and team members tonight, Mama!"

Sydney had already missed the fact that Robby's football meeting was tonight because Nate had distracted her. She wouldn't allow herself to be distracted anymore. "I'm excited!" she said to Robby, dropping the conversation about Nate, but today's events lingering in her mind. "Maybe we can get ice cream after."

"Yeah!" Robby bounced up and down, clearly delighted.

Beau must have sensed the anticipation in the air because he barked and then gobbled up his tennis ball, loping over to Robby and dropping it at his feet. Robby picked up the ball and opened the front door. "Wanna chase the ball, boy?" he asked. "Let's go!" Robby and Beau sprinted out the door toward the yard.

"Your face looked like a storm cloud when you came in," Jacqueline said. "Want to tell me what's going on?"

"Not really," Sydney replied, offering a weak smile. She never did like talking about things. "But I got a few responses done for my column and I'm ready to relax. Know what I think you and I should do?" She draped her arm around her mother, ignoring the fact that all the little moments with Nate were still buzzing through her mind.

"What's that?" Jacqueline grinned at her daughter.

"I think we should dig out the margarita mix and make ourselves some frozen drinks in the blender."

"I like this plan," her mother said. "We've got tequila in the cabinet."

They went into the kitchen and Mama plugged in the blender. "It's weird making drinks without Hallie," she noted. "The three of us are usually together when we do this."

"I miss her," Sydney said. "I hope she and Ben are having a blast."

"Has she texted you at all?"

"It's only been three days since they left," Sydney laughed. "I give her one more day before we get the text."

"I think she'll last five days. She and Ben are surely too...busy." She winked.

"No. She won't be able to stand not telling us what they're doing." Sydney grabbed the bag of ice from the freezer, topped up the blender, and poured in the margarita mix.

"I hope she brings something back for us." Mama handed Sydney the bottle of tequila. "I need a new keychain—one of those gold ones with the word 'Barbados' in brightly colored letters would be nice."

"I'd like a coffee mug."

"That's boring." Jacqueline smirked at her while salting the rims of two glasses. "You already have an entire cupboard of mugs."

"But I don't have one that says, 'I know you think I'm hotter than this coffee.'" She laughed.

Jacqueline rolled her eyes playfully.

"Or how about, 'I never intended to be the best sister, but here I am crushing it.'"

Her mother burst out laughing. "Ooooh," she said, putting a hand on Sydney's arm to interrupt her. "How about one of those woven beach bags—maybe one with an island picture intertwined in the rattan on the front. I'd like one of those."

"She needs to text us now," Sydney said with wide eyes as she hit the button on the blender, drowning out their conversation for a few seconds. When it finished mixing, she shook it around in a circle to get the slushy concoction off the sides. While she poured the margaritas into their glasses, she said, "Should *we* text *her*?"

"We shouldn't..." Jacqueline said before taking a sip from her glass. She eyed her phone, second-guessing her statement.

"You're right. It's her honeymoon. Let's leave them alone." Sydney held up her glass. "To this opportunity to be two Flynns instead of our usual three. We never get time with just the two of us and I'm thankful to have it."

"Cheers." Jacqueline tapped the rim of her glass against Sydney's. "Why don't we take our drinks outside and watch Robby and Beau play?" she suggested. "That way we won't be tempted to pick up our phones!"

With a laugh, Sydney followed her mother out of the kitchen, hoping she could put her memories of Nate's kiss aside and enjoy the moment.

They headed out the front door and then settled in the old rockers on the porch that overlooked the large expanse of wiry beach grass that made up the yard. Robby was at one end of it, running around in circles while Beau honed in on the ball that was in Robby's hand. Robby chucked it into the air, sending Beau in a frenzy of hopping and sprinting to retrieve it.

"Robby's so excited about football tonight," Mama said.

"He loves the sport. I know he can't wait for fall to get here so they can begin practices."

"I hope he gets Sam Baldwin again. He's such a good coach. I've asked him to put in a word if he gets a chance so that Robby can be on his team."

Sam had coached Robby when they'd moved back to Firefly Beach briefly after the divorce. Football had been such a help in getting Robby through the traumatic changes and disruptions that hit them when Christian left. At the tender age of five, he'd signed up for football that first year after his father had gone, and fell in love with the sport. A skinny child, Robby wasn't built for football, and he'd gotten hurt the first time he'd tried to play in the recreational league, so Sydney had urged him toward baseball. But Robby wouldn't hear of it.

"I know." Sydney took a drink from her glass, the icy cold of it a shock against the warmth settling on her skin. "He loves Sam. They had such a good season that year."

"It should be fun tonight." Jacqueline rocked back in her chair. "The meeting is a cookout and a picnic. I knew you were really busy trying to work, so I've already gotten some potato salad and a few jugs of sweet tea to bring. I signed us up for the easy stuff."

"Thank you for doing that," Sydney said, considering the fact that she still had to respond to *NY Pulse.* "It is taking me a little while to get adjusted, but I want to make sure that I spend enough time with Robby. I won't get this time back, so I really want to make sure I don't miss a thing. He's getting so big." She looked out at her son.

"It flies, baby girl," her mother replied, her doting eyes on Sydney. "You were in that yard with your hula hoops and batons just yesterday, I swear. I blinked and you landed in this chair beside me." She tipped her margarita up against her lips and took a slow drink.

"Watch this, Mama!" Robby called over to Sydney. He

tossed the ball high into the air, did a spin, and caught it on its way back down.

"Wow, good catch!" she said back to him.

"Wanna see me do it again?"

"Of course I do!" She was so happy just sitting on that porch with her mother. There was nowhere she'd rather be.

"I didn't want to bombard you with this right when you walked in," her mother said as they sat on the porch, their glasses long empty. "We should check on Uncle Hank. He's low today. I thought he was taking a nap earlier, but I found him in tears up in his bedroom."

"What's wrong?"

Her mother shook her head. "I'm not sure. Lewis tried to get him to tell him, but he wouldn't. He talks to you."

"Do you think he's worried about selling Starlight Cottage?"

"I don't know. Maybe you can get it out of him."

Robby poked his head out the door. "Mom, I can't find my football jersey for the picnic. Can you help me?"

"I'll go," her mother said, standing up and heading inside with her grandson.

Sydney went through the house and out to the back porch that overlooked the sparkling gulf and the towering lighthouse, its white brick reaching into the heavens, contrasting with the nautical colors of the gulf behind it. It was one of Uncle Hank's favorite spots at the cottage. He always sat out there when he was thinking things over.

"Hey," she said, sitting down beside him on the porch swing.

He didn't turn toward her, his gaze still on the white beach that snaked along the property, but he nodded, acknowledging her presence.

"Wanna tell me what you're thinking about?"

Uncle Hank let out a sigh, causing Beau, who had followed them out and was now sunning himself at the edge of the porch, to lift his head and assess the situation. Seeing no immediate threat, the dog put his chin down on his paws and closed his eyes once more.

"I've just been thinking about how things change," Uncle Hank said. He finally looked her way. "I understand that life continues to move forward, but it never bothered me until I was an old man." He rubbed his hands along his thighs, his fingers unsteady. "I keep trying to be normal in a world that doesn't work for me anymore. Clara's gone. The town I adore is about to plow through my favorite view. And I feel useless." His bottom lip began to wobble and he pursed his lips to keep it still, tears surfacing. "I'm being forced to sell this cottage—Clara's dream; the place we built together. I can't even have my home. What is my reason for being here?"

It was clear that Uncle Hank's mind had slipped back to the same sadness he'd felt when she'd first arrived in Firefly Beach after Aunt Clara's death. She understood how that could happen; she knew all too well how easily old emotions could bubble to the surface.

"This is just an idea, but do you think hearing someone else's perspective might help? Mary Alice could work through your feelings with you. She's really good."

He stood up with a huff, rocking the swing by the shift of his weight. "I don't need a counselor. I need my life back." He folded his arms, his weathered hands gripping his biceps so tightly that the ends of his fingers were white.

Sydney hadn't meant to hit a nerve. She'd only been trying to help. "She won't try to convince you that you don't need your life back. She'll just help you find a way to understand it that you hadn't thought of before, which can sometimes help you manage a little better."

His shoulders rounded. "I'm an old man, Sydney. I mean no disrespect, but I'm living in a world where kids are running my life, and sitting in a room with the little girl who used to sell lemonade with you on the corner isn't going to help me." He blew air through his lips. "I'll be fine," he said, but she didn't believe him.

Sydney stood up in front of him, wishing she could hear Aunt Clara's voice to soothe them both. "Uncle Hank, you're the wisest person I know. If I were battling with something big, what would you tell me?"

"I don't know." He shook his head.

"Yes you do. You've never just let us flounder when we have problems. You've gotten me through every single one."

He leaned on the railing, his arms stretched out, his fingers gripping the whitewashed wood. "I'd tell you to follow your heart, not your head. But that's just it: my heart is somewhere unreachable at the moment."

"So what does your heart say about Starlight Cottage?" she asked.

He dragged his finger affectionately along the railing. "It aches to keep it the same. For Clara. And for me."

"Then let's do everything we can to make that happen. I'll go with you to the meeting Friday." She took Uncle Hank's hand. "We can do this." A seed of resolution stirred inside her, and no matter what, she'd fight for Starlight Cottage until the end.

Chapter Fifteen

Sydney's phone lit up with a text as it sat on the table beside her computer while she tinkered around with the cover design for the wellness center. It was Malory.

Coffee?

With everything going on, Sydney had forgotten that she'd mentioned getting coffee with Malory at her party. She'd been busy working the rest of the day while Robby was at his friend's house, and she'd emailed *NY Pulse* magazine to give them days and times when she'd be available to discuss the content editor position.

With a couple hours before Robby's football meeting, Sydney decided it would be nice to spend some time with her friend. It was such a gorgeous evening that she decided it would be a perfect night to walk, so she texted Malory that she'd meet her at Cup of Sunshine in fifteen minutes if she was up to it.

Malory texted back:

Absolutely! Sliding on my flip-flops right now...

Sydney shut down her laptop and scribbled a quick note to her mom, letting her know where she was headed. Then she slipped on her sandals, grabbed her handbag and sunglasses, and headed out the door, deciding to take the shortcut past the lighthouse, down the beach, and along the coast.

The sea air wrapped around her like a warm hug, blowing her long hair behind her shoulders, and caressing her skin. Sydney walked through the yard toward the tree-laden area where she and Nate used to write in the shade of the palms. She ran her fingers down the spiny bark of a palm tree, remembering all the times she'd sat on a blanket under it, her notebooks spread out around her...

She walked further in, along the old path the people who lived on these lots had carved out to allow them to pass through until they reached the next clearing. She hadn't been down this path in years. The sun shined through the trees, casting long rays through their leaves, blinding her and then relenting as she walked along. Then suddenly, something caught her eye, making her gasp. A rusted thumbtack jutted out from one of the trees, a tiny torn piece of paper still speared into the bark. She touched it, remembering the notes she'd put up for Nate to give him inspiration. As she ran her hand over the remnant of it, barely even a visible piece of it left, she closed her eyes, hoping to hear Nate's voice calling her. Would he walk up behind her and pull her back to that time in her life when everything seemed to be perfect? She kept her eyes closed and waited, the shushing of the gulf mocking the silence.

She opened her eyes and started walking again. Every tree, every bend in the path ahead of her was like a graveyard for her memories, each one preserved in that space, lingering there and calling out to her to remember. She fought the swell of fear at the thought that all this would be a parking lot soon. Her memories bulldozed without a single thought. Suddenly, she wanted to run back to Starlight Cottage and plead with Uncle Hank not to sell.

When she finally emerged onto the main street in town, she surveyed the intersection. It was lined with tourists, the shop doors clogged with people, the stoplights congested and all the area picnic tables brimming, people spilling out of the outdoor dining areas onto the sidewalk, stopping foot traffic. She maneuvered around passers-by and made her way to Cup of Sunshine, plunging herself into the air-conditioned interior.

Malory waved from a table she'd saved for them.

"This is crazy," Sydney said, squeezing herself into a chair. "It's not even the weekend."

"It doesn't matter when it's late afternoon, in-season. All the vacationers are here for the whole week and they probably don't even know what day it is. On Sundays, I can hardly get in and out of the village with all the traffic leaving their rentals. It's a nightmare." She scooted a cup of iced coffee toward Sydney. "I got you an iced caramel latte."

"How did you guess my favorite?" she asked.

"Nate suggested it when I said we were getting coffee together." She offered a cautious smile. "He said, 'When in doubt, go sweet.'"

Sydney chuckled. "He always did know what I like." She took a sip, and settled in to the space between the two of them.

"How do you like being back?" Malory asked her.

"It's where I belong," she said. "The longer I stay here, the more I realize how much I need the sea air and the open spaces."

They both looked around at the coffee line that was nearly out the door, the trail of sand coming in on all their

feet, the beach bags—full to the brim—bumping into people. "Open spaces," Malory said, and they both laughed.

Then a man in line caught her eye and raised his hand,
his smile very familiar. She realized it was Logan, from the
wedding. She smiled at him.

"Who's that?" Malory said, her tone playfully suggestive.

"His name is Logan Hayes. I met him at Hallie's
wedding."

"He looks very happy to see you."

"He's really nice."

"You should go say hello...I would."

She noticed that Ariel Barnes was a few people behind
him. Ariel worked at the candy shop in town and she'd made
friends with Robby, offering him his favorite peppermint
spinner whenever he came in—a candy that would actually
spin on its stick. She'd talk to Ariel first. That would be a
great way to break the ice.

"Okay. Be right back. And while I'm up there, I'll mention that you're single..." Sydney teased.

Malory's eyes got as big as saucers, and then she looked
back at Logan, clearly considering, making Sydney laugh. "I
wouldn't hold it against you if you did."

Sydney stood up and went over to Ariel. "Hi," she said,
coming up behind her friend.

"Oh!" Ariel said, her two dark French braids swinging
madly as she offered Sydney a warm hug. "It's so nice to see
you!"

"Same. Robby is dying to get in for your peppermint
spinner."

Ariel gave a warm smile, her freckled cheekbones pushing her black-rimmed glasses up. "Any time. You know, I've
made a larger one now. And I found a way to get a rainbow-
colored flash light on the end of the stick!"

"That's amazing! He'll love it."

"Bring him in soon. I need someone to taste-test my new chocolate line."

"I'd be happy to do that for you myself," Sydney said with a laugh.

The line moved, causing them all to step forward.

"Well, it was nice to see you," Sydney said.

"You too!"

She walked forward in line as if she were headed back to her table and when Logan made eye contact, she stepped back over to talk to him. "Hey," she said, joining him in the line.

"Hey there." He offered her a warm smile. "It's so nice to see you."

"Same. Would you like to join us?" she asked, nearly sure by Malory's response to him that she wouldn't object.

"I wish I could. I was running errands and I'm grabbing a coffee for my mom on the way back to the cottage. But I demand a rain check."

Sydney grinned. "Absolutely. Well, it was great to run into you."

"I'll text you once I get home and we can set up a time." He looked around at the crowds. "Maybe not *this* time of day."

"Definitely not." Sydney said her goodbyes and then headed back to Malory, glad to have seen Logan again.

"Okay, tell me the date and time," Malory said once she'd returned to the table.

"Date and time?"

"Of my date with Logan."

They both fell into their usual laughter. Sydney was so happy to be back with her friend again. If everything could be as easy as rekindling their friendship.

*   *   *

"Robby! Did you get your football?" Sydney called upstairs as she scrolled through the email on her phone that had all the details for tonight. The kids were all meeting at the park where they'd receive their coaches and team assignments.

She was about to put her phone in her back pocket when the screen lit up, drawing her attention back down to a text. Sydney swiped it open.

It read:

Hey, it's Nate. I just wanted to warn you before you got here. I'm coaching for the Firefly Little League, and Robby's on my team. I just got the roster.

A barrage of conflicting emotions swarmed her: the thrill that he had her cell number and they were still somehow connected, the fear that she'd have to face him tonight after their talk on the boat today, the unsettling idea that Nate might be sticking around in Firefly Beach, and that he and Robby would be spending an entire football season together.

She texted back:

Thanks for letting me know. See you soon.

"Ready to go?" Robby asked, hopping down the last step from upstairs. He had his ball under his arm, his favorite jersey and shorts making him look more grown up than he usually did. He was visibly buzzing with anticipation.

"I sure am!" she said, sliding her phone into her pocket. "Let's go!"

* * *

Sydney opened the car door to let Beau out. She'd decided to leash him up and bring him with her since he'd been cooped up at Firefly Beach since Ben had left. She unhooked his lead and grabbed his tennis ball from the floorboard. "Ready?" she said to him.

Beau's feet were tapping unmercifully against the dirt, his tail swinging wildly in circles. Sydney chucked the ball across the field, and Beau went tearing after it. He retrieved it in seconds, and galloped back to Sydney, dropping it at her feet, his tongue hanging from the side of his mouth as he panted, his loyal eyes on her.

Sydney threw the ball again and Beau chased it once more.

"I know a little secret," she said once Robby had exited the car and walked around to her side.

"What is it?" he asked.

Beau dropped the ball and nuzzled Robby's hand until he picked it up and threw it again.

"I already know who your coach is and I think you're gonna be really excited."

At the end of the day, no matter what her problems were with Nate, one thing she knew without a doubt was that he'd be an amazing coach. He was so patient with Robby and he knew the game of football inside and out. Plus, the end of football season might provide her a nice, clean way to break the relationship with Nate and Robby. With Ben and Hallie staying primarily in Firefly Beach this year to be near family and prepare for their adoption, Ben would be right there to jump in and fill Nate's shoes. Then Sydney could finally cut him out of her life and move on. "Want to know?"

Robby's eyes grew round. "Who is it?"

Just then, she caught sight of Nate and turned Robby around, pointing toward him.

"Nate's my coach?" Robby broke into an enormous grin and went running toward him, Beau trotting after him. Sydney picked up Beau's ball and followed them.

"Hey, buddy!" Nate said. He reached down and petted Beau, the dog's tail spinning circles with pleasure. He met Sydney's eyes but then turned his focus back to her son. "Are you ready for some football this season?"

"Yes, sir!" Robby stepped back a few paces and lifted the ball into a pass position.

Nate put up his hands, catching the ball when Robby threw it. He tossed it back. "Let's go to the table and find out who else is on the team." He turned to Sydney. "May I take him?"

"Of course," she said, reaching down to take Beau's collar so she could hook up his leash. Beau sat dutifully and allowed her to get a hold of him.

As she let them go, Nate and Robby walked together, their backs to Sydney. Robby was looking up at his new coach, talking animatedly, the football under his arm, while Nate laughed at something he'd said. The sight of it pinched her chest.

All of a sudden, her phone went off, startling her. She peered down at the caller. "Ha!" she said to no one, wishing her mom was there to witness Hallie calling. She answered it immediately. "How is Barbados?" she asked without even a hello.

"Amazing! I got you a coffee mug."

Sydney smiled. "You know me so well."

"How's everything at home?"

"Apart from Robby running off with Nate, his new best friend and football coach, not much."

"What?!"

Sydney pulled the phone from her ear to save her eardrum. "Yes."

Hallie's voice came through muffled as she had evidently turned from the phone to relay this information to Ben.

"Sorry," she said, coming back to Sydney. "Ben and I are at the most incredible place right now having drinks. It's all pillars and white tablecloths with sparkling wine and the whole place hovers over the ocean. It's absolutely incredible."

"So why are you on the phone? You should be enjoying it!"

"I am! I just wanted to check in. Here, I'll put you on speaker. There's no one around at the moment and Ben wants to hear all about Nate and Robby."

"So have you two finally made up?" Ben's voice came through the phone.

Sydney started walking around the field with Beau in one hand and her phone in the other. "I wouldn't say we've made up. I think I've finally found some closure."

"I don't buy it," Ben said.

"Why not?"

"He's crazy for you. He's been in love with you since the day he rolled out of town."

She looked over at Nate in the distance. He was to the side of the team tent, kneeling down with a group of boys, smiling, making them laugh.

"He has a funny way of showing it," she said, Ben's comment making no sense at all. Why would he have left her and hurt her so terribly if he loved her? "I think you're mistaken. Nobody rolls out of town when they're crazy about someone."

"I'm not mistaken," Ben said. "But it isn't my place to get involved. I just thought he'd have told you, that's all."

Juliana waved from across the field and started making her way over to Sydney.

"Have you gotten Mama anything, Hallie?" she asked, changing the subject. She threw her hand up to Juliana.

"Not yet! I'm still looking..."

"You should get her a beach bag or a keychain," Sydney suggested, another grin surfacing at the thought of her earlier conversation with her mother.

"Oh, yes! I saw these cool woven bags at a corner market. I'll find her a really great one...I can't wait to see you."

"How's Beau doing?" Ben chimed in.

"He's missing you," she told him. "He loafs around most of the time. I've got him at the park with me right now while Robby's at his first football meeting. Here, talk to him. I'll put you on speaker." She tapped her phone screen.

"Hey, boy!" Ben called through the phone. "I'll be home soon, okay?"

Beau's ears perked up, and he lifted his head to sniff the phone, his tail wagging.

"He's rolling his eyes and telling me you'd better bring him back a new toy for the lack of ball-chasing he's had to endure in your absence," Sydney said with a laugh. Juliana had nearly reached her, so Sydney said, "I'm going to go, okay? But call me back later if you want to catch up some more."

They said their goodbyes as Juliana strolled up.

"May I walk with you?" Juliana asked from behind her sunglasses. She was wearing a form-fitting spandex workout suit with designer sneakers, her dark hair pulled tightly into a smooth ponytail at the back of her head, accentuating her high cheekbones.

"Of course." Sydney started to walk along the small track that circled the field while Beau jogged beside her. "No photographers today?"

"It seems like it was just the one..Not sure if they were after Nate or me. Sometimes they will do that when we are in remote places; someone will get word about where we are and they certainly aren't going to tell anyone so they can have the exclusive. When we didn't come out, he probably finally gave up."

"Dodging them all must be exhausting."

"Yes..."

"And you're sure it was someone from the press and not a hired photographer from your agency?"

"I am not sure," she said, her frown pulling down her features, showing her stress. "Nate said he told you about Seth." She pushed her dark glasses onto the top of her head and made eye contact with Sydney.

"Yes. I'm so sorry that happened to you."

Juliana peered over at Nate. "I am so thankful for that man," she stated, her whole body now turned toward him.

Sydney stopped walking to stand next to her, and Beau turned around to see what was going on. Then he sat, clearly waiting to keep going.

"He is easy to love," she said. "I fell head over heels for him, but he did not feel the same way for me, so we settled for friends."

Sydney was surprised by Juliana's admission. Here Juliana was, confessing that she'd loved Nate, and he hadn't loved her back. Sydney could definitely relate to that. How glamorous Juliana Vargas's life had seemed from the outside. Any bystander would assume she could get anyone she wanted. Sydney was learning that things definitely weren't always what they seemed. She and Juliana weren't all that different.

"I cannot see myself dating him now," Juliana said. "We have been friends for too long. But I always wonder who will have his heart in the end." She pivoted around to face Sydney. "Whoever it is, is a lucky woman." She let out a wistful sigh. "He is a good man."

"Do you think people change?" Sydney asked as she watched Nate running with the kids.

"I don't think people change entirely. They just learn more about what they are and are not capable of. And sometimes, you think you know someone, but you have not really *heard* them yet. My grandfather used to say, 'If you want to know someone, listen to their stories—every single one. Who they are is in their stories.'" Juliana slipped her glasses back down over her eyes and resumed walking.

"I definitely know Nate's stories," Sydney said, leaning more toward the idea that Nate was who he was and there was no changing him.

"Ah, but you have not heard them *all*."

"What hasn't he told me?" Sydney asked.

"I haven't heard them all either," Juliana said. "But when it comes to you, he definitely has stories to tell." She pressed her full lips together, seemingly thinking about something. Finally, she said, "He told me once that he loves you. I asked him how he could love someone he hasn't seen in ten years. He said, 'Because I know her soul.' That is pretty powerful."

First Ben and now Juliana. It didn't make any sense. "He left me," she said. "He just walked out on me, out of the blue, to pursue his music career. Not a call—nothing. Just gone."

"I'm afraid I have no answers for you," Juliana said. "He has never told me about this."

Perhaps Nate hadn't told Juliana that part of his little fairy-tale love story. Maybe Ben and Juliana were both wrong about him. After all, Sydney was the one who had

known him best. She should stop allowing others to cloud
her judgment.

"Will you ask him about this?" Juliana said.

"I don't have any questions about it," Sydney returned. It
was pretty clear to her what had happened that day and for
the years following. She deserved better.

Chapter Sixteen

When Sydney arrived at the wellness center to show Mary Alice a few ideas she'd come up with, her office door was closed. She checked her watch. Mary Alice had said to come by at nine o'clock. Sydney wasn't late. She was actually ten minutes early, so Mary Alice must have started her first session before the regular counseling time. On her way to the spare room they'd been using, Sydney had gotten both her and Mary Alice a coffee from Cup of Sunshine, but now she stood holding both cups, wondering how cold Mary Alice's would be in an hour when the door reopened. She walked into the small kitchenette area at the back of the office and set the paper cup on the counter. With nothing to do, she took her own coffee into the spare room and opened her email. Perhaps she could write a few responses while she waited, and get ahead.

Her skin prickled with anticipation as she saw an email from *NY Pulse* magazine. She opened the message. They wanted to talk today. She could hardly contain her excitement. Sydney looked up from her phone at the empty room, just dying to share the news with someone. This was the first big shot she'd ever taken with her writing. She

typed back that today would be great and she was eager
to hear what they had to say. Then she noticed she'd never
responded to mel4221's last email. She reread the last bit of
the message:

> ...She isn't coming back to me, and I can hardly manage,
> knowing that she was the one person in this life who com-
> pleted me. I haven't found anyone who can fill her shoes
> since. What if I've ruined everything by letting her go?

This was definitely difficult to answer, given the fact that
she replayed that last moment with Nate over and over in her
head, wondering the same thing. If she'd run after him that
day, would he have stopped the truck? Had he been waiting
for her to stop him? But she knew that she was overanalyzing
things. She'd given him a million opportunities to stay. It
had been his decision to leave her, and he'd been pretty clear
about it.

She hit respond and typed an email back.

> Hi Mel,
>   Do you ever wonder why someone so perfect for you
> actually isn't The One? I had a similar situation and wonder
> that all the time. What leads people in the wrong directions?

Sydney stared at her response. It wasn't really a response
at all, but more of a conversation she was starting with this
person. But the problem was, there wasn't an answer to this.
If there was, she certainly hadn't found it. She signed her
name and hit send.

Then she pulled up the spreadsheet with Mary Alice's bud-
get. Juliana wouldn't model for the cover, and she and Nate
would've been perfect, not to mention she probably could've

gotten them at a good price. She opened up a search screen on her computer and typed in a search for local models, but there wasn't a whole lot in the vicinity of Firefly Beach.

Before she could consider her options, her phone lit up, and to her complete surprise, mel4221 had responded again. She opened the email.

> I think it comes down to bad timing and wrong choices. Do you ever wish you could rewind the clock and start again? Would things be different?
> Mel

Sydney debated whether or not she should send another email to Mel, but as she considered this, she thought it might help the poor guy. He was really going through a rough patch, it seemed, and perhaps her personal experience could help him in some way. She typed back:

> I agree. Definitely wrong choices. And if I were able to rewind the clock, sadly I don't think it would change a thing. Our paths are a muddle of ups and downs, but in the end, they are our paths—we can't unwind them and make them cleaner or straighter. They just are the way they are. I hope someday you can find some closure.

She sent the message and set her phone down on the table, the conversation with this stranger sitting heavily. But in a flash, she got a single-line response.

> Have you been lucky enough to have closure? I haven't.

That was a tough one. She didn't dare tell him that she hadn't; that, years later, he may still be just as heartbroken.

But cutting through her thoughts was another message from mel4221.

If you could write a letter to him, what would you say?

This was getting personal. Quickly, she fired off an answer.

I don't think my love letter to him would impact your dilemma.

Another email came back to her:

Love? Did you say love letter? You still love him?

Shoot. Did she say "love"? She reread her message and gritted her teeth. She hadn't meant to say that, but it must have just come out with her honesty. What could she say to his question, other than the obvious? She sent back an answer:

Yes. I will always love him.

She hated to dash Mel's hopes that he could move on, but she was just being honest. Sydney waited for his reaction to her answer, but her phone sat silent, the back-and-forth suddenly over. Then suddenly, a final response, and what it said surprised her.

I'm happy to know you still love him. I feel the same way about her. Thank you for chatting with me and for making my day.

Well, that went better than expected, she thought. But then a second email came through.

One day soon, I'm going to show her how much I love her.

While Sydney liked the romantic idea of this guy professing his love to the girl of his dreams, she did worry that things might not end the way he hoped. She opened another email to warn him. She considered telling him how her own situation hadn't worked so well, but then she reconsidered. It would be a long story, and she didn't want to bring Nate into this. And what if she deterred him, and it kept him from rekindling things with this woman? It would be best to let time take its course. With a sigh, she deleted the draft.

Mary Alice's door was still closed, so Sydney decided perhaps she should come back another time. She peeked into the lobby to see if anyone was waiting, and to her surprise, Juliana was on the sofa reading a magazine.

"Hello," Juliana said, raising a long, lean hand at Sydney. "I am early."

"I'm sure it's fine," Sydney said, moving over to her. "You okay?"

Juliana folded her hands, her shoulders tense. "The photographer must have been Seth's. He texted me and said if I did not go back and finish out my contract, he would have me in breach of the agreement."

"Oh no." Sydney sat down next to her, giving Juliana her full attention.

"I'm scared of him," Juliana whispered.

"Is there any way to work for him without actually being in the same place?"

Anger flashed in Juliana's eyes. "He does not want my work. He wants to make my life miserable. No one tells him no."

"How is he able to do this?" Sydney said, concerned for her new friend.

"Look at the life he gave me. Aspiring models die for that kind of life. They will put up with a lot and they will keep it quiet." She crossed her legs, her delicate sandal dangling from her painted toes. "I noticed how most of them kept their distance from him, but I was too naïve to read the signs and when he became friendly with me, I fell right into it. He loves the power of making people into superstars and he will not allow me to be successful if I am not working for him. I am worried he is going to hurt me…"

Sydney covered her gaping mouth. "Oh my God," she said, aghast.

Juliana's eyes glistened with fear but the noise of Mary Alice's door opening caused her to wipe her face clean of any worry she had.

Mary Alice came walking briskly toward them behind the couple that was leaving. "Oh my goodness!" she said when she saw Sydney. "I haven't had a minute to spare. I'm so sorry."

"No worries at all," Sydney told her. "We can catch up later."

"Thank you," she said with relief. "You're welcome to work here in the office today, if you need a quiet place."

"I actually have a call," Sydney said. "It might be good to take it here."

"Absolutely!" Mary Alice said. Then she turned to Juliana. "Hello. I'm so sorry you've had to wait." She peered down at her watch. "Oh good, I'm not too late." Mary Alice pushed a smile across her face. "Come on back."

It was time for her call from *NY Pulse*. She was oddly calm about the whole thing. It was so incredibly out of her league that she couldn't even feel nervous about it. The idea that she could beat out her competition with no real experience, on a single submission, was ridiculous, so she kept her excitement in check. She was more curious to hear what it was about her writing that had interested them.

"Hello, this is Sydney Flynn," she said, answering the call.

"Ah, hello, Sydney. My name is Amanda Rains. I am the editor-in-chief of *NY Pulse*. How are you?"

"I'm doing well, thank you," she said, her heartbeat rising at the thrill of speaking to Mrs. Rains herself. She'd read about her after submitting, and her experience in the field was unmatched.

"I'm glad to hear it," Amanda said with authority. "I have to say, I read your submission personally, and I was blown away. The intimacy you created in drawing connections between your family and the elements of renovation actually brought me to tears at one point. I loved the idea of the new layers of paint not covering over, but *protecting* the old, sealing it in, the way we internalize our family values. It was incredible. It's *exactly* what I'm looking for."

"Wow," Sydney said, unable to manage anything else.

"If you're still interested in the position, I'd want to give you a couple more writing tasks to see what you've got, with a pretty quick turn-around to get a feel for what you can produce under a time-limit. And if you can do it, the next step would be to fly you up to New York for a formal interview. What do you think?"

Sydney's hands were getting sweaty now. This was huge. Probably the biggest opportunity that she'd ever gotten in her life. And she hadn't even really been trying. It was just a whim, a sort of writing lottery she'd entered with Hallie. She'd never thought for a second she'd actually get a call...

"Would you like some time to think it over?" Amanda asked into the silence.

"Oh," Sydney said, realizing she hadn't answered. "I'd love to try to write the pieces for you," she said, thankful, now, that she was well ahead on her column articles for the *Gazette*.

"Perfect. Shall I send them to the same email from your original submission?"

"Yes, that would be great." Sydney's mind buzzed with the reality that this was actually happening.

"Lovely. I'll get them out to you today. It was so nice speaking to you."

"Great talking to you too," she said. "Thank you for this opportunity."

"You're welcome. I can't wait to see what you send me."

Sydney finished the call and sat in the middle of the empty room at the wellness center, stunned. Had that really just happened? She couldn't believe it. But once the excitement had worn off, a new fear set in. Was she ready for something like this? Chances were that she might not get this kind of opportunity again. Did she have what it takes?

Mary Alice knocked on the doorframe of Sydney's open office door and held up the coffee she'd left in the kitchen this morning. "Did you know you left a full coffee on the counter?" she asked, looking completely ragged. Her normally neatly tied-back hair was wispy, her cheeks red, her eyes tired.

"It was for you," Sydney said with a half smile.

"Oh, I'm so sorry," Mary Alice said, coming in and setting it on Sydney's desk before dropping into the chair across from Sydney. "I was so busy. I've got more patients than I have time to see." She ran her hands down her face and squeezed her eyes shut before looking back at Sydney. "It's a good problem to have, but I'm not sure what to do." She leaned forward and popped the lid off the coffee, obviously deciding if it was worth drinking the ice-cold, five-hours-old beverage. She must have decided against it, because she sat back in the chair with a huff. "My mom's coming to pick me up for dinner," she said with a smile. "I need a nice night out."

"I love your mom," Sydney said. The memories came to mind of Mrs. Chambers bringing them cupcakes with their names on them after field hockey games and dressing up for Halloween in the most extravagant costumes just to make them all laugh.

"She's going to be very excited to see you," Mary Alice replied. "She's asked about you a couple of times since you've been back."

"We should all get together soon." Sydney closed down her computer for the day. "I'll walk you out and tell her hello."

"You're welcome to grab Robby and meet us for dinner tonight," Mary Alice offered.

"Thank you, but I should probably get home and make sure Mama doesn't need any help with dinner."

Just then, Mary Alice's mother, Susan Chambers, walked through the door. She had the same friendly eyes and bobbed hairstyle she'd always had but her amber brown locks were graying now.

"Oh, Sydney," she said, her arms stretched wide to embrace her. "I have missed you, my sweet girl." She pulled Sydney into a bear hug, the floral scent of her perfume registering as one of the markers of Sydney's childhood. She pulled back. "Are you coming to dinner with us?"

"Probably not tonight," Sydney said, "but another time, I promise."

"I'm going to hold you to that." She fluttered her hands in the air, some sort of excitement hitting her. "We should have all of you kids together! Nate's back, you're here. We could get Malory to join us . . . It would be just like those days when I had you all in my kitchen after school, hanging out."

"Maybe we could," Sydney said. But she really wasn't ready to spend a night reminiscing about old times. It would only serve as a reminder of a life path she hadn't taken.

"Have you seen Nate since the wedding?" she asked. "Mary Alice told me he would be there."

"I have, actually," Sydney said, purposely not elaborating to keep the conversation light.

Susan fluffed one of the pillows on the sofa nearby, her mothering instincts still on high alert. "I'm so glad," she said as she reached for the stack of magazines, straightening them. She looked around the office waiting room where they were standing. "You know, he's the reason Mary Alice came back to Firefly Beach."

"Oh?" Susan's statement had completely stunned Sydney.

"Yep," Susan said with a doting look to Mary Alice. "He was the one who talked her into giving up her job, moving to Firefly Beach, and starting her own practice."

"Nate? Nate *Henderson*?"

"Yes," Mary Alice said with a nod. She gathered her bags and slid them up onto her shoulder.

Sydney walked with them to the door. "I'd love to hear that story."

Mary Alice cut off the lights. "I'll tell you one day, but I can't tell you *everything*. Patient confidentiality and all . . . But, as an old friend, not a counselor, I urge you to try to get him to open up."

As Sydney drove home, Uncle Hank's words went round and round in her head: *We all make mistakes, Sydney.*

Could Nate have changed for the better? What had Mary Alice meant by "everything"? She couldn't tell her *everything*, she'd said. What didn't Sydney know? And after all, she wasn't so sure she wanted Nate to open up. If he *had* changed, he was going to have to convince her beyond a shadow of doubt that he had, because it would take a whole lot for her to let him into her heart again.

Chapter Seventeen

Frustration slithered through Sydney as she parked her car next to Nate's old truck. It had a shiny new paint job, but she could tell it was the same one he'd had all those years ago by the beach shop sticker in the back window.

She still remembered when he'd put that sticker on. They'd been on the beach all day. Sydney lay next to Nate on her towel in the sand, the warmth of the sun playing with her consciousness.

"Let's get ice cream," Nate said, rolling over onto his stomach, pulling her from her dreamlike haze that drowned out everything but the rushing surf and coastal wind. He leaned over her, his shadow allowing her to focus on the adoration in his eyes as he looked at her.

"I don't want to get up," she said, hoping he'd look at her like that forever.

He leaned down and kissed her. The salty taste of his lips was a sensation she'd never forget. It was the taste of every summer she'd spent with him.

He took her hands and pinned them playfully above her head. "You know you want some mint chocolate chip," he said.

"Stop." She giggled as she squirmed away from him. "You're all hot and sandy."

"Hot for *you*," he said, pulling her to him and nuzzling her neck.

"Get off," she squealed with laughter. "There are families on the beach."

"And they'll all know I adore you." He kissed her again.

She wriggled to a sitting position and he ran his fingers through her hair, pulling her to him for another kiss. "This is my ploy to get a cup of double chocolate swirl," he teased, kissing her over and over.

She laughed. "Let's go," she said, relenting and standing up.

They gathered their things and headed to the ice cream parlor, where they got ice cream cones—giant waffle cones with piles and piles of ice cream. Beside the ice cream parlor was the beach shop, and they walked the aisles of the store, licking their cones.

"I need to have these shades," Nate said, slipping on a ridiculous pair of blaze-orange sunglasses.

Sydney laughed and took them off him. "Don't hide that gorgeous face," she said.

He grabbed her with one arm, his ice cream coming precariously close to a rack of T-shirts. "I love you," he said, looking into her eyes. A grumpy shopkeeper glanced over at them from his spot at the register.

"Wonder what happened to *that* guy today? We should buy something so we can try to make him smile," he said, looking around.

"I'm not sure that's possible," she said quietly. "He looks like he's having the worst day ever."

Nate grabbed a sticker from a pile on one of the shelves and took it up to pay for it. "Hang on," he said to the guy and ran back to where he and Sydney had been standing to grab the orange sunglasses. "These too," he said, putting them on the counter. "The lady secretly loves them," he whispered, but the guy just rang up the items and handed him the bag.

When they got outside, Nate handed her the bag. "Wait right here," he told her. Then he strode off toward the ice cream shop and after a few minutes returned with a giant sundae.

Sydney eyed the dripping vanilla scoops with chocolate sauce and sprinkles. "Still hungry?" she kidded him.

He offered a mischievous grin and nodded toward the door of the shop for her to go back inside. Nate walked in and set the sundae on the counter. "Whatever kind of morning you've had is gone. All you have ahead of you now is sunshine and a sundae."

A tiny smirk broke through at one corner of the man's mouth. "I can't find my cat," the man admitted. "She's lost."

"What's her name?" Nate asked, sobering.

"I named her after the day I got her because I think she saved me." He looked down at the ice cream. "Her name is Sunday," he said, meeting Nate's eyes.

They both shared a moment, realizing that Nate had told the man that the only thing ahead of him was sunshine and a *sundae*.

Nate got a description of the cat and promised he'd look for it. And then when they got outside, he put the shop sticker on his truck. "I want to remember this," he said, "because when we first went in, I thought that guy was just having a bad day, but he was suffering." He smoothed out the sticker and looked at it for a while. "I want to remind myself not to take people's reactions at face value. Everyone needs someone to hear them."

Coming back to the present, Sydney could almost taste

the ice cream on her lips, and she realized she'd been standing at Nate's truck for quite a while. She went inside and followed laughter, walking straight to the kitchen where she found Nate and Robby sitting at the table together, hovered over a piece of paper.

Sydney dropped her keys on the table and peered down at them. "Is that math homework?" she asked.

Nate looked up. "Hey, Syd," he said as if it were totally regular for him to be sitting at the table with her son. "Yes," he answered finally. "Robby texted me so I came over to help."

"You texted?" she asked her son.

"He told me to text any time," Robby said.

"He told you to text any time," she repeated for clarity she knew she wouldn't get. "And you texted him on your emergency cell phone that I got you?"

"It *was* an emergency. I had five word problems tonight. They're really hard and Uncle Hank didn't know how to do them either." Robby had had a tutor for the summer, after falling behind in school a little bit last school year. She came over once a week to review with him and then she usually left him a few assignments to complete. With Sydney having so much on her plate with moving back to Firefly Beach and taking care of Uncle Hank and the cottage, and her mother being a lost cause at math, Uncle Hank had been stepping in as much as he could. But sometimes, given his health, he just wasn't up for it.

Sydney shifted her attention to Nate. "You gave Robby your number?"

"I gave it to the whole team," he said, pointing to the football team roster that she, herself, had pinned to the fridge with a magnet after the informational night.

"Look," Robby said, turning the homework paper around. "Nate knew how to do them all."

"But do *you* know how to do them all?" she asked.

"Yeah, Nate is a really good teacher! He even made me two new problems to solve on my own and I did it!" He grinned fondly at Nate. "Are we done now?"

"If you feel like you've got it," Nate said, reaching down to rub Beau's head as the dog sat up in response to Robby climbing off his chair.

"Okay," Robby replied. "I'm gonna go out on the porch with Uncle Hank and everybody."

"Wait, don't you want some dinner?" she asked.

"I already ate," he said. "Nate made us all burgers on the grill." Robby ran over to the door and let himself out, taking Beau with him.

"*You* hungry?" Nate asked once they were alone.

"I'll just make a sandwich," she said.

"Nonsense. I've got a bunch of food left." He stood up and walked over to the fridge, like he owned the place, pulling out a plate of burgers covered in plastic wrap.

Sydney wrestled with the two sides of her mind. Part of her wanted to sit down with Nate, asking him about what Mary Alice had said, and the other half wanted to get him out of their kitchen and on his merry way.

"I really just want a sandwich," she said, her fear of letting him back into their lives winning out.

"Okay, I'll make you a sandwich." He slid the burgers back into the refrigerator.

"I don't want you to make me a sandwich," she stated, taking the loaf of bread from the pantry and setting it on the counter, her frustration with herself getting the best of her. She couldn't deny the fizzle of happiness that had shot through her when she saw him at the table tonight, and she should be stronger than that. "I've got it," she said, snatching the pack of cheese that he'd just gotten out of the refrigerator drawer.

He held up his hands in playful surrender. "I come in peace." When she didn't return his lighthearted banter, he added, "I have no other motive than to help Robby with his homework. *He* called *me*, remember?"

Sydney tried to unscrew the lid on the mayo to give her fingers an outlet for the nervous energy pulsing through her, but she struggled to get it open. "And you just decided to make an entire dinner for the family while you were here." She twisted with all her might, the whole situation heating her face.

"Your mom bought hamburger patties at the grocery store earlier and Uncle Hank needed help starting the grill to cook them. She asked if I'd help him." He eyed her struggle with the mayo and held out his hand, but she kept the jar pinned against her as she continued to twist unsuccessfully. Finally, her shoulders relaxed in concession.

"I'm sorry I snapped at you on the boat," Nate said. "I was aggravated with myself; it wasn't directed at you." He gently took the jar from Sydney and opened the lid, handing it back to her. "Look, I know it's been a very long time… I've been coming on pretty strong since I've been back… You've moved on, and rightfully so."

He stopped talking as if he were giving her one more chance to deny it, to tell him he was the one, and she'd been waiting for him to show up, but she wasn't about to say a thing. She didn't trust herself to open her mouth. She would inevitably follow her heart, and that hadn't worked very well for her in the past. She turned back to her sandwich, twirling the knife around in the jar of mayonnaise.

"I'd like to wipe the slate clean."

Sydney looked up at him, honesty swimming around in those blue eyes of his, making her curious. "And how do you propose to do that?"

"I can't change the past," he said, looking into her eyes. "And I can't predict the future. But I have *this* moment in unspoiled clarity, and I don't want to mess it up. It's perfect exactly the way it is, so why don't we just *be* for a little while? No expectations, no consequences."

"That sounds like something Aunt Clara would say... And the start of a song idea," she said, thawing toward him.

He raised his eyebrows. "Maybe it will be. Hurry up with that sandwich and you can help me write it." He grinned. In that one look, the Nathan Carr persona was completely gone, as if Firefly Beach had worn it off him the way the tide smoothes a seashell. His jagged edges were softer now.

"I can't," she said. "I'd like to spend some quality time with Robby—I haven't seen him all day. Then I have work to do."

His face lit up. "How *is* the new job going?"

She dared not tell him that she'd gotten interest from *NY Pulse*. "It's going great," she said. Why had she just done that? She knew why. She didn't want Nate to know that she might blow her first ever chance at writing full-time professionally.

Nate was staring at her as if he were assessing something.

"What?" she asked, turning back to the sandwich to avoid eye contact. He could see through her; he always could. She laid a piece of cheese and a few cold cuts onto the bread and set the sandwich on a plate, carrying it over to the table.

Nate plopped down beside Sydney, not taking his eyes off her. "Is the job not what you thought?" he asked, a clear attempt to decipher her inner turmoil. "I always pictured you writing about specific topics of interest..."

Sydney buried her insecurity deeper and lifted her chin. "What are you talking about? I said it's going great."

"Yes, but you're blinking more than usual, and that means that you are completely lying..." he said with a grin.

He was clearly making light of the situation but hitting a nerve instead. He'd tapped right into her self-doubt. What if she failed at this? She swallowed the lump that was forming in her throat, fighting the tears as they surfaced.

"Oh, Syd," Nate said, his face sobering, wrapping his protective arms around her like he used to when she was upset. "It's okay," he soothed.

She closed her eyes and buried her face in his chest, inhaling the familiar scent of him, drawing her back in time. A wave of calm engulfed her for an instant, but then she thought about the magazine and wondered if she was completely out of her league.

"Tell me," he urged her softly.

Nate was the only person she'd ever been able to be vulnerable with, the only one whom she'd open up to. Perhaps it was the old feeling that came back being in his arms or she was finally having some sort of breakdown, but she blurted, "I was given the opportunity to write a few pieces to see if I'd be a good fit for a magazine in New York." Tears surfaced unexpectedly as the fear became all too real.

Nate lifted her chin and wiped her tears, smiling down at her. "*This* is the girl I remember," he said fondly.

Confused, she waited for more explanation.

"The girl who gets upset when she hasn't built an empire by her first day on the job," he said, huffing out an affectionate laugh. "It's only a couple of pieces. The people reading them will know that your comfort level will build as you go. You'll get there. And I think they'll see the potential. Your writing is incredible, Syd."

His encouraging tone was like finally catching her breath after being under water.

"Do you know what the difference is between you and all the people who fail?"

Sydney shook her head, drinking in his reassurance.

"Motivation."

"Lots of people are motivated," she countered. "You put too much faith in me."

"Yes, people are, but they don't have the level of motivation you have. Look at you: you're in tears before you've even written the pieces. And you think it's because you aren't qualified, for some ridiculous reason, but I think, deep down, it's because you *want* it. And I know you. You won't sleep at night until you get it. Those wheels will turn relentlessly," he said, tapping his temple, "until you get an idea that satisfies you. Remember that little exercise you used to do to help me think?"

"The messages on trees?"

"Yes. It worked because I need to move and I'm visual. But you're introspective. Look inside yourself and break it down one thing at a time."

"If I'm breaking it down one thing at a time, it isn't just the *NY Pulse* job. I have to come up with a cover for Mary Alice's magazine, and I'm having a little trouble with it too."

"Tell me what you're thinking."

She told him about her idea for a couple on the cover, and the more she said her ideas out loud, the more vibrant they became. No one could tap into her frequency like Nate could. She'd forgotten how great he was at pulling ideas out of her, and she could always do the same for him. They were great together. *Were*, she reminded herself.

"I don't have anyone to do the shoot for the cover photo, though," she said. "I've contacted a few modeling agencies and talent agencies, and I've seen some headshots, but finding someone close enough to Firefly Beach who can live up to my visual image is tough. Do you think there's any way we could get Juliana to agree to do the shoot, or would it bring back too many painful memories?"

"I think it's worth explaining it to her," he said. "This would be more informal than her typical shoots, right?"

"Yes. I've emailed the local photographer Gavin Wilson and he's agreed to do the shoot. We'd use mostly natural light, and the beach, so the set would be minimal. I was hoping to have the two of you, hand-in-hand, walking down the beach." She threw in that last bit just to be indulgent.

"You want me to be in it?"

"The back of you, yes."

"So you and I would work together?" There was a playful suggestiveness in his eyes when he said it.

"For that *one* day." She wasn't going to totally give in to his charm.

"I like the sound of that," he said. "We'll ask Juliana. Want me to text her right now?" He pulled out his phone.

Sydney put her hand on his to stop him, and her gesture worked because his movements became still. He let go of his phone and twisted his hand under hers, peering down at her fingers as if they were some sort of delicate seashell that might break if he handled it incorrectly. The tips of his fingers stroked her palm before she pulled her hand away, her heart thumping like crazy.

"Right," he said, on an inhale, and then cleared his throat. "Work. What's the first topic?"

"Sorry?" she asked, trying to regain her focus.

"The first topic you have to write for the magazine? We're trying to work through your problems, right?"

"I'm not sure yet," she said. "I wish I could talk to someone who's done this sort of thing to pick their brain on structure and length before I start writing."

Nate picked his phone back up and began to scroll through his contacts, stopping on one. "I must have someone who can give you a quick pep-talk." He studied the screen, scrolling up. "If not, I've got a massage therapist…" He gave her a smirk, scrolling again because he obviously knew it was a stretch.

Sydney rolled her eyes and leaned over to look with him. When she did, she caught sight of Mary Alice's name in his phone—no last name, just her first name as if she were one of his close friends. *How odd*, Sydney thought. It wasn't *that* odd. They'd known each other since childhood, but they hadn't been close growing up. The phone contact, coupled with what she'd just learned about him talking Mary Alice into moving back to Firefly Beach, gave Sydney pause.

"See anyone interesting?" he asked, his brows pulling together as he looked at her. Only then did she realize she'd been staring at his phone.

Curious or not, it wasn't any of her business. It was better just to let it go.

Startling her, Nate's phone came to life. "One sec," he said, standing up and walking over to the doorway. "Hello?" His broad shoulders were hunched just slightly as he leaned forward to take the call. "You're kidding…" He began pacing slowly, a smile crawling across his face. "When does he want me there?… Absolutely. Talk soon." Nate ended the call and came back over to the table. "I've got a pretty big writing retreat to go to."

"Writing retreat?"

"Yeah. When an artist wants to make an album, sometimes they might ask a few songwriters to collaborate. We all go to a specific location together for a week or so and hash out a bunch of songs. This time, it's Malibu."

"California?" she asked, more so out of disbelief. Nate's reality was that he found it completely normal to leave suddenly and head to Malibu for a couple of weeks—all in the name of work.

"Yep. It's for a major country music star who's coming out of retirement, but it's sort of under wraps, I was told, so I'd better not say." Nate mimed zipping his lips. "I have to leave tonight."

"You're just going to drop everything and go?"

"I've gotten pretty good at managing schedules on the road," he said. "I'm totally used to this sort of thing. I do it all the time."

"Just like that? Will Juliana be okay? What if that photographer comes back while you're gone?" she asked. "If we call you, will you come home?"

"I have to silence my phone when I'm writing. I completely go off the grid. But Juliana knows how to handle herself with the press."

"That guy Seth wouldn't come to Firefly Beach to find her, would he?" Sydney fretted.

Nate shook his head. "I doubt it. He's a busy man and he doesn't strike me as the type that would spend his energy chasing people around. I won't let anything happen. And if she needs support, Malory's here, and Mary Alice will help her through any issues until I can get back."

"And when will that be?" she asked.

"I'm not sure. Probably whenever we have enough songs written. Sometimes we can get on a roll and be done in a few days; it just depends."

Robby ran past the window and a stab of fear shot through Sydney. What would Nate do if he had to leave during football season this fall? Certainly, he couldn't just disappear for an unspecified amount of time with absolutely no contact. Had he given any thought to this at all? Living in Firefly Beach wasn't the same as the big cities he'd become accustomed to. Here, if he wanted to be a part of the community, people would count on him to be there when they needed him.

"You look worried," he said, pulling her out of her thoughts. "If anyone needs anything, I have an assistant named Cameron Ross. He'll be coming into town in about two days to oversee the building on my lot while I'm working. I'll text him and ask him to come earlier."

The mental image of Nate sending his assistant to Robby's game when he couldn't make it slid into her consciousness and suddenly, when Sydney looked at Nate, all she could see was Nathan Carr. "That won't be necessary," she eventually said.

"No, really. He'd be okay with it."

"I'm sure he would." Sydney stood up and tipped her plate, sending her sandwich into the trash.

Nate followed her with his gaze as she dumped the plate into the sink. "You didn't eat," he said slowly, something brewing in that brain of his.

"I'm not very hungry anymore. I'm going to go out with Robby and the family."

"I haven't finished helping you with the magazine," he said.

"I don't need any help."

She would do this on her own because that was what she'd become great at doing. She hadn't needed Nate in the years he'd been gone, and she didn't need him now. He was right: the only clarity she had was this moment, and this moment wasn't any different than the other moments she'd had with Nate since he'd been back. They had become two very different people.

Chapter Eighteen

Sydney took in the picturesque view through the French doors of the living room this morning as she sat on the sofa with her coffee. The gulf was striped in bright aquamarine and electric blue, and the sun beamed while the palms danced in a light breeze. Sydney couldn't wait to get ready for the day and head to work.

She'd slept like a baby. But this morning, the uneasiness of Nate's absence settled upon her when she looked at the clock and guessed he'd already left for Malibu. He'd stayed an incredibly long time last night, playing with Robby and talking with Uncle Hank about some options for Starlight Cottage, none of which did she want to hear unless they involved stopping the development and maintaining the land surrounding them. To avoid any more lengthy conversations, she'd stayed out on the porch with her mother, and then she'd run into town to get a few things her mother had forgotten at the store, until she knew he'd be gone. Any later, and he'd miss his flight.

She'd fallen asleep with Robby while tucking him in and blindly made it to her room sometime in the middle of the night. It wasn't until she'd come back into her bedroom and raised the blinds that she'd seen the note that had stopped her cold. She walked over to the dresser and picked up the plastic ring with the purple stone that sat on top of the paper. Hesitantly, she slid the little band onto her finger and peered down at it. So many dreams had been wrapped up in that toy ring. But that wasn't what was bothering her right now. What was eating away at her was the message on the paper beside it. In Nate's familiar writing, the note simply said:

> When I get back, I need to tell you something.
> Love you, Nate

No, no he didn't. He didn't need to tell her anything. He needed to just let her move on already. Too much had changed between them. And every time she considered her feelings for him, they were all based on what she knew of the past, not what she saw in front of her now. But she couldn't ignore the niggling curiosity of what it was he had to say. She looked down at the ring, the memories surrounding it assaulting her. What could he have to tell her that hadn't already been said?

"Hey, Mama," Robby said from the doorway, rubbing his sleepy eyes.

"Good morning." Sydney walked over to him and wrapped her arms around his tiny frame. "Did you sleep well?"

"Mm hmm," he said, before a yawn engulfed him. When he finally opened his eyes, he touched the ring on her finger. "I showed that to Nate last night."

"You did?"

"Yeah. We were playing that word game that Uncle Hank has. When it was my go, I got a really hard word so I ran to Uncle Hank and asked him to explain what it was. I was trying to get Nate to say 'costume jewelry' and Uncle Hank said that was pretend jewelry that was less expensive than real jewelry. I wasn't allowed to talk, so I remembered you had that ring! Wasn't that good thinking?"

"Yes, it was!" she replied with forced enthusiasm. "Did Nate guess the word?" she asked carefully, mortified that he'd seen the ring and dying to know Nate's reaction after she'd told him she didn't have it anymore.

"He looked at it really weird for a long time and then he guessed the word was 'love.'" Robby squeezed his eyes shut and shook his head, giggling. "You *could* give someone a ring if you love them, but gross." He wrinkled his nose at the idea, making her laugh.

Sydney slipped the ring off her finger and set it down on top of Nate's note. "Come on," she said, "let's get you some breakfast."

Sydney sat at her desk in the old sewing room. The sewing room used to double as an extra bedroom, but in the renovation of Starlight Cottage, Sydney had replaced the twin bed with a soft, seashell-colored cream sofa and rearranged the furniture, keeping Aunt Clara's sewing machine that she'd used to make some of the pieces she'd designed for her company Morgan and Flynn as a focal point on one wall while adding a small desk in the center of the room. She stared at her computer screen.

This was what she knew: Nate dropped everything to run off and write—it was his job to do that. He said he did it all the time, and, being an incredibly successful songwriter, he probably had to. The magazines reported that he never stayed in one location for very long, and, given what Sydney knew of his attention span, they were most likely correct. He lived a life where he was followed by photographers and hounded by the press...

Sydney tapped her pen against her bottom lip. She

wanted to run into his arms when he got back, but everything in her brain told her she needed to get over him once and for all or he'd haunt her for the rest of her life. What could she do to take her mind off him, though? Here she was at her desk at work, needing to get a move on with figuring out this magazine, and he was filling her head. She had to have something else to think about...

Slowly, she looked down at her handbag on the floor, leaning against her desk, and an idea came to her. In that instant, she realized that Nate kept trying because deep down, she still had hope that they could be what they were, and she allowed him to have glimpses of it. As much as it would hurt, she had to give Nate a solid message that he needed to stop. It was the only way that she could get him out of her head so she could move forward in life.

Sydney grabbed her cell phone and pulled up Logan's number on a text screen. She typed:

Hi. This is Sydney. I was wondering if you want to get together again sometime.

She stared at the message, considering, and the more she thought about it, the more she knew she had to do it. She hit send.

The word "read" appeared at the bottom of her message, alerting her that Logan had seen the message, and a cold shiver coursed through her. *He seemed nice*, she told herself. *He was funny.*

Logan's text came in:

Love to. Today work?

Yes, she answered. She could take a late lunch and meet him in town.

How about 1:00 at The Fruity Fish?

She hadn't been to the local juice bar called The Fruity Fish in ages. It would be nice to stop back in. Maybe she could even grab a take-out menu to see if Robby would like any of their smoothies.

Logan came back to her:

See you then!

Logan emerged through the throng of vacationers strolling through town and met her in front of The Fruity Fish. He was much more casual than he'd been when she'd seen him last, wearing a T-shirt and sunglasses, his thick crop of dark hair attractively messier than it had been before. He broke into a gorgeous smile when he saw her.

"Hey," he said, greeting her with a friendly hug. "It's great to see you."

"Shall we go inside?" she asked.

In response, Logan opened the door for her and allowed her to enter, the cool air welcoming after being in the midday heat. Every table was occupied. As usual, the place was crawling with tourists, wide-eyed and buzzing over the selection of beverages listed above the juice bar, their arms full of Fruity Fish mugs and T-shirts that said "Eat your veggies" with a cartoon smoothie bending at the side, a smile stretching across the cup.

The owner, Sanders McCoy, waved to them between juice cup flips and straw catches. He was known for his acrobatics when making juice drinks. In fact, Aunt Clara had tried to get her and Nate a job there after they'd shown her their lemon-juggling routine.

They joined the line to put in their orders.

"Do you see an open seat?" she asked Logan. He was taller than she was, so perhaps he could get a better view over the crowd.

He took off his sunglasses and tipped his head up, scanning the room. "Nothing." He looked down at her, the corners of his eyes creasing with his smile. "Where can you get the worst food in town?" he asked.

She smiled. "Even there, it'll be full of tourists this time of year." She really should've thought this through a little better, but her mind had been on Nate instead of planning a great spot. Her tummy growled.

"Was that your stomach? You're hungry," he said.

"A little," she replied, trying not to let on that she was absolutely starving.

"I'm not trying to be creepy, but my place is just a couple minutes' drive. I could make you lunch. And I *do* have coffee."

Sydney had to be back at work in an hour. And going to Logan's house was a little more involved than grabbing a cup of coffee with him. She froze with indecision.

"Did I mention that I'm Ben's sound designer? I have a summer house here that's been in our family for years. It's on the beach in the next village." He held up his hands. "I promise I'm not a crazy person or anything. In fact, my mother is visiting at the moment, so she'll be there too."

It sounded better by the second.

Logan pulled to a stop in front of a cedar-shingled bungalow that sat on stilts in the powdery white sand. It had a modest but elegant front porch with two rocking chairs on either side of a bright orange front door displaying a wreath made of seashells and starfish.

"When you were getting in the car at the coffee shop, I texted my mom to tell her we were coming," he said as they got out and headed up the steps of the cottage. "Fingers crossed she's dishing us up her famous chicken salad."

Logan slipped his key into the lock and let Sydney inside. The small space was open and airy, decorated in the classic beach style: lots of white and nautical blue. She eyed the small wicker bench in the entryway and ran her fingers over the navy blue and white striped pillows propped up on it. Like a smaller version of Starlight Cottage, the kitchen was along the back, and a wall of windows afforded a view of the stretch of white sand, dotted with dark blue umbrellas, which didn't disappoint.

"Oh my stars! Logan found a friend," teased a smartly dressed woman with a gray bob of hair and a friendly smile as she greeted them. The woman swished forward in her flowing linen trousers and loosely belted shirt. Her delicate jade bracelets jingled on her wrist as she held out her hand to introduce herself. "I'm so happy to meet you. I'm Delilah Hayes, Logan's mother."

"It's nice to meet you," Sydney said, already enjoying the lift she felt being with someone who had no ties to her past. Like Nate's suggestion to live in the present moment— it certainly was a comfortable place to be. Even Sydney's ex-husband had grown up with her, and there was always the element of shared experiences that could be a blessing but at times, also a curse. Whether this meeting between herself and Logan went anywhere from today was yet to be seen, but this was a clean slate from which to build.

"Logan never brings girls to the house," Delilah said, beckoning them into the kitchen where she had plates made already with croissant sandwiches and fresh pineapple garnish.

"Maybe it's because I never had your chicken salad to offer them," he said with a wink.

"Yes," Sydney said, playing along. "I was actually just walking by, minding my own business, when Logan came up to me and offered me chicken salad. I completely changed my plans."

Delilah laughed and patted his shoulder, handing him a plate.

"Mom, are you hungry? You should join us," Logan offered.

"Yes, please do," Sydney replied.

"I'd hate to intrude," Delilah said, wiping the crumbs from the counter with a dishrag.

Logan silently consulted Sydney and she offered her consent. It would be nice to have someone else to take some of the pressure off.

"Nonsense," Logan said. "We're just having lunch."

Delilah whipped up another sandwich and sat down with the two of them at the small farmhouse-style distressed wood table. She scooted a bowl of lemons to the side so they could all talk. "How do you two know each other?" she asked.

"Sydney was at Ben's wedding," Logan told her.

"Ah, Ben. I adore him." Delilah handed Sydney a paper napkin, still getting settled but not wasting a minute of conversation time. It reminded Sydney of Aunt Clara. She used to be just like that, talking and genuinely listening as she puttered around the house. "Life is too short not to have conversation. We're built to be with one another, not alone," she said once.

"I'm Ben's new sister-in-law," Sydney explained. "But I've known him since we were kids."

"Oh!" Her eyebrows rose in interest. "So that makes you one of Hank and Clara Eubanks's nieces?"

"Yes," Sydney said.

"How lovely. I never knew them, but I've heard what wonderful people they are. I know how much Clara has done for the community of Firefly Beach. And I've also seen Starlight Cottage in all the magazines—it's incredible! Your Aunt Clara was so talented."

"Yes, she was."

"I'd heard they're planning to put in that public beach access right beside the cottage. How does your family feel about that?"

"We're all really upset about it." Sydney picked up her sandwich. "My Uncle Hank attended the last meeting and he's going to the one today."

Delilah shook her head. "Logan, don't you know someone who could help change their minds?" She leaned forward, as a thought clearly came to her. "What about that guy from the music business—the famous guy on the board of supervisors for Firefly Beach—the one that I pointed out in the local paper this morning? Do you know him at all? Couldn't you bend his ear a little?"

"Nathan Carr? I don't know him... And I doubt I could change his mind anyway. I think he's heading up the whole thing."

All the blood rushed out of Sydney's face.

"Ben knows him... And *you* were talking to Nathan at the wedding, right?" Logan said to Sydney. Logan's voice plunged through the fog that had filled Sydney's mind. She struggled to pull herself back into the conversation.

"Uh, yes. I know him."

"Maybe you could talk to him?"

Sydney could kick herself. She'd let Nate in, allowed him to manipulate her thoughts, and her worst fears were confirmed: Nate had only come back into her life because he wanted something. He was hoping to convince Sydney and the family to sell Starlight Cottage so he could put in the beach access. Everything was coming together—the empty lot where he'd leveled his parents' cottage that sat vacant because it was in the line of houses that needed to be torn down for the beach access. The fact that he was building his new house further out so he wouldn't have to be near the mess he was going to cause with the influx of tourists. Was that what he wanted to tell her when he got back?

"It's just an idea," Logan said, tearing her away from her complete panic at the thought that Nate had deceived her. She'd never have thought he'd stoop so low.

Sydney forced herself back into the moment and forced a smile. "Yes, I could definitely talk to him," she said. Oh, she certainly would talk to him. She planned to give him a piece of her mind and push him out of her life once and for all.

"You okay?" Logan asked, concern written on his face.

Sydney scrambled to gain composure. "Yes. I'm totally fine. It just makes me so sad that Starlight Cottage is facing this, you know?"

"I can't imagine," he said with a compassionate shake of his head. "I'll tell you what. There's a little ice cream shop down the road, and I'll bet it isn't nearly as busy as the one in Firefly Beach." He raised his eyebrows in suggestion. "We can't fix the big things in life sometimes, but we can take a second to free our minds of them. Wanna go after lunch?"

Sydney was grateful for Logan's kindness. "I can't think of anything better."

Chapter Nineteen

Juliana walked up the steps to Starlight Cottage, sitting down in the rocking chair beside Sydney's and crossing her legs.

"Thank you for coming," Sydney said. "I didn't know who else to call."

Now in the shade of the porch, Juliana pushed her sunglasses up on her head. "What is it?" she asked, her eyes wide.

"Remember the magazine I'm working on? I need someone great for the cover," she said. "It would be a very informal shoot..."

"I am sorry," Juliana said with a frown. "I do not want to work in this field anymore. It has too many bad memories for me...I am sure you can find someone else to do it."

She'd thought about asking Logan if he'd do the shoot. He definitely had the right build. She just needed a partner for him. "I don't know anyone else," Sydney admitted.

"Yes, you do. *You* do it."

Sydney laughed, the idea completely taking her by surprise. "I wouldn't be natural at modeling, I'm afraid."

"What if I coached you?" Juliana offered. "I can show

you how to use the sunlight, the way your limbs should move when you walk so the shot is clean, if you're doing an action shot. I can position you and the other person to be sure you're at the best angle."

"I don't look the part..."

Juliana chuckled. "I will style you. You're gorgeous! I will do your hair and make-up."

This magazine cover was sure to be a complete disaster if she didn't take charge right now. "I need it to look professional."

"Why don't you let me do your hair and make-up and dress you in something elegant? Then you will see."

Sydney deliberated. She wished she had Aunt Clara to ask about these sorts of things. She wasn't any good at this. She put her forearms on the arms of the chair and started to rock it, thinking. *What would Aunt Clara do?* She would hustle. Aunt Clara used to always say, "Real success comes from a good hustle, and when something you really want doesn't go your way, you don't pout about it; you make it happen—you just have to get creative and hustle a little more than you expected."

"Okay," Sydney said.

"I am so happy!" Juliana said. "We could also call your photographer to do some shots."

"Great idea. I'll give Gavin a call." She felt a swell of excitement, and tried not to think about how long the road still was to getting this publication ready. *Baby steps*, she told herself. "What time can I come over?"

Juliana twisted the watch on her thin wrist around to view the time. "Want to do it now?"

"My mom and Uncle Hank took Robby to a movie so we'll have a few hours to work."

"Perfect!"

* * *

When Juliana said, "Let me grab my make-up bag," Sydney hadn't been ready for the suitcase-sized tote that Juliana loaded into Sydney's car at Malory's. Juliana lumped it on Sydney's bed next to where she was sitting. She then set up a circular tripod with white lighting and shined it on Sydney's face.

"You need all this for a shot of two people holding hands?" Sydney asked, peeking into the bag. It was filled with different combinations of make-up colors, nail polishes, hairstyling kits—everything anyone could ever need and then some.

Juliana scooted the bag over and sat down beside Sydney. "The shot is only one element of a great image," she said. "Before we put anything on your face at all, we need to know what we are painting."

"What do you mean?"

"What is the product you're trying to sell?"

Sydney tied her hair back with a rubber band. "The wellness magazine."

"What emotion or question do you want from your reader when he or she sees this cover? What will make them pick it up?"

Sydney contemplated this for a second. She'd been so consumed with the minutiae of each of the pieces that she realized she hadn't given thought to the overarching theme of the whole thing. "I'm not sure if it's a question per se," Sydney said, thinking out loud, "but more of a curiosity. I want people dying to know what's inside that will better their lives."

Juliana sighed a long, luscious exhalation of happiness. "You think like a writer," she said. "You are an emotional thinker. I love that. We need to tap into it."

Sydney had never really considered that her thought pattern was any different than anyone else's. She'd just gotten used to pondering things in this way from being around Nate. She hadn't really dissected the "why" of things in a long time. Perhaps it was the fact that, since Nate had left, she hadn't had anyone ask the right questions.

"I have only known one other person who thinks that deeply about everything he does," Juliana said.

Her comment made Sydney feel exposed, and her cheeks heated right up. "Well, if it's Nate, let's move along," she said. "He's a colossal distraction, and I need to focus on the magazine right now."

"Yes, you are right. Let us focus." She pulled a curling iron out of her bag and plugged it in, setting it on the dresser. "What is the title of the magazine?"

"It's called *A Better You*."

"So my interpretation of this is clean lines, simplistic, stripping away all the baggage—nothing but fresh, youthful happiness. We need a visual representation of mindfulness, wellbeing, and joy. Minimal make-up, loose hair that allows the sunlight to flow through it, lightweight clothing, perhaps bare feet. How does that sound?"

Sydney was surprised at how much more there was to Juliana's creativity and spirit than what she put out in the public eye. "I love how you work," she said.

"Thank you."

Juliana gave her a meek smile that was different than the vivacious looks she'd offered the cameras over the years.

Juliana rooted around in her bag and pulled out a wide tray of varying colors. "I'm thinking we will play up the colors that you already have naturally. With your auburn curls, we want cinnamons and coppers for your eyes, a light, shiny nutmeg for your lips." She dabbed her finger

in one of the colors and swiped it on the back of her hand.
"Like this."

"That's beautiful," Sydney said. "These decisions seem
to come naturally for you. In seconds, you can choose the
right colors. It would take me hours of discussion at the
make-up counter in town."

Juliana smiled and motioned for her to close her eyes.
"I could do it in my sleep," she said as she applied Sydney's
eyeshadow.

As Juliana worked on Sydney's face, her brushes and
sponges moving effortlessly, various creams and powders
dabbed on the back of Juliana's hand, Sydney said with a
little laugh, "It takes a lot to look natural, doesn't it?"

"Yes," Juliana said, returning the amusement in her
words. "At the end of the day, it is like art: we play with
colors and textures and light…" She dragged a wide brush
across Sydney's forehead. "What we want to do is give your
natural skin the texture and color it needs to look just as
beautiful on camera as you do in real life. But to do that, we
have to speak the language of the lens in terms of reflection
and shape."

"You sound like my friend Gavin. He's the photographer
for the shoot, and he has an art gallery in town. Have you
been there yet?"

Juliana shook her head.

"He's incredibly kind, and I think you two would have a
lot to talk about. Of course you'll meet him soon anyway if
he comes to take those shots you suggested."

Juliana seemed happy at the thought of meeting someone
else in Firefly Beach.

"Do you like it here?" Sydney asked out of the blue.

In this moment, Juliana had relaxed so much that she was
nearly unrecognizable from the images she posted on her

social media feeds. Her hair was in a loose ponytail at the back of her neck, her face naturally youthful and glowing without any make-up. She had on an unassuming white T, the front hem tucked into the waistband of her faded jeans. She was still incredibly beautiful, but her mannerisms were relaxed and small, as if the bubble of fame that encapsulated her had deflated over her time here, leaving just the raw beauty of her. At her heart, she, too, was just a small-town girl, trying to make her way.

"I love it here."

"What do you love about it?" Sydney asked, curious.

Juliana got out a small brush and plunged it into a tube of lip-gloss. "I love that people are kind when they have no ulterior motive. They are kind simply in the hope that you will be friendly in return. I feel valued here. In that way, it reminds me of my home." She unwound the cap on a tube of mascara. "Look up for me."

Sydney couldn't deny the tiny seed of hope that Firefly Beach would have the same effect on Nate. Maybe over the years, the sea would wash that big image right off him, diluting Nathan Carr, and he'd be the boy who'd looked into her eyes with all that love so many years ago. That is, if he didn't completely ruin Starlight Cottage before then, she thought, her blood boiling. She decided that it would be too much to ask even the heavens for Nate to come around.

Juliana got to work on Sydney's hair, twisting and curling large pieces of it. "I envy you," she said as she unclipped a curl, the lock bouncing down Sydney's cheek.

"*Me*?" Sydney asked. "Why?"

"You know what you want. He loves that about you. He thinks the world of you."

"How could he?" she said in a knee-jerk reaction. "You don't betray people you care about."

"Betray?" she asked.

Sydney shook her head. "He . . . It isn't important," she lied.

"Nate tells me you are a very talented writer. He said he never imagined you doing anything but writing. And here you are, working on the magazine for the wellness center and he tells me you are also writing for a column."

Just like her view of Juliana—things weren't always as they seemed. "I don't know if I'm cut out for the job yet."

Juliana's face crumpled in concern. "How could you not be?" She ran her fingers through Sydney's hair to comb it out.

"I was given the opportunity to apply for a magazine position that would be pretty close to my dream job. But at times, I feel like I'm shooting too high for a girl who's spent most of her time as a mom, doing part-time work to pay the bills. I don't have the clout I need to pull it off."

Juliana's hands stilled as she turned inward, thoughtful. "You know, I would never have believed I would leave my little village in Argentina for the bright lights of Los Angeles. That was something of movies, not real life. On my first shoots, I was not performing the way they'd hoped, and another model pulled me aside and gave me some advice. She said, '*None* of us belong here. We just pretend like we do until it becomes who we are.'"

Sydney grinned. "Fake it till you make it."

"That's right. But it is more than that. You have to believe that at some point, you *will* belong. You just have to be creative with how to build yourself up from the bottom."

"You know what? You're exactly right."

Juliana turned Sydney around in front of the mirror and Sydney's jaw nearly dropped to the floor.

"Oh my gosh," she said as she viewed the stranger in her reflection.

"You are beautiful."

"How did you do that? I don't even look like myself. Well, I do, but it's like some heavenly version of me. You are so talented... You know, you wouldn't have to model to work in the business. You could do something behind the scenes. You could teach people how to model, teach them about color and light."

"I wouldn't know where to begin," Juliana said.

"Fake it till you make it."

Both women laughed at Sydney's comment, but Sydney could see a sparkle in Juliana's eye at the possibilities.

"Mama, is that you?" Robby asked when he and Jacqueline entered the cottage and slid their flip-flops off at the door. Sydney was still wearing the make-up Juliana had put on her.

Uncle Hank came in behind them and shut the door while Sydney's mother pushed the shoes to the side to get them out of his path. "You could win the Miss Firefly Beach pageant looking like that."

"Yes, she certainly could," Jacqueline said, her eyes round.

Sydney bent down to give Robby a hug. "Juliana thinks I should be on the cover of the wellness magazine. She did my make-up so I could see if it would work."

After Juliana left, Sydney was so energized by their conversation that she was ready to take charge of her life. She texted Logan to ask if he would be interested in doing the shoot with her. He was beyond excited, and he invited her to dinner after the shoot tomorrow. Sydney had said she'd go; but Nate's deceit weighed heavily on her mind, casting a cloud over everything. No matter how hard she tried to push it out of her mind, it wouldn't budge.

Chapter Twenty

Sydney and her family waited to cross the intersection at the overcrowded traffic signal, beachgoers flooding the center of town. When the walk sign finally flashed, Sydney guided Robby across the street and then entered the town hall through the double front doors, following her mother, Lewis, and Uncle Hank, along with the gathering of others opposing the public beach access. The building they were in was a historical landmark, part of it having been the first permanent structure of the village. The old wood floors creaked beneath their feet as they all headed deeper into the cool air-conditioned space.

Uncle Hank's smile was replaced by a serious expression of concentration, his eyes fixed on the door at the end of the hallway where they were all going. The family had decided, along with the other residents that would be affected by the public beach access, that everyone should attend to show their disagreement. As they took their seats, Sydney tried to overlook the fact that, even with them all present, their numbers weren't terribly overwhelming. What she also hadn't had the heart to tell Uncle Hank and her family was that Nate was behind the plans. The icy cold feeling that had pelted her over and over in the early days after he'd left

Firefly Beach slithered back in at the thought of his betrayal. It was nearly more than she could bear.

An older woman by the name of Sheila Fox lowered herself warily into one of the three chairs on the small stage and tapped her microphone, causing it to squeal in protest.

"I thought the entire board would be here tonight," Sydney whispered to Uncle Hank as board members filled the other two chairs on stage. The idea that Nate would head this thing up and not even bother to attend any of the meetings sent a bitter taste through Sydney's mouth. How convenient that he would disappear for the final discussion before the vote to essentially ruin Starlight Cottage.

"As Firefly Beach grows, there seems to be less and less personal interaction," Uncle Hank said under his breath. "And I think the board members are just doing this so we feel like we have a voice."

Sheila stood up to the clearing of throats and shifting in chairs. "Thank you for joining us tonight," she said into the microphone, her amplified voice echoing in the church-like room full of empty chairs, only the first few rows sparsely occupied. "If you'll bear with us, we'd like to inform you all of our considerations for the project at length before we take any of your questions." Sheila opened a hand toward the man in the chair at her right. "Forrest Baker will mention the current state of affairs regarding traffic through Firefly Beach, leading to the proposal by the board," she said, before turning to her left, "and Joyce Powell will give you the impact on your wallets with the suggested tax increase as well as the projected revenue the project will provide."

The crowd sat, hushed and waiting, some with arms folded, others with eyes clamped on Sheila, chests filling with air in anticipation of the next part.

"I will begin with an overview..."

What if, for some unknown reason, Sydney wasn't meant to stay in Firefly Beach? It certainly seemed like the odds were against her: Nate's constant presence would only drive her crazy, the future of Starlight Cottage was in jeopardy, and, even though she'd managed to look on the bright side, the magazine for Mary Alice still wouldn't have gotten off the ground were it not for Juliana's help. She wondered if she should go back to her old paralegal job in Nashville, where she'd been just fine before.

"There will always be forward movement," Sheila's voice filtered back into Sydney's consciousness. "We have to prepare for it, whether we like it or not. Change is inevitable and, at times, uncomfortable. But we *must* move forward." Sheila paused dramatically to the silent staring eyes of the crowd surrounding Sydney. With a hesitant breath over the speakers, she said, "I'm going to turn the microphone over to Forrest who will give you the breakdown of traffic through the main thoroughfare as well as the proposal for how to alleviate that traffic."

Forrest Baker walked over and took the microphone from a relieved Sheila and began pacing the stage, his long, thin strides making him look as though he were gliding. "Last meeting, we discussed the proposed zoning for the project. With that now cemented, it's time to look forward to the project at hand: alleviating the overcrowding on our main street while building up the area with more shopping surrounding the new public beach access..."

"I'm bored," Robby whispered to Sydney. "I wish Nate was here so we could draw."

A pinch caught in the back of her shoulder. "What about Ben?" she asked.

Robby grinned up at her, nodding. "He'd be fun too, but Nate likes *all* the stuff I like."

Sydney leaned close to Robby's ear. "I'm not sure Nate will be around a lot," she said, ignoring the churning in her stomach. "Maybe I can draw with you." She dug around quietly in her handbag for a pen and a scrap of paper.

"What do you mean?" Robby looked up at her with concern in his little eyes.

"Well, he travels a lot, and I'm not sure how long he'll be in Firefly Beach."

"But he said—"

She shook her head and waved him quiet with a kind smile, hating Nate for the pain he would cause her son. "We'll talk about it later, okay?" She drew a tic-tac-toe board on the back of an old receipt and handed him the pen. "You go first."

Joyce Powell gave them all the financial breakdown while Sydney played games with Robby. The entire time, the fear kept creeping in that Robby was going to be devastated when Nate was no longer welcome. There was no way she was going to let him back in to their lives after this. Now, all the kindness he'd shown was in question. Had it all been to sway them to sell their property? Would they knock it down to build shops like the ones that surrounded the current public beach? She scanned the faces in the crowd, noticing that Malory wasn't there. She remembered now that he was building something for her on his land.

"Once the final two residents agree to sell, the project *will* move forward," Joyce said. "I hope that after tonight, you have some buy-in as to the positive economic and aesthetic impact the public beach access will have on Firefly Beach. It will essentially give us our streets back. Now, we will all take your questions."

"Are we one of the remaining two?" Jacqueline asked Uncle Hank, clearly worried.

He shook his head. "We've been approached to sell, but we aren't in the actual development line. We'll lose our view, but we can stay."

"Who approached you to sell?" Jacqueline asked.

"I got a letter from the board."

An icy thorn of anger poked Sydney's insides. Nate wanted them to sell, didn't he? It seemed pretty darn obvious now.

Attempting to ease Jacqueline's nerves, Uncle Hank replied, "They probably just heard that I'd been asking around for real estate agents and thought I was interested."

"And are you?" Jacqueline asked. "Are you *really* interested in abandoning the dream that Aunt Clara built for us all?"

Sydney feared that her mother's emotion would upset Uncle Hank, but she knew Mama wasn't snapping at him. She was just making sure that he understood what he was considering. Starlight Cottage was a part of their history, an extension of Aunt Clara, and the only legacy left by her in Firefly Beach.

"Nate offered to sell us a piece of his property," Uncle Hank said, clearly considering this as the words left his mouth. "We'll talk about it later." He shifted his focus back to the stage.

A tingling sensation crawled over Sydney's skin. She did *not* want to be any closer to Nate than she had to be, and once Uncle Hank and her family found out about Nate's involvement in the—

Sydney's thoughts were interrupted by a buzzing wave of noise from the crowd.

Joyce put the microphone to her lips. "I'm delighted that we could get our intentions across with this meeting. With the two of you agreeing to sell tonight," she said, her gaze on the owners of the final two cottages on Sydney's street, "we will be able to move forward. Our board will be preparing a step-by-step guide of the process that will be online to keep you informed as we go."

"What just happened?" Sydney said to Uncle Hank.

Uncle Hank had also missed the conversation while they'd been whispering back and forth, but unlike Sydney, his level-headedness had kept him from panicking, and he'd been able to jump right back into the conversation. "Looks like it's a go," he said. He tipped his head back, searching the ceiling, as if he were trying to find Aunt Clara up there.

They all needed her help right now.

The crowd was restless and Tom McCoy, the owner of the old fruit stand and one of the final two cottages to sell, got up on the stage and took the microphone in an obvious attempt to calm any fears. "I was approached by a board member a few days ago," he said into the microphone, his eyes suddenly finding Sydney. Why was he looking at her? "He gave me a price I can't refuse, and also let me know that it would be in my best interest to sell. I've known him since he was a boy and while I'm nervous about the change, I have to trust him."

Sydney had to close her gaping mouth. The only person on the board that Tom knew like that was Nate. Fire coursed through her veins and her hand shot up into the air.

A look of surprise washed over Tom's face. "Yes?" he asked.

Sydney stood up, ignoring her mother's confused glances. She called out over the two rows of chairs separating them: "And what stake does this board member have in the project?" Her eyes narrowed.

Tom shrugged, helpless, his shoulders slumping as he shook his head in surrender.

"*How* is this in your best interest, Tom?" she nearly pleaded.

He just shook his head, mute.

Sydney felt like she was moving down a dark tunnel, the room closing in on her. She hadn't gotten this feeling since seeing Nate's truck driving away from her that day. Once again, Nate had managed to take all her joy with him. She'd tried her best not to let him hurt her again but he just had. He'd torn her heart out. Her anger withering to sadness, she sank back down into her chair in silence.

After Robby had had his bath, Sydney tucked him into bed and kissed his forehead.

"When is Nate coming back?" he asked her.

Sydney took in a deep breath of air to keep her shoulders from tensing. "Ben will be home in two days," she suggested instead, praying that he would refocus his attention on the man who would never hurt him.

Robby broke into a smile. "I miss him. And Beau misses him too."

Sydney nodded. "We all miss him. I miss Aunt Hallie a lot."

Robby's tired eyes grew round as a thought entered his mind. "Isn't Ben friends with Nate? Maybe when Ben gets back, the three of us could go fishing!"

"Maybe," she said, trying to soothe him to sleep. She couldn't tell him outright that she never planned to let him near Nate again. He had no regard for anyone's feelings.

"You look sad, Mama," he said. "You can go fishing with us if you want to."

She ran her fingers through the strands of hair on his forehead, brushing them back affectionately. Robby would be devastated if he knew that Nate was no longer going to be in his life, and the idea of yet another man leaving him would make things worse.

"Ben has another friend named Logan. Maybe he could go fishing with you all," she heard herself say. She had no idea why she uttered Logan's name, except for perhaps her hope that Robby could like someone who couldn't hurt him. The more she considered this, the stronger the idea became. Ben would eventually be wrapped up in the family he would start with Hallie, and Nate would be out of the picture.

Logan was kind and funny. Maybe he could be a role model for Robby.

"Who's Logan?" he asked.

"I met him at the wedding," she said. "He doesn't know a lot of people here. Maybe you should include him. He'd probably like that."

Robby's gaze was cautious.

"Maybe you could meet him first," she suggested. "You and Ben could show him all the good fishing spots."

"And Nate," he corrected her.

She smiled to cover her worry. "It was just an idea. We can talk more about it later." She kissed his cheek and tucked the blankets around his little body. "I love you."

"Love you too," he said, closing his eyes.

"Sleep tight."

Sydney turned off the lamp by Robby's bed and let herself out of the room, the uncertainty of the situation settling heavily on her. Before she joined her family, she had an idea. It was time to give Logan a quick call.

"Sydney, it's nice to hear from you," Logan said as Sydney closed herself into her bedroom and lowered herself down on the four-poster bed. She smoothed her hand over Aunt Clara's sand-colored linens.

"I had an idea," she said to him.

"Tell me." His voice was gently eager to hear what she had to say.

"When we have dinner tomorrow night, how about we do a picnic instead?"

"A storm's coming in, so the temperature will drop a little by tomorrow night. It would be perfect."

"One more request," she said. "I'd like to bring my son, Robby."

"Oh?" He didn't sound taken aback, which was good. He was more curious.

"I've been so busy this week, and I don't want to leave him with my mom again. She's done so much for me since I've gone back to work—she needs a break, even though she'd never say so, and I need some quality time with Robby. You could come to Starlight Cottage and we could go down to the beach once the fireflies are out, maybe do some fishing."

Her shoulders relaxed when she could almost hear his smile on the other end of the line. "That would be fantastic. I'll gather up all my fishing supplies."

"Thank you so much," she said, relieved.

"I can't wait. . . . and maybe when Robby goes to bed, we can grab a drink somewhere?"

"That sounds great." For the first time in a while, a quiet optimism settled over her.

Sydney said her goodbyes, and then settled in, under her covers, leaning against the headboard with her laptop balanced on her legs. She stared at the email she'd opened and viewed her two topics for *NY Pulse*. The first one was titled "A Love Letter." She opened a blank document and rested her fingers on the keys, pulling into herself to think of possible angles for this topic. There were so many people she could write a love letter to—she even thought of Mel and his lost love—but the more she thought about it, the more she realized that she needed to write one to herself. She started typing.

To the girl who wonders

To the girl who wonders where she went wrong, sometimes there's no right or left, only forward. To begin the journey you want, all it requires of you is to take the first step. To the girl who wishes things could be different, ask yourself, "Different from what?" Different from the empty space and time in which you live, the void yearning to be filled with your dreams? It can be different. Look up at the stars, find your light, and pull it into your void. To the girl who wonders if there's love out there...

She took a deep breath and tried to collect her thoughts. This was a tough one. How did she really feel about love? As she considered this, her phone pinged with an email from mel4221. She opened it.

Hi Ms. Flynn,
    I was wondering what you thought about my last statement that I was going to show the person I love how much I love her. Do you think that's a good idea?
    Mel

Goodness. What should she say to this? Maybe she should just be honest with him.

Hi there,

I was just pondering the idea of love for an article I'm writing. I was wondering if, for those of us who love people we can't be with, are there others out there for us who can make us happy? Is the idea of "the one" something we've made up? Perhaps there are many people we could be with?

Ms. Flynn

She got an immediate response.

I believe in "the one." And the reason is because I think we're wired that way. I'm a pretty regular guy. I'm rational at work, in my friendships, with people I meet. But she makes me irrational. She makes me want to give her whatever she needs to understand how much I care about her. How can we feel so strongly for one person if we were built to simply let our love go and find someone else?

Sydney could definitely relate. What she didn't write to mel4221 was that when she'd typed the words "to the girl who wonders if there's love out there," all she could think about was Nate and the disappointment he'd caused her. She yearned for things to be different because it would be so easy to love him. She already did. But he'd betrayed her in the worst way, and there was no coming back from that.

I don't know…

She hit send, the whole conversation making her feel lost and confused. The truth was that Sydney *had* found someone else. She'd gotten married and started a life with that person, but she'd never really let her love for Nate go. Her phone lit up.

If you don't know—sorry to ask such a personal question, but I'm curious—does that mean you still feel you could have something with him? I guess I'm hoping that my theory about The One is true...

Sydney didn't want to give this person false hope. She typed back:

How long were you two together?

Mel answered.

Four years...So, is he still special to you?

That was definitely enough time to know if he loved her. She knew that much from being with Nate. However, Sydney wasn't going to get into her issues regarding Nate with a total stranger. The thing was that no matter what he'd done in the present, she'd had four amazing years with Nate, and he'd changed her for the better. She responded.

He'll always be special. I really hope you figure out what to do about your own situation. I wish you luck.

Her phone lit up with one last email.

Thanks. I'm gonna need it. One day soon, I'll tell her everything.

Chapter Twenty-One

"Thank you for agreeing to do this," Sydney said to Logan as he stood, holding a slew of fishing rods and a tackle box while simultaneously appearing more groomed than she'd seen him since the wedding. His hair was freshly washed and perfectly combed, and his outfit matched the specifics that Juliana had given him over the phone this morning for the photo shoot.

He stared at her as if he were speechless for a while before finally saying, "Wow. You look..."

He lost his words again, making her feel self-conscious in all the make-up. Juliana had been meticulous with her makeover, taking all morning to get it just right. Sydney nervously pushed a perfectly curled tendril out of her face.

"Gavin's out back," she said.

"Oh, you two look gorgeous in those outfits," Juliana said, as she strode up to them from the hallway. She'd chosen the white sundress that Sydney had worn to the Easter church service last spring and dressed it down with a pair of wedge sandals and dangly shell earrings from Sydney's jewelry box. Juliana had explained to him on the phone that the color for the shoot was going to come mostly from the gulf, and everything else should be muted and color-coordinated in the same shade as the sand. Gavin had agreed with this completely because the soft colors of their clothing against the shoreline would give her a lot of options for text overlay on the photo once it was formatted for the cover.

Juliana had struck up a conversation with Gavin almost immediately, both of them talking a mile a minute about camera angles. He invited her to have a look at his gallery downtown, and she laughed, telling him she'd already been in. Gavin's art and photography gallery had gotten so popular with the tourists that he'd hired two people to work for him, which allowed him more time to do things like this. But it also meant that he missed moments in the shop like Juliana Vargas browsing around, looking at his work.

"Let us go outside," Juliana said, starting back down the hallway while beckoning them to come along. "We'll want to get our shots. A storm is brewing off shore."

Juliana had been soft-spoken around Sydney most of the time she'd known her, but when she was working, she was an entirely different person. She was in her element. Her hair was pulled back from her face in a ponytail secured by a silk scarf, and she had a camera around her neck. She'd told Sydney this morning that she planned to take some shots herself to get a feel for how the outside lighting affected the make-up, and her hair would blow across the lens were it not for the ponytail.

When they got outside, Logan leaned his fishing rods against a tree near the pier and they all walked over to the area of the shore where Gavin had set up a small set.

Gavin threw up his hand in greeting. "Hey there," he

said when they'd approached. He shook hands with Logan, introducing himself. "I'll be shooting the cover of Sydney's fantastic new magazine today," he said with a smile, always encouraging.

Sydney shook her head, her modesty coming through. Or perhaps it was the rampant imposter syndrome she felt taking on this project. "It's only a small magazine," she said, "for the wellness center patrons."

Gavin's smile widened. "We have to start somewhere. One day, we'll all look back on this moment and say, 'Remember when…'"

"I don't know," she said teasingly, but really simply expressing her insecurity.

Juliana cut in. "From what Nate tells me, you are an incredibly talented writer. He still reads over old writings of yours that he has."

That was the old Nate, Sydney thought. But Juliana's comment did strike something within her: she didn't believe in herself anymore. Gavin was right: we all have to start somewhere.

"Will you have them walk this way?" Juliana asked, getting right to work, swinging her arm along an imaginary path and bringing Sydney's attention back to the photo shoot. "It might be good light from the sun if it hits them at the side—it would create depth, I think."

"It would be easy to shoot too," Gavin agreed. "We'll just have to watch how the shadows fall on their faces."

"We can tilt your speedlight out of the shot but toward their faces," she suggested.

"Brilliant." Gavin tilted the large screen toward them to shield some of the direct sun.

Juliana put her camera to her eye and peered through the lens, taking a shot. She pulled back to view the screen.

"Oh!" she called out. "It's exquisite. The lighting is perfect."
She guided Sydney, leading her over to the spot she wanted.
"If you can stand here, face the wind so your gorgeous hair
flows behind you, that would be perfect. Logan, come over
beside her and take her hand."

Logan stepped up beside Sydney and lightly touched her
fingertips before clasping her hand. She looked up at him,
and before she could process anything at all, the camera
went off, causing spots in her eyes.

Gavin peered down at his camera. "That's a great shot,"
he said. "Sorry." He beamed over at Sydney. "You two just
looked so perfect in that moment that I stole a photo. Just
perfect."

Juliana laughed. "Those are the best shots," she said.

"The cloud cover from the storm coming in is also allowing fantastic lighting," Gavin said.

This creative process was sort of like Sydney's writing. It
was all about forming ideas and emotion around parameters.
Her parameters were written language, but both Juliana's
and Gavin's were light, wind, and movement. She could see
how certain expressions and lighting would affect the over-
all feel of the picture just like her choice of words did.

"When you walk, Logan," Juliana said, "turn your other
hand to the side and relax your fingers like this." She demon-
strated the position she wanted. "It feels unnatural but actually looks more normal on film than your regular pose…"

The entire time they worked, Gavin moved around them
snapping photos. The freedom to think outside the normal
day-to-day that Sydney felt as the shoot progressed gave
her a buzzing need to start writing. She couldn't wait to get
back into the house. Tonight, once everyone had turned in,
she was going to write the remaining piece and send it to *NY
Pulse*.

* * *

Robby sat on the dock quietly between Sydney and Logan, his feet swinging above the water, his eyes on the spot where the fishing line met the water's surface. He wasn't as open with Logan, but he'd agreed to come out and fish with them, which was encouraging.

"I've got some homemade raspberry lemonade in a cooler in the truck," Logan said, reeling in and setting his rod on the dock. Ben's dog Beau, who had been lounging beside them, stirred and his ears perked up. "My mom made sure she didn't leave me empty-handed before she headed back home to North Carolina. She packed a whole bunch of snacks." He leaned in to Robby's view. "Including her famous chocolate chip cookies. I asked her to be sure to leave some behind so I could bring them for you."

Robby's gaze slid over to Logan.

"Want me to go get them?" he asked.

Robby nodded.

Logan was so kind, and thoughtful. His mother seemed lovely, and it was clear that she'd raised a wonderful man in Logan. But something held Sydney back. Her feelings were totally cut off. Her head told her that he was a great catch, and he seemed interested in her, but any time she tried to stir up affection for him, it just felt forced. She couldn't deny the comparison to Nate. Even with everything against them, it was easy for her to love Nate. More importantly, she reminded herself, perhaps it was because she knew deep down that she needed to focus on herself.

Beau wandered over to Sydney and dropped down at her feet. "One more day," she told him. He looked up at her as if he knew that she was talking about Ben's return. His head popped up and turned to the side, then he got to his feet.

Robby handed his fishing rod to Sydney, scrambling up the dock toward Logan. But her heart slammed around in her chest when he ran past Logan to Nate, who'd just come over the hill. Logan turned around and they greeted each other, walking together toward Sydney. She reeled in Robby's line and got up to face them. Nate had a new football in his hand.

"Robby, go long!" he said, and he tossed it into the air. "I brought that back for you. All the way from Malibu." Robby ran up to him and he tousled Robby's hair before throwing it again as her son sprinted across the yard to catch it.

"Hey," Nate said when he reached Sydney, but his gaze devoured her. She realized then that she still had her hair and make-up done from the photo shoot today. He seemed to be assessing the situation, his gaze darting from her hair to Logan and the blanket they'd spread out on the grass, the cooler in Logan's hand...

"Hi," she said, not wanting to make a scene. The last thing she wanted to do was to make Logan feel uncomfortable.

"You're... going somewhere?" Nate asked, clearly trying to make sense of her appearance.

"Juliana got a hold of me," she said, allowing a smirk. "I had the photo shoot with Logan today and he's staying for a dinner date tonight."

Nate's jaw clenched just slightly, as he regarded Logan. Sydney suddenly felt a rush of empowerment. She was making him uncomfortable. Having Logan there was evidently spoiling his plan of sweet-talking her into thinking she was doing something wonderful by selling Starlight Cottage and moving in on his land. Perhaps she wouldn't set things straight at all about Logan, and Nate would give up and go back to LA where he came from.

"You're back so soon?" she asked.

He clamped his eyes on her and the pain in them almost made her falter, taking her back to long summer drives next to him with the windows down and the ache in her heart that she felt when she was headed back to school, away from him...She stood her ground, lifting her chin.

"I wrote four songs for them," he said. "But then I told them I had to get back. I had important business to attend to."

Like convincing my family to give up Starlight? she wanted to say, but it wasn't the time.

Logan set the cooler down on the blanket and beckoned Robby over. "Here are the cookies I promised," he said with added excitement for Robby's benefit.

Robby set the ball down in the grass and took the cookie from him, kneeling down beside him, nibbling.

"Good, right?"

"Mm hmm," Robby said.

Nate stepped into Sydney's view. "Can we talk?" he asked, that hurt she'd seen on his face now clear in his words. He gave Logan a discreet look of appraisal.

"I can't," she replied, forcing herself to be strong. "I have company."

He nodded, his gaze fluttering over to Logan, his jaw clenching again as a cloud pushed its way in front of the sun. "I'm sorry to interrupt. Maybe you can come over later?"

"Logan and I are going out for drinks."

"Tomorrow, then."

"Hallie and Ben come home tomorrow, so I'm sure I'll want to see them and hear all about their honeymoon."

He took in a deep breath and let it out slowly. Sydney knew she couldn't put off talking to him forever, and she did want to give him a piece of her mind, as well as find out why in the world he would do this to Starlight Cottage. But she also needed time to figure out how to approach the situation.

The last thing she wanted to do was to break down and cry the way she felt like doing every time she thought about it.

"Syd..." he said in a quiet plea, playing on her emotions, but this time, she wouldn't allow him to get the better of her. "I need to tell you something," he said into her ear.

"It's clear that you do," she replied. "But whatever it is, I don't want to hear it." She took a step back. "We're being rude to Logan. He's here to spend time with me and Robby, and I'm being a terrible hostess." She didn't give him time to reply, turning away from him and sitting down on the blanket. But she did allow herself one quick glance over her shoulder to see him slowly walking away.

Chapter Twenty-Two

"Glad to see you," Wes said over his shoulder as he led Sydney and Logan through the throngs of tourists.

The beach-goers surrounding them were the same every summer: they had settled in for a good seafood meal before their sleepy-eyed jaunts along the main street, dipping in and out of candy and souvenir shops before finally turning in for the night, sunburned and exhausted. All of them were seemingly oblivious to the clouds that were rolling in. The wind picked up, signaling the calm before a quick summer storm. The harsh weather warnings promised for this evening that they'd been reporting on the news hadn't materialized yet but Sydney had lived along the coast long enough to know that the strip of gray on the horizon moving quickly toward them would not remain silent before it blew over. "How's Uncle Hank?" Wes asked.

"He's doing well, apart from the public beach access that is going in down the road from us."

"I'd heard," Wes said, offering a chair to Logan. Their table sat at the edge of the outside deck of Wes and Maggie's restaurant, close enough to feel the coastal breeze as it gently danced across the gulf between gusts that blew in sporadically. The red flags had been raised on the beach, alerting swimmers to potentially rough waters. "Rumor has it that someone's bought all the lots around the public beach access and the plan is to build commercial retail shops. It's supposed to bring in high-end merchants."

"The purchase didn't go through the board? I assumed the county acquired them."

Wes frowned. "I'm not sure." He leaned in to keep the conversation between just them. "It's all being kept hush-hush because people are going to be upset when they find out that our little village is going to be overrun by tourists. I like the business—don't get me wrong—but we can hardly keep up *now*."

Sydney knew only one person whose description included the words "high-end" and "hush-hush." And pounding at her temples was the realization that the one in question was also now on the board of supervisors...

"I definitely need your Passion Punch," Sydney told Wes as she took a seat across from Logan. She clarified for him: "It's got rum, strawberry daiquiri mix, and a splash of pine-apple and coconut. It's divine."

"Great memory!" Wes said, waiting expectantly for Logan's order.

"Make it two," Logan told him. When Wes left to fill their drink requests, Logan leaned forward, putting his fore-arms on the table between them. "Judging by your drink order and the way you closed right up after seeing Nathan Carr today, I'd venture to say something is bothering you. Want to tell me what it is?"

"Not really," she said, shaking her head.

Wes brought them their drinks: large hurricane glasses with painted umbrellas sporting starfish and brightly col-ored flip-flops stabbed through maraschino cherries.

She leaned back in her chair and smiled kindly, honing in on the shushing of the waves as they lapped up on the beach behind them to give her calm. Even at their harshest, gulf waves were like little angry children stomping their feet in a storm. But the gray clouds on the horizon that were creeping closer were another matter.

"I certainly don't want to pull you in to Nathan Carr's drama," Sydney said. "He doesn't deserve our time. You and I had an amazing photo shoot, and we need to celebrate that." When he didn't seem convinced, she let her smile fall. "I'm sorry if I wasn't myself after Nate showed up at the house. He's really upset me," she told Logan honestly. "But I don't want it to impact tonight."

"Might be too late," Logan replied, looking over her head.

Sydney turned around to find Juliana and Nate walking up to them. The trouble with this town was that Nate would have a pretty good idea of where Sydney would be. Didn't he have the decency to let her enjoy her night?

"I'm so sorry to interrupt," Nate said.

"Well, you definitely have," she snapped quietly so as not to sound totally awful to poor Logan.

She eyed Juliana for help, but Juliana shrugged as if to say she'd already tried. Sydney took a large gulp of her drink, the alcohol zinging down her throat. She needed to calm herself down before she said something to Nate that no one else would need to hear. She'd known when he'd gotten here that he was a self-centered, selfish man. She should've listened to her gut.

"I need just one minute of your time and then Juliana and I will go have dinner," he said, nodding a second apology to Logan. A gust of wind whipped through the deck, rustling the light items on tables, and a few paper napkins went somersaulting through the air as a man dropped his fork to catch them. Vacationers were starting to catch on, an unsettling buzz pushing through the crowd as another gust of coastal wind blew in.

Sydney gritted her teeth and wriggled up from her chair against her will. "I'm so sorry," she said to Logan. "I'll be right back."

"Logan and I can talk about the shoot today," Juliana said as she sat in Sydney's seat, clearly trying to lighten the mood.

Sydney mouthed a thank-you, her cheeks burning with irritation, and then followed Nate down the restaurant stairs at the back of the deck leading to the boardwalk that stretched over the dunes and down to the gulf. Nate walked all the way to the water's furiously foaming edge, and Sydney kicked off her flip-flops, joining him.

"What is so important that it couldn't wait for me to have a drink?" she asked, raising her voice above the wind picking up.

He turned to her, his face full of emotion, the wind rippling his white cotton shirt as he folded his arms. "Why didn't you tell me you still had the ring?"

"What?" She was getting more irritated by the second. "I was having drinks with someone, Nate! You can't just interrupt my night over some stupid toy ring that I happen to still have!" She turned away, ready to stomp back up the beach when he caught her arm, spinning her around.

"I couldn't let you go a third time," he said, a crease forming between his eyes with his emotion.

She stared at him. "Third time? What are you talking about?"

"Robby said you were on a date, and I nearly fell apart. I haven't had enough time to make things right, and I can't lose you again."

"Robby?" she asked, taken completely off guard, totally forgetting his comment about letting her go three times. "I thought he was asleep."

"He had a bad dream and your mom told him you were out with someone and you'd be back soon. He tried to text you, but he didn't get you, so he texted me. He was worried you were on a date. To calm him down, I promised to play football with him tomorrow."

Stunned, Sydney pulled her phone out of her pocket and realized her ringer was off. She had three missed texts. Guilt ran rampant inside her, knotting her stomach. She quickly texted Robby back, even though she knew that he was probably asleep by now, and put her phone back into her pocket. Another explosion of wind blew off the gulf, whipping her hair into her face. She pushed her hair back.

"You are *not* playing football with Robby tomorrow," she said. "I'll put his mind at ease about my night out." The dark clouds had completely filled the sky above them, plunging them into an early dimness that usually didn't fall upon the coast for several more hours, but she barely noticed.

"I know Hallie and Ben are coming back. I wouldn't get in your way. It might be nice to have someone play with Robby so you and your sister can catch up."

"Okay," she said, closing her eyes in a feeble attempt to alleviate her growing frustration. "I'm having drinks right now. Or I'm supposed to be. Yet I'm out on the beach with you instead. You said you needed *one* minute. You've already used your time." She turned around to walk back toward Logan, mortified that she'd left him as long as she had.

"Okay!" Nate said, running ahead and getting in front of her. "One minute."

"No!" Sydney replied, now completely exasperated. She'd told herself she wouldn't allow him to distract her and here she was, right back with him. "You had your minute. And all the minutes between the day you pulled out of town and now. I've given you more minutes than any human being should ever give someone who leaves someone they love like that," she said, her voice cracking under her emotion. "And I'm done, Nate." If she wanted him totally out of her life, now was her chance. Using her momentum, she'd drive the nail in the coffin. "You know why I still have that ring? Because it reminds me every day of a life I don't ever want."

There. She'd finally said it out loud: she would never love Nathan Carr. He had to know that because the truth of the matter was that he couldn't go back to being Nate Henderson again—no matter how hard she wished it would happen.

Nate's arms fell limp at his sides, her words wiping his face clean of all emotion except for the glassiness in his eyes and the shock that had turned his skin pale. He suddenly looked broken, like the life had been sucked out of him. Seeing him like that made her want to wrap her arms around him and tell him how much she still cared for him but she reminded herself that it wasn't Nathan Carr she was still in love with.

A crack of thunder sounded above them. She'd been so involved in their conversation that she hadn't noticed how quickly the storm was coming in. Lightning flashed, reaching a jagged finger to the sea.

He slowly sat down in the sand. "Go ahead," he nearly whispered, either oblivious or indifferent to the incoming weather. "I need a minute." He wiped a tear that spilled from his eye, ripping her heart out. Why did things have to be so complicated? She wished they could go back to the day before he left; she wished he'd have chosen to do a lot of things differently. But he hadn't. And they both had to live with that.

"Nate, what did you expect? Your choices in life are completely opposed to mine. At every turn, I disagree with them. You make me frustrated and upset all the time. You *have* to let me move on."

He looked up at her. "Is it the way I left all those years ago? Because I was just a kid, and there were reasons... But I've even messed *that* up."

He wasn't making any sense.

"I wish I could go back to that day..." He shook his head once and closed his eyes, as if to hurl the thought from his mind. "Everything I do pushes you away. I just wish I could show you how much you mean to me. I wish you could know how *I* see you."

What did he mean that he wished he could go back to that day? His motives had been pretty clear. Sydney recounted everything that had been burned in her memory that day: how he wouldn't even look at her, the way he brushed her off, telling her there was more to life than Firefly Beach, how he never once looked back. She wanted to believe that he was sincere, but the fact that he was on the board kept coming back into her mind, challenging her feelings and screaming at her to use her head. She opened her mouth to confront him about it, but Logan was waiting and with the roll of thunder and the biting wind from the storm that was coming, it was time to call it a night. She needed to get back, and nothing they said right now could alter reality.

"I need to get back," she said, her tone softer now. Despite her anger it hurt her to see him in pain.

She didn't only need to get back to Logan, she needed to get out of the past and back to her life. And she had to make the decision to separate her feelings from the boy she once loved and the man right in front of her now.

Chapter Twenty-Three

"What in the world are you doing?" Sydney called out her bedroom window. In the light of early morning, Uncle Hank was on the beach, banging away on some sort of wood contraption. Her head still pounding from the emotion of last night, she squeezed her eyes shut with another *bang*.

With the rush of the tide, and a boat going by, he didn't hear her, so she shut her window, slipped on her flip-flops, and went out in her pajamas to see what exactly it was that he was doing. He'd woken her up from a sound sleep and she didn't want him to wake up Robby and the rest of the house.

"What are you making?" she asked, hopping over a piece of driftwood to get to Uncle Hank.

The occasional blowing clouds made the lighthouse behind him look as though it were swaying. The storm had gone as quickly as it had arrived last night, leaving a crisp blue sky behind scattered hazy clouds that drifted past now and again.

"I'm making a birdhouse," he said with another slam of his hammer. He'd constructed an enormous box of wood and he was nailing the last piece onto the front. It had holes drilled in it to fit against the grid of wood that he'd built inside. "Clara had always wanted one and I'd never gotten around to building it for her." He picked up another nail and lined it up, with focused determination.

"How come you aren't building this in the woodshed?" she asked.

He looked up, out of breath slightly from bending over, small beads of sweat on his forehead. "Your Aunt Clara used to draw out her designs while sitting on this beach, so I wanted to build it out here where she could give me inspiration. I did the cuts in the woodshed but then I carried it all out to the sand—this was her place."

She couldn't help herself. "And why are you deciding to build it now?"

"I didn't sleep last night," he said, his voice heavy. "At all. The bed felt emptier than it has in a long time. I'm failing her by giving up Starlight Cottage." He lifted the large box and set it upright. "This is old wood from when we had the gazebo built all those years ago. It had been the one place in the house she and I designed together, and, through the years, it was there that we went whenever we wanted to talk. I wanted to put it up out there, so the birds would fill it." Uncle Hank stood back and took a look at the birdhouse, brushing a bit of sand off the top. "She loved the sound of birds in the morning. Putting this up would bring life to the gazebo again. When I sit out there, it's so quiet now. Her humming is gone. Her little chatter about whatever was on her mind is absent."

Sydney could hear Aunt Clara now. She'd told her once, "The birds singing are a constant reminder of life outside our walls, of a whole world out there, and the peace it can have if we all slow down enough to recognize our strengths. You'll never find an anxious bird, worried about where its next worm will come from. They just get up every morning singing and then do what they do best. And they're always fed. That's really all any of us should do."

"If I fill the silence with birds, then I won't feel so alone. I'm hoping to feel like she's with me."

Sydney looked out at the end of the pier where the gazebo sat as if it were suspended above the water. It was the place she'd first found a broken Uncle Hank a year ago, when they'd all arrived to finish carrying out Aunt Clara's wishes. Now it made sense as to why he'd been out there that day.

"So you've made the decision to sell?" she asked, fear swimming around as she waited for the answer.

"It's not a decision," he said, frowning. "My hand has been forced. If I stay, I'll be staring at a parking lot. All the property between us and the main road has now been bought up—the rezoning signs are posted. I saw them this morning on my walk. It's happening whether we like it or not." He peered down at one of the boards and inspected where it met another. "I want to hang it up in the gazebo and then take it with me when I move so that wherever I go, I'll have something left of Starlight Cottage."

"Where will we go?" she asked, feeling the emotion rising in her throat.

"I'm going to ask Nate about his land," he said.

She still hadn't told Uncle Hank about Nate's involvement in all this. "I need to talk to you about something," she said, taking a deep breath, steeling herself.

Uncle Hank's hands stilled and he turned to her.

"You might not want to live on Nate's land, once you hear this. Why don't we go over and sit down on the pier... Nate's on the board of supervisors," she said once they'd reached it. "He's also the one who bought all the lots surrounding the public beach access. I'm wondering if it was because he had more money than the county to offer the sellers. He wanted to make it a sure thing."

Disbelief slid across Uncle Hank's face as he sat on the edge of the pier, needing to steady himself. He looked wounded by the news rather than angry, his gaze submitting to the hurt and dropping to his folded hands in his lap.

"My guess is that Nate's moved back to Firefly Beach to invest in all those shops that are going up around the public beach access."

"He's not a developer," Uncle Hank said, clearly trying to make sense of this.

"No, but he grew up here. Who was his childhood best friend? Do you remember?"

"Colin Ferguson." Uncle Hank's eyes grew round. "The contractor who built the new waterfront hotel down the road."

"Yep." The whole thing gave her a bad taste in her mouth. She'd have never thought that he'd stoop this low. "I'm thinking he's offering us a spot on his land to relocate us so he can get us out of the way to build with Colin. I don't know for sure, of course, and I plan to give him a piece of my mind and find out what's going on, from his mouth, but I can't see any other reason for him to do this."

Uncle Hank put an unsteady hand against his face, and rubbed the white stubble on his cheek in thought. "I just can't believe this."

"I can't either."

The pain she'd seen on Nate's face last night had been etched into her mind. It was so confusing. What was also baffling was the intense ache that she felt at the finality of that moment on the beach. As angry as she was with him, there was a tiny irrational part of her that adored seeing him.

She missed him so much it hurt. Sydney pondered the

undeniable pull she had toward him despite her attempts to drag herself away. What was becoming abundantly clear was that the reason she hadn't really been able to make the kind of life she really wanted for herself was because she'd always imagined Nate in it. Nothing had ever felt as right as the two of them together. It was her coping mechanism to hide her absolute sorrow that she wouldn't ever get the future she'd always hoped for.

She wanted to believe that he was the same wonderful man he'd been when they were together, and that there was some other reason for his actions, but her head told her there couldn't be another motive. There was no Nate Henderson. Why else would he be doing all this?

Sydney's mind was still swimming about Nate and the way he had deceived them all. There was a part of her that felt like she needed to get some closure on all this, but she didn't know how. She sat on the bed in her bedroom, staring at the view of the palms through her window, thinking. Her gaze slid down the panel curtain to her handbag on the floor, the napkin with Logan's number peeking out from it. Already having his number in her phone, she got up and plucked the napkin from her bag, dropping it into the trash. When she did, something occurred to her: she was still heartbroken about Nate, searching for closure she'd never gotten. Not even now.

One thing was certain: she couldn't move forward until she got over Nate, and she needed to be honest with Logan about that. She grabbed her cell and called him.

"Hey," he said, recognizing her call.

"Hi," she returned.

"I'm glad you called. I was wondering if you wanted to

grab some dinner. But I'll cook. I think we should find something preferably inside and in a location where we won't be interrupted."

She could feel his smile on the other end of the line, making this more difficult but definitely necessary.

"About that interruption last time," she began.

His voice became serious. "You don't have to say anything," he said. "I wondered... Things aren't finished with you and Nate, are they?"

"Oh, they're finished," she said. "But it's complicated. I just don't want to drag you into the middle of everything. You deserve better than that. I just need some time to figure out what I want and where I'm going, you know?"

"I totally get it," he said, as kind as ever. "But if you ever want to get that dinner, it's a standing offer."

"Thank you for being amazing," she said.

When Sydney got off the phone call, she needed to take her mind off everything, deciding to help Uncle Hank install the birdhouse at the end of the gazebo. It was so big that they'd almost needed help, but eventually they'd managed it. Her biceps and shoulders ached from holding it up so long, but she also wondered if the pinched nerve she felt now was exacerbated by the stress of thinking about Nate. Even though she'd tried to push it out of her mind, his involvement in the public beach access had gone round and round in her head the entire time she'd been helping Uncle Hank.

Her inner thoughts were interrupted by the sound of a truck pulling into the driveway and Beau racing across the yard. Hallie got out of the truck and yanked her large suitcase from the vehicle, the thing landing with a thud onto the driveway. Ben got out the driver's side and ran around to greet an ecstatic Beau, who was alternating between whimpering and jumping up to Ben's face.

Hallie put a hand up to assist her pink visor in shielding the sun and caught sight of Sydney and Uncle Hank. She came jogging down to them, her slim frame tanned under her brightly colored T-shirt and shorts. She threw her arms around both of them, squeezing Sydney and Uncle Hank into a bear hug.

"I'm so happy to see you!" Sydney told her, giving her an enormous embrace.

"I missed you so much," Hallie said, her cheeks rosy from too much sun. She let them go, completely ignoring the fact that Sydney was still in her pajamas. "We had so much fun, Syd! We went snorkeling and we took a speedboat ride to this amazing restaurant right on the water..." She threw her hand to her chest dramatically. "The pool had personal cabanas with their own wait staff, and everything was included!"

"I knew I should've hidden out in your suitcase," Sydney teased.

"I've brought a little bit of it home with me," she said, waving her hands in the air in excitement. "I brought goodies! Who cares that I've been up since 4:30 for my flight home; I'm still in an island frame of mind! I've got piña colada mix in my bag and lots of presents for everyone. Let's go inside. Where's Mama?"

"That sounds amazing! And I need to check on Robby anyway. He should be up by now, and if he isn't, I'm going to wake him up so he can see you," she said as they walked, on either side of Uncle Hank, linking arms with him. "Hey, Ben!"

Ben raised his hand, a big smile on his face. He picked up their bags and took them inside.

Robby, who was having breakfast at the kitchen table when they came in, jumped up at the sight of Hallie and Ben and ran over to them.

"Hey, buddy!" Ben said, ruffling his hair and giving him a big hug. "Whatcha been doing while I was gone?"

Robby looked up at him, an enormous grin on his face. "Football and fishing and drawing and school work! Lots of stuff!"

"Sounds like you've had a busy week. Did Uncle Hank do all those things with you?" Ben took a seat at the table while Hallie ran over to give Mama a hug.

"No, I was with Nate! Isn't he your friend?"

Curiosity consumed Ben's face, and then he looked oddly excited. "Nate Henderson?" he asked, looking over at Sydney with suggestive delight.

"You mean Nathan Carr," Sydney corrected. "And yes."

"Sooo…" Ben said, clearly dying to know the details.

Sydney discreetly shook her head to let him know that there was no news with the Sydney-Nate situation, which seemed to confuse him. Strangely, he looked down at her hand and then made eye contact again. What was that all about?

"Have you talked to Nate at all, Syd?" he asked her.

"Plenty," she answered.

"Aaaand did he tell you…?" He eyed her as if she could read his mind.

"How he feels? Yes." She didn't want to get in to this in front of everyone.

"And what did you think about that?"

At this point, Ben and Sydney had Uncle Hank, Lewis, Hallie, *and* Jacqueline's attention.

"I'll tell you later," she replied. "Hallie said she has piña coladas."

They'd all left the kitchen table littered with empty piña colada glasses and scattered gift bags, their gifts of seashell necklaces, straw hats, and key chains sitting by their places, while they sat outside on the porch watching Beau run into the surf, shaking himself off and diving in again, clearly delighted his human was home. Ben and Robby were in the yard, and Jacqueline, Hallie, and Sydney had been catching up on everything.

"Where's Uncle Hank?" Hallie asked.

He'd gone in for a second and Sydney just now realized he'd been gone for a while. "Maybe he fell asleep after Lewis went home," she said. "I'll go in and check on him."

Sydney went inside. "Uncle Hank?" she called into the empty downstairs. "Uncle Hank?" she walked into the front sitting room and peered through the window to the porch—nobody was there. Where was he? "Hello-o!" she said, to no answer. She looked out at the road to see if he'd perhaps gone out to get the mail and had gotten stuck chatting with Lewis or something, but it was empty. She climbed the stairs to check up there.

When she got to the top, she heard a whimper in Uncle Hank's bedroom. She rushed down the hallway and knocked on his door, pushing it open. "What's the matter?" she asked, coming over to him and taking his hand. He sat on the bed, hunched over, his head hanging low while his back heaved with sobs.

"With Hallie and Ben home, it just hit me."

"What hit you?"

"I've already lost Clara. I can't lose Starlight Cottage too. It belongs in our family. Where will we all gather together once it's gone?" He took in a jagged breath. "And I'm worried they're going to level it if we let it go." His lip trembled. "I've tried to act like it's no big deal, but I'm losing the last bit of myself. I'm too old to start a new life somewhere. I should be slowing down and basking in all the memories of this gorgeous place."

The sound of Robby's voice outside the window cut through their conversation. A car had pulled into the drive. Sydney tipped her head up to see Nate—he'd come over in some sort of ridiculously expensive luxury car. This was all *his* fault. And he didn't seem to be bothered at all by the fact that he was disrupting the lives of everyone who used to support him in this house.

"I'll be right back," she said with determination. This was it. She was going to tell him once and for all, get everything out into the open right now. Sydney marched downstairs and out the front door, breezing right past Ben and Hallie. She poked her finger into Nate's chest. "We need to talk," she snapped.

"Hey, Robby," Ben said, clearly gauging the situation. "Let's go play football."

"Okay!" Robby ran over to Ben and the two of them went over to the yard. Hallie followed them, but she didn't leave without first giving a look of question to her sister. Sydney brushed it off kindly and then turned her dagger-of-a-stare back to Nate.

Opening the door to his shiny black Mercedes SUV, Nate gestured for her to get in. Without a word, she slid into the seat, her lips set in a pout. He got into the driver's side and shut the door.

"I know just where we can talk," he said. With a rev of the engine, he pulled out of the drive.

Chapter Twenty-Four

Sydney sat silently while Nate drove. They must have driven for at least twenty minutes, but she didn't notice. She was too busy seething. She'd absolutely had it. As soon as they got wherever he was going, she was ready to lay into him. He couldn't do this to her family.

Nate pulled onto a long, winding gravel road, propelling them deep into the woods. He put the windows down, allowing the earthy scent and the warm wind to fill up the car. Sydney's hair blew into her face and she tucked a tendril behind her ear. When they'd made it far enough down the path that the main road was no longer visible, he stopped the car right in the middle of the road and got out. She followed him to a small patch of grass that had formed in a natural clearing. A few beams of sunlight slid through the opening in the canopy of trees, illuminating the area. Nate sat down on the ground and patted the space beside him.

She wanted to ask where they were, but it didn't matter. This was about Starlight Cottage and Nate's selfish act to take it away. She sat down across from him instead.

"Why are you *really* back in Firefly Beach, Nate?" she clipped.

He stared at her.

It was obvious that she'd put him on the spot. "Cat got your tongue?"

"I've tried to tell you," he said.

"No, Nate. You haven't."

The skin between his eyes wrinkled in a way that she'd always found adorable whenever he didn't understand something, but she forced herself to push whatever fondness she had for him aside.

"Why don't you start by telling me about the lots?"

"The lots?" He looked deeply into her eyes as if he were trying to figure out how much she knew. Well, she knew it all.

"Yeah. The lots. How's Colin Ferguson these days?"

His initial confusion slid off his face, replaced by a cautious interest. "He's good," Nate said guardedly.

"Anything you want to tell me? Maybe, say, how you and Colin are about to rob me and my family of our home for your financial gain?"

The confusion was back again.

"How could you, Nate?" She stood up to hide her emotion. He came up behind her and put his hands on her shoulders. Usually, she'd flinch, but she didn't have the energy anymore. A tear fell down her cheek.

He turned her around and offered her a tender smile. "Come with me," he said gently into her ear. The fact that he wasn't even the least bit defensive had her questioning his reaction, so she walked back to his vehicle. He opened the door and she got in.

Another few minutes down the gravel road led them to another clearing, but this one was outlined by turquoise coast, and sitting right in the middle of it was a brand new white farmhouse with a porch that wrapped all the way around the structure, rocking chairs on painted gray decking, enormous windows showing off the stylish beach décor inside, and an incredible view of the glistening gulf, its water lapping lazily onto the bright sand, a white sailboat bobbing out on the horizon. It was literally the house she'd always dreamed of.

Nate shut off the engine and went around to her side to open her door. She stepped out and tipped her head up to view the massive house. "Is this yours?" she asked, her curiosity getting the better of her.

"For now," he said.

She regarded him with questions in her eyes. It would be just like him to build something beautiful like this only to go back to LA, but his demeanor was telling her something else that she couldn't decipher.

"Let's go in." He held out his hand, but she didn't take it, so he gestured for her to lead the way to the massive glass-paned double door, reaching around her to open it once they had climbed the porch stairs.

The décor of whitewashed wood and textured fabrics was just as she would've chosen for herself, but then again, Nate had always had wonderful taste. They used to talk about what their life together would look like once the two of them had made it big.

"I want to give you a big, white farmhouse," he'd said back then, rolling onto his belly, grabbing her wrists and pinning them gently to the grass she was lying on. He kissed her. "With a big porch going all the way around it for all of our kids," he told her, playfully. He broke her hold, wrapping his arms around her waist and nuzzled her neck, making her flinch and giggle.

"Not until I have a big, fat diamond on my hand. You'd better make an honest woman of me first," she'd said, giggling as he tickled her. "And we'll be famous, so I want more than that."

He looked into her eyes, that familiar smirk on his lips. "Whatever you want," he said softly. "Tell me."

"It has to sit right on the beach, with rocking chairs so we can grow old together there."

"I can't wait to grow old with you." He rolled her over so that she hovered above him. He ran his finger softly down her face and kissed her again.

"And we should have a giant barn for parties. I want to get married on the beach and have our reception in the barn."

"I'll do anything you want," he said lovingly.

Both of them were silent, speaking volumes with their eyes.

They'd never questioned it; it had always been a "when" rather than an "if." From the look of this house, he hadn't changed his mind about what he wanted.

"Would you like something to drink?" he asked, tearing her away from the past, and the memories that hurt her to relive. Nate crossed the driftwood-colored hardwoods to the expansive kitchen that overlooked a rustic living area.

It was all so beautiful that she'd forgotten for a second why she was there. "No, thank you," she replied, but he went to the fridge anyway and poured two glasses of iced tea.

"Please," he said, offering her one and pulling out a chair at the oversized bar that separated the space between the kitchen and living room.

Sydney sat down, wanting to move things along.

Nate lowered himself on a barstool beside her and wrapped his hand around his iced tea. "Would you like to tell me why you think I want to take Starlight Cottage from you?"

She turned toward him. "I know you're on the board, Nate. Stop trying to avoid this."

A small smile twitched around his lips. "Is that why you're so angry with me?"

Was he serious right now? She hopped off her barstool and cut her eyes at him. "Yes, Nate," was all she could get out for fear she'd reach over and shake him by the shoulders. Frustrated beyond belief, she walked over to the large glass doors that overlooked the pearly white sand and the restless waters beyond.

Nate came up behind her, looking over her head at the view. Then suddenly, his voice was at her ear, causing goose bumps down her arm. "I *am* on the board," he said softly. "And I've bought all the lots for the public beach access, which I will be donating to the county."

She felt the prick of tears. Finally, he'd admitted it. But even worse than the realization of the truth, was the fact she knew there was no more Nate Henderson left. He was now entirely Nathan Carr, because Nate Henderson would never have done this to her. She wiped a tear away quickly, but Nate turned her around before she could clear the emotion from her face.

"You asked me why I came back to Firefly Beach," he said, wiping another of her tears. "In order to truly answer that, I have to explain why I'd ever left in the first place." He took her hand and walked her over to the sofa, gently pulling her down beside him. "If you'll give me your time right now, I want to tell you everything. I've been trying but I haven't gotten it right. I need you to give me this. You don't owe it to me, but I'm asking you. Let me tell you everything."

"Okay," she finally said, literally praying that some miracle would fall from the sky and make everything better.

"You are an incredible writer," he said. "You got that writing opportunity to travel the U.S., remember?"

She nodded, hanging on his every word. She wanted to know why he'd left, in his own words.

"But what about the chance you didn't explore? Your

professor gave you two opportunities that year: the one in the U.S., but also one to live in Africa for two years, and you never filled out the paperwork."

What did any of this have to do with why Nate left? "I couldn't leave Firefly Beach," she said with a disbelieving laugh.

"I know that—you told me. But why? What was the reason you didn't want to go?"

She didn't want to admit it now, after everything. He had to know the answer to that already. But she needed him to be honest with her, so she decided she should be too. "It meant that I had to spend two years away from you." She stared at him as she said it, driving home the fact that she hadn't wanted to spend even two years away, let alone a decade. He needed to know how much he'd hurt her.

He leaned in, his fingers brushing hers. "I couldn't allow you to give up your dreams because of me. I never expected to be the successful writer of the two of us. Going to LA was my cover for removing myself from your life so that you could go on and do amazing things without me holding you back."

This revelation hit her like a ton of bricks. All these years, she'd thought he saw her as lesser when really he thought she was more. A tidal wave of emotions flooded Sydney as she sat in front of Nate, completely exposed. "When you left, you never even looked back. Not once," she challenged him, brushing a tear away. "I waited, staring at your rear-view mirror for just one tiny indication that you cared at all that you were tearing my heart out as your truck headed down the drive. You never. Looked. Back."

Nate leaned into her personal space, peering down at her, his hand resting on her arm, his eyes brimming with emotion. "There was a moment where I didn't know if I could make it out of the drive. I had to force my foot to stay on the gas, because I knew that I'd never feel for anyone else the way I felt for you." His touch moved down her arm until his fingers found hers and finally came to rest intertwined in her own the way they used to do without even thinking about it, all those years ago. "If I'd have looked back, I would've faltered." He bowed his head as if the memory of it had stolen his breath and he needed a minute to recover. "I thought I was doing the right thing, giving you the space you needed to be great."

"I didn't need space to be great, Nate. I needed *you*."

"I thought I was in your way." He shook his head. "You're the best writer I've ever known. Why didn't you continue, Syd?"

"I couldn't do it without you," she said, the ache burning her chest like it had the day he'd left.

"That's not true. You don't need me to be great."

"But I have to be happy to write, and you made me the happiest."

"I was just a boy from Firefly Beach. I never really expected to be anything more than that. And I knew how much you wanted to stay with me. It terrified me because your talent overwhelmed me. I didn't want you to wake up one day, stuck in this little town, wishing your life could've been different. I knew the only way to make you move forward was to cut ties. In my young brain, I'd thought it had been the right thing to do. But the more I tried living without you, the more I wanted to prove myself, to prove that I was worthy enough to be with you. When I looked at you, I knew I needed to be something great. For you."

"This doesn't make any sense," she said, breathless.

"I've been walking around quietly heartbroken, missing you for years. I stayed quiet when I wanted to speak. I stayed away when I wanted to run to you." He lightly ran his thumb over her hand. "You said you kept our ring to remind you of what you don't want, and all my fears came true." He hung his head and took in a deep breath before letting it out. When he looked back up at her, his eyes glistened with tears. He cleared his throat.

"That's not...I didn't mean it."

His eyes found hers. "This house, the boat outside, the truck that we used to ride in—it's all for you. I came back for you. I thought I lost you when you married Christian. I even called you, but I felt awful for meddling in your life when you'd moved on...I lost you once when we were young, and again when you married Christian. I wanted to give it everything I had this time. I wanted to do it right."

Sydney swam out of her feelings, trying to keep her head in check. "Then why in the world would you get on the board of supervisors and put Starlight Cottage in jeopardy?"

"I got on the board to talk some sense into them. I talked Colin out of building in the area, and I bought all the lots myself so that they would be forced to listen to me. The empty lots are going to be a natural preserve. There will be parking, but it will be inconspicuously placed. The view from Starlight Cottage won't change. I've been working with the county on hiking trails and water access for kayaking, planting trees, and landscaping out to the road. I've been calling people about it since the wedding. I didn't want to say anything in case I couldn't make it happen, but it passed with a vote of fifteen to two."

Sydney stood up and clasped a hand over her mouth in utter shock. It felt like a ten-year weight had been lifted, as if she were waking up from a terrible nightmare. How could she have gotten it so wrong: it had been Nathan Carr who'd been the imposter all along.

"I wish you'd have said something all those years ago..."

He nodded. "It was the worst decision of my life. I had to go to therapy for years just to stop the stress of it from eating me alive. That's how I was in touch with Mary Alice. I needed someone I could trust. I had run into her after college, and we'd shared what we were doing at the time, so when I needed a therapist, she was the one I turned to because I knew she would keep it from the press. She urged me to call you, and I tried, but I just didn't know if you'd want me in your life after what I'd done to us."

Sydney looked around the room, processing all of this. *That's* why Mary Alice's name was on his phone...

He rose and put his face right in front of hers. "I did it all because I'm totally in love with you."

"Nate, I'm so sorry," was all she could get out. She felt terrible that she'd misjudged him. All those times she'd thought he was being awful and selfish... Then all of a sudden, she noticed his frown and the disappointment on his face and she realized he thought she was apologizing for not feeling the way he did about her. "No," she said, taking his hands. "I'm sorry it took me so long to understand."

His face lifted and he squeezed her hands in his.

"I haven't stopped missing you since the day you left," she said.

With a *whoop*, Nate scooped her up into his arms, laughing with happiness. Then he looked into her eyes and pulled her close. "I've been wanting to do this for a long damn time." Agonizingly slowly, he pressed his lips to hers, and in that one kiss, he made up for all their lost time. His lips moved urgently on hers, his hands unstill, finding all the places they used to roam the last time his fingers had been set free upon her. She reached up, and ran her fingers through the back of his hair, the feel of him better than anything in the world.

Gently, Nate pulled back, the effort clearly quite difficult for him. He took his phone out of his pocket and typed something. Then, as he set his phone down on the counter, hers buzzed to life. Suspiciously, she pulled her phone from her back pocket and peered down at the email push notification.

I told her everything.
Love, Mel

She looked up from her phone, confused.

"I wanted to talk to you when you weren't so angry. I wanted to hear what your real thoughts were…"

"Mel?" she asked.

"Short for Melody, the name we wanted for our little girl."

She swallowed. "And what's the significance of 4221 in your email address?"

He lifted his eyes to the ceiling, and then shifted his gaze around the room. "It's the address of our new house," he said, spreading his arms wide.

"*Our* new house? Nope, I'm not shacking up with anyone who hasn't made an honest woman out of me," she teased, recalling their old memory. "My ring is back at Starlight Cottage."

Nate grabbed his phone again, and started typing something, his action jarring and pulling her out of the moment. Was he responding to something in the middle of their conversation? The fear that Nathan Carr was still present came rushing back, despite everything.

"Come outside with me?" he asked suddenly. "Let's take a walk."

He grabbed a pad of paper and a marker from the drawer and led her through the floor-to-ceiling glass doors that opened up, exposing the entire room to the beach. The warm breeze blew in like an old friend as he took her hand and led her across the deck and down the stairs to the sand.

"Where are we going?" she asked.

"You'll see." He led her around the house and down the path they'd driven, into the mass of trees. The brush had all been cleared and shade-grass planted, the tops of it cool against the sides of her feet as she walked in her flip-flops.

"What was the message you sent from your phone just before we left?" she asked casually.

He stopped and faced her, looking down at her with a grin on his face. "It was nothing," he replied. He leaned down and kissed her.

"Then why won't you tell me?" she pressed playfully as she got up on her toes and looked him square in the eye. "You'd better tell me," she said when he laughed instead of answering her. "I'm small but I'm feisty! I can take you down." She hit her best karate pose, making him laugh even harder.

"You have nothing on me," he said, tossing his notebook and pen into the grass. He grabbed her around the waist, lifting her up and making her squeal.

She wrapped her legs around his torso to hold on while she tickled his sides, causing him to collapse from the weight of her, both of them tumbling together onto the soft grass.

"I know your weakness," she said, still giggling. She reached out and tickled him again.

Taking her hands, he trapped them across her chest so she couldn't move. "I can still defend myself." He then pulled her hands around him as he hovered over her. "I don't want to, though," he said tenderly. "I'm all yours..."

Abruptly, he looked at his watch and stood up, grabbing her hands and pulling her to a standing position.

"What's going on?" she asked.

He took her hands again. "I need you to close your eyes. Will you trust me?"

She nodded, almost unable to follow his command because of the way he was drinking her in like he used to do. Finally, she closed her eyes.

"Okay, don't move or look until I tell you to. Promise?"

"I promise." She didn't move a muscle, all of her other senses on high alert. She took in the clean cotton scent of him when he kissed her forehead, the warmth of the sun on her skin, the rustle of the palm trees in the coastal wind. She could feel him rushing around her, breezing past her.

And then finally, he said, "Open your eyes." She allowed her blurred vision to sharpen on Nate. He was a ways from her, still holding the marker and the pad of paper. But as her scope widened, she started to notice little pieces of white paper stuck beneath the triangular bark of the palms between them. "Start there," he said, pointing to the tree closest to her.

Slowly, she paced over to it. Nate had written a message on it like they used to do at Starlight Cottage. Sydney plucked the paper from the bark and read, "I love you." She looked out at him and smiled as he stared at her with that adoring look that melted her in an instant. He pointed to the next tree.

Another note: "I never want to live another day without you."

Nate gestured toward the next tree. Holding both the pages in her hand, Sydney went to the third note. "Everything that you achieve in life, I promise from this day forward to be by your side to cheer you on." Sydney's eyes clouded with tears and she blinked them away to go to the next tree. She read the next one. "I want you with me for every sunset and every sunrise for the rest of my life." There was one more tree between Sydney and Nate and he stepped up beside her as she read the last message. It said simply, "Take my hand." Nate held out his hand and Sydney placed hers in his.

"Follow me," he said, leading her toward the back of the house. When they got to the beach, he kissed her. "Wait right here." Then he nearly sprinted across the yard and up the steps, rushing into the cottage. She caught sight of a white van, driving away around front just as he came back down to the shore out of breath. He took a minute and then smiled at her. "Ready to go inside?"

Sydney took his hand and walked beside Nate, climbing the steps where she got the first glimpse inside. She gasped, throwing her hand over her mouth. Every surface of the entire open area was filled with red roses, gardenias, and flickering candles. "What's going on?" she asked, breathless, as he led her into the center of the room, the fragrance filling her. "How did you do all this?"

"I've had the florist on standby since the wedding. All I had to do was text him and he'd be ready."

"You've had this planned since Hallie and Ben's wedding?" she asked, looking around at all the stunning bouquets.

"Somehow, I was going to get you back. Even if I spent the rest of my life trying. This house is yours whenever you want to move in. And as for making an honest woman of you . . ." He reached into his pocket and gripped a small black velvet box while taking her hand with his other. He got down on one knee. "Sydney Marie Flynn, will you marry me?" He opened the box to reveal an emerald-cut solitaire that was big enough to blind someone if she went out in the sunshine wearing it.

"Yes," she said, tears pricking her eyes. "It's incredible."

"I asked you to wear the plastic ring until I could get you the best ring money could buy. This is it." He took it out of the case and slipped it onto her finger, the weight of it substantial, but at the same time, like it was meant to be there. Then he stood up and gazed into her eyes. "Mrs. Nate Henderson. I like it."

"Not Mrs. Carr?" she questioned.

He shook his head, placing his hands on her face. "Definitely not. Just the real me and the real you." He leaned in and pressed his lips to hers. "I love you," he said into her ear. "I'm madly in love with you!" Nate scooped her up, spinning her around.

All of a sudden, when he set her down, something came to her: she remembered how Ben had looked at her hand when he'd come home. "Does Ben know about this?" she wriggled her finger with the solitaire.

"Yeah," he said with a grin. "I told him all about it when I came home for the wedding. I already texted him too. Everyone's coming over. They'll be here in just a few minutes."

"Everyone?"

"Yep. Your whole family, Malory, and Juliana. Ben's explained everything to them. He's telling them about my involvement with the board and the *real* reason I came back." He trailed his hand down her cheek. "He's rounding them up now."

"Where will they stand with all the flowers?" she giggled.

He leaned in and nibbled her neck, clearly unable to keep his hands off her. "Let's get in the truck," he said, taking her hand and moving toward the front door. "I've got something else to show you."

Nate locked up behind them and led her to the old truck she'd spent so many days in. He opened her door. "After you, my dear," he said dramatically. He kissed the top of her hand and ran around to his side, getting in. As she sat in his truck now, it felt just like it had all those years ago, all the pain associated with it leaving her like a grain of sand in the wind.

They left the beach and started down a narrow gravel path through the woods in the other direction.

"Are you kidnapping me?" she teased as they pushed on further into the middle of nowhere.

"Absolutely." He gave her a wink, leaning his elbow on the open window like he always had, his other hand resting on the top of the steering wheel. "I'm never letting you go again." She scooted over so that she was right next to him on the old bench-style seat. He eyed her with a suggestive look on his face. "I should've thought this whole family gathering out... I want you all to myself."

"There's plenty of time to be by ourselves," she said, kissing him on the cheek.

He nodded. "We have our whole life ahead of us."

She put her head on his shoulder.

When the truck came to a stop, next to a line of familiar cars belonging to her family and friends, they were outside of an enormous red barn with white trim. Nate got out and opened her door before running up to the barn and sliding the large panel to open the space. Inside, it was finished with hardwood floors and an enormous chandelier hanging from the vaulted A-line ceiling. "What is this?" she asked, coming up beside him and waving to everyone inside.

Lewis was there and Uncle Hank. Mama and Robby were both grinning like crazy, and Hallie had her hand on her heart lovingly as she stood by Ben and Malory. Juliana was grinning from ear to ear.

"Well, by day, it's a whiskey distillery. And by night, it's a private concert venue…I thought we could get married on the beach and have our reception here, if that's what you still want to do."

Robby ran forward and put his arms around them both. "Hey, buddy," she said, her two realities colliding. "I want to tell you about Nate," she said.

"Ben told me!" Robby said excitedly.

"Oh?" she asked. "What did he tell you?"

"He said that Nate loves the two of us very much and that he's going to take care of us and play all the football I want!"

Nate and Sydney both laughed, their attention moving over to Ben, who shrugged with a guilty smile.

"He's right," Nate said. "Football all day, every day! But right now, we have a party to go to."

As they went inside the barn, Sydney noticed a table full of boxes of pizza and bottles of soda. She looked at Ben questioningly.

"It's the best I could do on short notice. I know you've never been a big planner, Nate, but thirty minutes would be difficult for anyone," he said with a laugh. "The rest of the town should be here in about an hour. Fingers crossed they can find the place. But I do have a surprise." He pointed to the corner of the barn, and Uncle Hank pushed a lever on the wall illuminating a small stage. The back door opened and one of Ben's super-groups that he produced, Sylvan Park, a band that recently had been selling out whole stadiums, walked in and took their places on stage.

Sydney clapped a hand over her mouth. "How did you manage this?" she asked through her fingers.

"They're on vacation down the road in Seaside at the moment, and they owed Nate and me a favor."

The lead singer tapped his microphone, the amplifiers on the walls thumping. "This is a song that Nate wrote for

Sydney. It's on our next album. You all are the first to hear it live. I hope you enjoy it. It's called 'It Was Always You.'"

> *Rest your head tonight*
> *In your bed tonight,*
> *Close your eyes*
> *And think of me*
> *I'm out here all alone*
> *Hoping you hear me,*
> *Wishing you knew*
> *It was always you…*

Nate took Sydney's hand and walked her out under the chandelier to dance with her. As they moved to the music, he whispered in her ear, "It was always you." And Sydney danced with Nate Henderson for the rest of the song, and forever.

Epilogue

"You know I don't like you flying to New York in your state," Nate said to Sydney, kissing her as they sat together on the porch swing at their cottage. "*NY Pulse* will have to wait for our little Abigail to make her appearance."

They'd decided to name their baby girl Clara Abigail after Aunt Clara instead of their original choice of Melody. Abigail and Robby were going to grow up in Firefly Beach, and it was only fitting that the next woman in the family carry Aunt Clara's name. Abigail would have her whole life ahead of her to choose what she wanted to do, but one thing was for sure: Clara Abigail Henderson would be born into a strong line of creative and innovative women. And Nate and Sydney would be right there with her to help her along the way.

Sydney waved to Robby, who was chasing their new cocker spaniel mix they'd named Bentley down the beach. Bentley was their gift to Robby to celebrate the fact that he was going to be a big brother. Nate pulled Robby aside. "You know, I was a big brother, and there's a lot of responsibility that comes with taking care of your sister," he'd said. "I think you might need some practice with that. Wait right here."

While Robby waited in the front yard of their new home, Nate let Bentley out of his crate and opened the door. The little puppy went racing across the grass toward Robby, his big red bow flapping in the wind, tackling him and knocking him over with puppy kisses.

Sydney set her laptop aside. "I have just a few meetings to wrap up before I stop completely. But I don't have to fly to New York this time. Amanda is coming to me. She didn't want me flying either when I'm due in two weeks." Sydney rubbed her belly fondly, her wedding band and solitaire sparkling in the summer light.

Only a week after her engagement to Nate, she'd gotten a call from Amanda Rains of *NY Pulse* magazine, offering her the content editor position. She'd been able to work remotely, and her work had been so successful that over the last year, she'd been promoted to Senior Content Editor.

"Should we go?" she asked, standing up as Nate folded down her laptop to take it inside. She called Robby and the puppy Bentley, beckoning them back up to the house.

"Juliana's flown in for the baby shower," Nate said, peering down at his phone. "Your mom just texted to say they're home from the airport."

"Oh my goodness!" Sydney hadn't seen Juliana in a year and she couldn't believe she'd come all the way from Argentina just to see her.

After her contract had ended, Juliana had gone back home to her family farm, away from the paparazzi, where she'd opened a small studio for aspiring models. Before she left, she'd gone to the media about Seth, causing a firestorm. He would never work again. Between losing so many models over the last year after Juliana's admission and his legal fees, he barely had a cent to his name. Before going home, she'd told Sydney that what was most important to her was making sure that the girls she worked with knew that they were worth more than just their faces. She explained her new approach to modeling, where they would get instruction in how to pose and walking techniques, but also self-esteem classes and information on what best practices looked like in the industry. She was loving the work, feeling more fulfilled than ever.

"And Uncle Hank has made a key lime pie." Nate eyed her.

Sydney threw her head back, laughing. Uncle Hank and Lewis had taken a culinary class focusing on desserts. Uncle Hank had truly enjoyed it, and he'd been making pies for the last eight months or so.

"Hallie said not to worry; she'd had her team decorate in lime green anyway."

Hallie and Ben were expecting their first adoptive child to arrive in mere months. And the birth mother had just told them she was having a girl. Hallie and Ben decided to name her Violet. Both cousins Violet and Abigail would be born in the same year, and Sydney and Hallie were having a joint baby shower for the two of them.

"Nate!" Robby said, out of breath, his bare feet sandy and a football in his hand. "Will we be able to bring this?" He tossed it into the air.

"Absolutely," Nate said, catching it above Robby's head before Robby could reach it. "There's only so much cake one man can eat in a day…" He winked at Robby. "Go long!"

A Letter from Jenny

Thank you for reading *The House on Firefly Beach*. I hope it got you longing for those endless summer days, ocean views, and the sound of island music and fresh-fruit cocktails!

If you'd like me to drop you an email when my next book is out, you can sign up here:

www.ItsJennyHale.com/email-signup

I won't share your email with anyone else, and I'll only email you when a new book is released.

If you did enjoy *The House on Firefly Beach*, I'd love it if you'd write a review. Getting feedback from readers is amazing, and it also helps to persuade other readers to pick up one of my books for the first time.

If you enjoyed this story, you can read about Hallie and Ben in my novel *Summer at Firefly Beach*. And if you'd like even a little *more* summertime on the beach, do check out my other summer novels: *The Summer House* and *Summer by the Sea*.

Until next time!
Jenny

Acknowledgments

To my husband Justin, for his steadfast support, as he listens to all my wild ideas, I am forever grateful.

To my friends and family, I am thankful from the bottom of my heart for all the positivity and encouragement they provide. I am so appreciative of the creative people I've met here in Nashville, and delighted that I was welcomed into their circles. I am continually inspired by the people who surround me in this business.

Thanks to the folks at Bookouture. An enormous thank you to my editor Christina Demosthenous, who jumped right in and never missed a beat with me. To Oliver Rhodes, I am eternally grateful. I am so thankful for everything he's given me.

About the Author

Jenny Hale is a *USA Today* bestselling author of romantic women's fiction. Her novels *Coming Home for Christmas* and *Christmas Wishes and Mistletoe Kisses* have been adapted for television on the Hallmark Channel. Her stories are chock-full of feel-good romance and overflowing with warm settings, great friends, and family. Grab a cup of coffee, settle in, and enjoy the fun!

You can learn more at:
ItsJennyHale.com
Twitter @JHaleAuthor
Facebook.com/JennyHaleAuthor
Instagram @JHaleAuthor

Can't get enough of that small-town charm?
Forever has you covered with these
heartwarming contemporary romances!

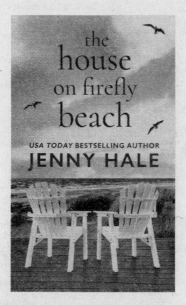

THE HOUSE ON FIREFLY BEACH
by Jenny Hale

Sydney Flynn can't wait to start fresh with her son at her sanctuary: Starlight Cottage at Firefly Beach. That is, until she spies her childhood sweetheart. Nate Henderson ended their relationship with no explanation and left to become a successful songwriter—only now, he wants to make amends. But when a new development threatens her beloved cottage, can Sydney forgive him and accept his help? Or will the town they adore—and the love they once had for each other—be lost forever?

Discover bonus content and more on
read-forever.com

THE LITTLE BOOKSTORE ON HEART LAKE LANE
by Sarah Robinson

Single mom Rosie Dean loves her unruly life. But between raising twins, running her struggling bookshop, and secretly writing a parenting advice column, she refuses to think about dating...until her high school crush returns to Heart Lake for the summer. Even though Evan has grown into a huge grump, he's still *supersexy*, and soon sparks begin to fly. Will one steamy summer convince them to give love a second chance? Includes a bonus story by Annie Rains!

SECOND CHANCE AT THE ORCHARD INN
by Heather McGovern

Chef Aurora Shipley spent years working her way up the ladder of L.A.'s restaurant scene, but when her sisters needed her, she dropped everything to help. Now that things have settled, it's time to return to the city—before her high school sweetheart can stir up any more memories best left forgotten. But Jude has always known there's no one like Aurora, and this time he's strong enough to fight for her—and their future together. Includes the bonus novella *Only Home with You* by Jeannie Chin!

Meet your next favorite book with @ReadForeverPub on TikTok